SALLY AND HER HOMEMAKING

DODD, MEAD CAREER BOOKS

Would you like to know how the authors and subjects of Dodd, Mead Career Books are chosen? Each year, hundreds of suggestions for career novels are received, but only a very small number of these finally become books. The reason for this is that every Dodd, Mead Career Book must pass a severe four-point test before it can even be considered for publication. If you would like to know more about Dodd, Mead Career Books, their authors, their aims and their accomplishments, ask for an interesting free booklet. Address your letter to Dodd, Mead Career Books, 432 Fourth Avenue, New York City.

SALLY AND HER HOMEMAKING

By

MAY WORTHINGTON

AUTHOR OF
Sally and Her Kitchens

ILLUSTRATED BY

MARGUERITE BYRAN

DODD, MEAD & COMPANY

NEW YORK   1942

COPYRIGHT, 1941
By DODD, MEAD AND COMPANY, Inc.

Published August 1941
Second Printing September 1942

PRINTED IN THE UNITED STATES OF AMERICA
BY THE VAIL-BALLOU PRESS, INC., BINGHAMTON, N. Y.

Acknowledgments

My grateful thanks to Mrs. Willis B. Anthony and to Mrs. Louis Kulcinski of Fitchburg, Massachusetts, for their pet recipes; to Mrs. Anthony especially for her inspiring demonstration of how to paint a kitchen! Marjorie Mills and her assistant, Sally Larkin, of the *Boston Herald* gave most graciously of their time and information, as did Janette Kelley, head Home Economist of Lever Brothers Company, Cambridge, Massachusetts, and the staffs of the *American Home Magazine* and of the *Herald Tribune* Institute of New York City.

To all of these go due praise and gratitude from

THE AUTHOR

KEENE TEACHERS COLLEGE
Keene, New Hampshire

Contents

PART I

PART II

PART I

One rubber plant can never make a home,
Not even when combined with brush and comb,
And spoon, and fork, and knife,
And gramaphone, and wife;
No! Something more is needed for a home.

One rubber plant can never make a home;
One day did not suffice for building Rome.
One gas log and a cat
Can't civilize a flat;
No! Something more is needed for a home.

ANONYMOUS.

CHAPTER I

Miss Kitury's Kitchen

"WHAT grist for our mill this morning, Miss Lewis?" Miss Katherine Kitury, editor of Miss Kitury's Kitchen, the homemaking column of the morning and evening *Star*, hung her hat and coat on a hook behind her desk, which occupied a corner of the busy city room. Typewriters clickety-clacked all around. Early reporters pounded out their assignments—fire, murder, or sudden death; war abroad, and defense at home; the doings of the great and the near-great, petty intrigue and power politics—"All the news that's fit to print," as one famous paper claims.

Sally Lewis was seated at an adjoining desk, still piled with unopened mail. If there were faint lines of anxiety about her young eyes never seen there before, if she seemed somehow a bit older than on that afternoon in late June when she had so joyfully said good-bye to her lunchroom job at Manfred Junior College, expecting to be married within the week to Alexander Merrill of Honolulu days, she was certainly no bigger.

By dint of sitting near the edge of the chair and tucking one slim foot around the other she could touch bottom, but only by dint! But, then, she had always found it hard to keep her feet on the ground—in more ways than one, her friends often teased. Standing—or sitting—in any one spot for long never had suited quick-moving and impetuous Sally!

She was now opening envelopes with a flip of the paper knife, busily sorting and arranging their contents. Some letters went into a wire basket, some under the paper weight, others were clipped together, more went into a folder. She swept the empty envelopes into the wastepaper basket and her fair curls bobbed as she looked up with a quick morning smile for her "boss."

"Mrs. Sanderson of Somerville wants to know how to take coffee stains out of her best tablecloth," she offered with a chuckle, "and Miss Halloway who runs the Stepping Stones Tea Room says she puts four or five coats of Valspar varnish on her kitchen tables and counter tops. Makes them slick and smooth. 'Wipe off like a dish' says she. I'm going to remember that idea myself—and, oh, yes, there's a good-sounding recipe for nut cake from somebody up in Maine, and several others for desserts there under the paper weight. We made a grand haul this morning," indicating the stack on the desk. "So far, ten entries have come in for the cooky contest you are planning for that Sunday edition later on. That's good, isn't it? Mrs. Somebody Else writes that your column is a real help to her and she says to tell the woman whose fern is getting ratty to water it with cold tea now and then! Aren't they funny?" Sally laughed. "I love to read their letters. This pile here is for you," and she passed over a neatly clipped batch.

Katherine Kitury had been inwardly enjoying her young assistant's fresh enthusiasm. "Any comeback from that Crescent Cereal Company?" Her capable hand ran through the letters Sally handed her.

"Here it is." She scanned it quickly:

Dear Madam:
    Your letter of the sixteenth at hand. We regret your refusal to advertise our Golden Hearts on your radio hour. We shall offer our business elsewhere.

"Oh, they will, will they?" Her blue eyes snapped. "You see," she explained at Sally's look of inquiry, "I turned down an offer from them yesterday to do a daily 'plug' for their cereal and I was a bit curious to see how they'd take it. They don't take it, of course. They say sweetly that they'll do business with someone else—less fussy, they mean. Well, let 'em, say I." Miss Kitury gave the letter a toss. "I hate to lose business, but I can't boom anything I don't like, and that mixture certainly stuck in my throat. Too much like sawdust for my taste. Well, never mind. I guess there's enough in the mill without worrying over that." She dismissed the matter with a wave of the hand, as she sat down at her desk.

"Just how far along did we get yesterday? Tomorrow's column is all set, isn't it, for both morning and evening editions?"

"The proofs haven't come up yet," Sally answered.

"Not yet? What's the matter with Mike? Nine o'clock. Why don't you run downstairs and get them yourself? But hand me that folder for Friday before you go, and I'll see if I can get things together there." And Miss Kitury settled to her job of writing two quarter columns of good advice to housewives.

Sally skipped down the narrow back stairs to the composing room. She loved these peeks into the inner workings of the big newspaper. So strange, so different from anything she had ever known. The rows of linotype machines clacked as the men busily rapped out their material. She gave a swift glance at some long tables covered with forms—sample pages of the paper set in type. Here was one of the household pages for a week or so ago! "Silver cake—Mrs. S. T. Best, Vt.," her eyes caught in passing.

"Oh, yes, Mrs. Best. 'We are so grateful for this unusual cake recipe. It was kind of you to send it. We hope you will write us again soon,' " Sally quoted her answering letter, as she made her way toward Mike's desk. The big foreman, coat off, pipe going like a smokestack, looked up with a twinkle as she approached.

"You here again? Let's see what I did with your story." He fished in the basket on his desk. "Here you are," handing over the familiar pages.

"Tell Miss Kitury I didn't see any slug on that second page but I guessed it was her's from the pies 'n things."

Slug? "Only slugs I know about crawl in the garden," Sally thought to herself. She thanked him for the proofs, and looked quickly on page two—then back to page one. "Kitury's Kitchen" in upper left corner. Nothing in that corner on page two except Mike's penciled scrawl. "So that's a slug, is it? Bet I could pick a fancier name for it than that! Guess I'm the girl that left it off, too, come to think of it," she remembered ruefully. There were many things to keep in mind on this job, she bethought herself anew, as she turned to go.

"Guess we won't bother to send the galleys up any more. Kinda nice to have something pretty and fresh to look at once in a while," Mike spoke to her retreating back.

Sally turned, waved a gay acknowledgment for his compliment and climbed the stairs.

"Nice old fellow." She slid into her chair and picked up her pencil to check the proofs against the next day's "story."

Miss Kitury's columns were rattling along at a great rate under her sure hand. Oftentimes they were made up of answers to questions asked by her readers the week before; of clever hints sent in by her enthusiastic followers; of easy ways of doing things—how to take the work out of housework. Some days she told them about odd and unusual eating places tucked away in the city's back streets; of outstanding tearooms cleverly decorated or uniquely simple, successful because their managers had imagination and a flair for food. And always she wrote in an easy and informal style. She was visiting with her friends—the homemakers of New England.

Her "editorials" done, she must then get together some especially good recipes, four or five always, for each morning and evening edition, besides organizing her script for the afternoon broadcast—"and in case anybody thinks that's as simple as it sounds, let her try holding the interest of fickle woman day after day and see!" Miss Kitury often sputtered. This was her morning's stint, day in and day out —and double on Thursday, when material for the Sunday page must be ready. She tried always to keep at least two jumps ahead—just to have a little leeway in case anything happened—but many a morning in the years gone by, when she and the column were new and she had no assistant, she had worked frantically against the deadline. Those were the days when she had worried about running out of ideas and recipes, when she had combed the cook books and the few household magazines then available. Finally she had hit on the idea of making her column an exchange with her readers, inviting them to share all short cuts to easier housekeeping that they themselves had used, the quick tricks and the trump cards of their own game. She urged them to discuss the problems that troubled them, wrote these up in her column next day, and invited anyone who had an answer to send it in.

But that was years ago. Now the worry wasn't that the well might run dry. Merciful heavens, no! But over the flood that daily deluged her desk. How to keep up with it? How to get inquiries answered, either by radio, through the morning or evening paper, or by letter, so that each woman received personal recognition, thanks for her help, or assistance in her need.

Miss Kitury was herself an ardent apostle of the gospel of good housekeeping, of hospitality, of good food. Everything about the topic interested and intrigued her. She was a friendly and outgoing person. She wanted earnestly to help lift womankind from the drudgery of *housework* to the romance and fun of *homemaking*. To this end her clientele must be encouraged. They must be shown the light, made somehow to feel that they belonged to a special sisterhood. She knew that these women were thrilled, that they were proud and flattered to see their names in print, or hear them on the air, and she, Kate Kitury, saw to it that they were not disappointed. She wasn't Irish for nothing! A bit of blarney, a little "soft soap" as her mother, née Bridget O'Leary, would have called it, got for her what nothing else could have done: it kept her mail family coming. She enlisted their help, she praised their response—for they were indeed the geese that laid for her the golden eggs!

Sally, from her chair nearby, stole an admiring glance at the arresting figure beside her—at the thick wavy hair, smartly bobbed—at the strong fingers flying over the typewriter. Miss Kitury was that breezy, informal type that wears sport clothes with flyaway dash and verve. She fascinated Sally, who herself was no slow-poke. She, too, had enthusiasm and spark a-plenty, but Miss Kitury had personality plus, it did seem, backed, furthermore, by a special brand of assurance—her degree from the school of hard knocks, she would have said. Apparently everyone knew Kit Kitury. Everyone hailed her from afar. They marveled at her boundless energy, admired her cleverness, and grinned at her quick retorts. Sally, filled with admiration and fired with zeal to emulate, had looked on in wonder many times during the past month since she had come to substitute for Miss Kitury's regular assistant, away on leave. She liked her "boss" very much; she liked this very different job; she wished fervently that she did not have to give it up. . . . The worried look came again to her face. But there! She gave herself a shake. Since she did not yet quite dare look forward very far, she would just have to take the days as they came for a bit longer and be thankful she had a job, even for a short time, while her courage gathered for the next jump.

There was work to be done right in front of her. She had sent the galleys back downstairs but there were piles of letters still unanswered; the scrapbook to bring up to date, where were pasted the "stories" cut from each day's paper; recipes to type and file. She swung around to her desk. Thank goodness she had learned to use a typewriter in high school. Anyone would be sunk on this job without such a very necessary skill. She had discovered that before she had been there a day. She opened a letter now from a town in New Hampshire.

"My word!" she exclaimed, half to herself. "This woman is sending directions for making soap."

"What's that about soap?" Miss Kitury leaned back in her chair for a minute.

"This Mrs. Johnson—no, Johnsbury—says she makes her own soap always and tells how. My mother used to make soap on the farm when I was little, I remember, but I didn't know anybody ever did it any more!" Sally explained.

"Just what I need! Somebody was asking me about making soap the other day—where on earth was I speaking? D.A.R. meeting, I guess. That will just fill this column and

show Mrs. Daughter that I didn't forget her either." Miss
Kitury held out her hand for the letter.

"Let me type the directions for you first. The writing's
terrible." Sally swung to her machine and wrote out Mrs.
Johnsbury's instructions for the simple, homely task.

"Easy, isn't it?" she said as she handed over the card.

"Thrifty trick, too, and an old-time one that will appeal
to all good New Englanders." Miss Kitury chuckled as she
bent over her writing.

The morning raced on toward noon.

"What's the date today?" Miss Kitury reached for her
calendar suddenly. "There's a luncheon this noon at the
Barbarole—given by the Longwood Garden Club—that I
promised Jane Berry I'd attend and report on, and I forgot
it completely! Made an appointment with that advertising
fellow from the A. & M. Stores. I've got to see him, too, that's
all there is about that. Sally, you'll have to go to the luncheon for me. Do you good to get out." She smiled at Sally's
astonished look. "You're all right just as you are." Her eye
ran over the neat blue dress and white collar. "Everybody
wears street clothes and besides there'll be a crowd, so you
won't be noticed anyhow. Take your notebook along for
they often have something unusual and interesting to eat
and clever table decorations at these affairs. Keep your eyes
and ears open and tell me what you hear and see. Better run
along now. Here's your ticket. You won't need to rush back,
so have a good time."

Miss Kitury watched the slim figure through the doorway. "Sweet child, and smart," she said to herself. "But I
wonder . . . Sometimes she sparkles and a gay little laugh
comes out when she forgets herself. Always she's quick as
a wink at seeing what I want and her ideas are good, but so

often there's a worried look about her, as if she didn't see how she could pay her rent, or something! She looks so young, too. If it isn't money that's the trouble, it's a man, I'll bet a cent on that! Both, maybe. Either one can be worry enough, heaven knows—but taken together they've been many a maid's undoing, as I all too well remember!" And Katherine Kitury shut her desk down with a bang.

CHAPTER II

"*Tough Enough*"

MISS KITURY did not know how near she had come to the truth. She did not know that every night for many months Sally, too, had wondered and worried and wondered again—ever since that night in June.

It still rose vividly before her whenever she shut her eyes. She had been awakened by knocking on a door near the guest room in the Merrill home, where she was staying for the week prior to her marriage to Alex. She had so wanted to be married at her own home in the state of Washington, but she did not have money enough to get there—none to be exact—and Alex was not for waiting any longer. His mother had insisted that she stay with them, so there she was.

"Alex, call the doctor, *quick!* Your father—" Mrs. Merrill's frightened voice brought Sally out of bed with one bound. Turning on the light—feet into slippers, housecoat on—out into the hall—to see Alex in bathrobe running toward the telephone, his mother standing in the bedroom doorway, her face ashen.

"What has happened? Can I help?" Sally was beside her in a second.

"It's Father—his heart. I've done everything I know. We'll just have to wait for the doctor." Mrs. Merrill went back into the bedroom. And they waited—an eternity it seemed—Sally's hand clasped tight in Alex's. The doctor came at last—and stayed. And then followed days, days of agonized waiting. Nurses arrived and the tranquil life of the household was gone. Alex's face grew drawn and white and his mother scarcely left his father's side.

Sally tried in every way to help. Beds, sweeping and dusting, trays and meals, dishes and laundry—at least she knew about these and she flew from one to the next. Her home economics training at college, her experience in the dining hall at Haiilani School in Hawaii, the year in the lunchroom of Manfred Junior College, not to speak of a very practical bringing up on the farm, all came to her aid now. Besides, she had earned her way through school doing all these jobs. She could do dishes blindfolded! And mopping a floor. If she only had a dollar for every time she had done that she would have a real hope chest now, instead of one small shoe box!

"What I do, you not here?" Hilma, the Finnish maid, wiped perspiration from her face, as they ploughed through the accumulated washing one morning. Hilma had been in the family a long time but these last weeks had tried even her stout heart.

"I'll turn the wringer, Hilma. You put clothes through." Sally grinned.

"What I do myself, I not here?" she wondered. And as the weeks grew into months she wondered more, for it became increasingly evident that a long siege was ahead.

"Dr. Anglin, tell me honestly, what do you think about Mr. Merrill?" Sally caught the doctor as he was leaving one day some weeks later. She told her own story briefly, who she was, why she was there.

"Well, Mr. Merrill is holding his own—a hopeful sign. But it will be a long pull at best—and uncertain."

"Long? Months *more*, you mean?" Sally's heart sank lower.

"Many months—probably a year—and absolute quiet. No strain. It will take Mrs. Merrill's undivided attention and her son's, too. No wedding bells." The doctor looked keenly at the young, anxious face before him. "Tough, eh?"

Sally blinked fast. A faint smile, meaning nothing. "Tough enough."

She sat down in the quiet hall to think.

How could any world have changed so fast?

She could not stay in Alex's home too long. Order and routine were pretty well established now. Hilma could manage. Mrs. Merrill didn't need her—not really. One less to think about. She must talk to Alex. Poor dear. He'd take it hard. But his mother did need him, as the doctor said. She could see that. She couldn't be a burden. She must take care of herself. That had been rooted and grounded in her ever since she could remember. She must find a job. Twenty-five dollars—just that much she had in her pocketbook. Munificent margin to marry on, wasn't it? Would it be enough to tide her over? Riches if . . . Yes, *if!*

She gathered herself together at last, went to wash her face, to powder her nose, to make her plans—to talk to Alex.

"Tough enough," she muttered as she climbed the stairs.

"But, Sally, what will you *do?* Your old position at Manfred is filled by now, isn't it?" Alex and Sally were standing by the sun dial in the garden that evening, Alex upset and unconvinced. Sally's finger absently traced the lettering — I c-o-u-n-t o-n-l-y s-u-n-n-y h-o-u-r-s— ("The thing must have stood still in its tracks for weeks, then!" part of her mind registered.)

"Worse luck, yes, but Dean Ardwell will fix me up. And, anyhow, Miss Lawrence is always needing someone to pinch-hit in the lunchroom at college. She told me to come back if I ever needed to," elaborated Sally swiftly. She could not bear that distressed look on Alex's face!

"Please, dear, don't feel so badly," she begged. "I'll be all right. You've no idea really what a smart and versatile woman I am," she twinkled. "I'm sure it's best. It will only be for a year and then next spring or summer—when your father is well again—why. . . ."

"You're a game little sport, Banty! Come here to me!"

And the next day Sally had packed her possessions and said good-bye.

Mrs. Merrill took Sally's face between her two hands.

"You're a sweet and a good girl. I don't know how I would have managed without you these weeks. It's a great pity your plans have been all spoiled like this, but you are young. It won't hurt to wait. Later on, when Father is better . . . Good-bye, dear. Take care of yourself. Write often. Alex will be lonely."

Sally kissed her quickly and ran.

"I'll go to the Y.W., Alex. That's a good, inexpensive place and very convenient," Sally directed as they drove toward the city. "One of the secretaries I used to know in Hawaii is there. That will be a help. Remember Miss Booth from Palmhurst? She was a good scout. Runs the cafeteria in this big branch on Harvard Street now." Sally spoke with a cheerfulness she was far from feeling. Anything to keep Alex from slumping.

In a corner of the big lobby, he hugged her tight.

"I hate to leave you here, Sally. Write every day and tell me everything that happens. I'll be down as soon as I can, but if you get stuck, telephone. Good-bye, sweet." And he was gone.

Thank goodness it was night and she could go straight to bed, where no one could see her. What a narrow cot—like college days. Sally shut her eyes resolutely. "For four cents

I could cry good and hard," she thought to herself. But she did not dare spare the four cents!

She did write Alex often in the weeks that followed. She told him the truth, but not the whole truth. She trusted she would be forgiven for the things she failed to mention. No use worrying him any more than he was already. For jobs were scarce in September. School positions were filled by that late date. Dean Ardwell was distressed. She had no openings at all right then. She would surely keep her good pupil in mind, she wrote. Sally registered with more agencies —business and professional—dreading to see her precious dollars vanish for fees, but hoping. She made the rounds of all the teaching agencies where, fortunately, she was still a member from the year before. Then she waited. But nothing happened. So she started forth every day, visiting each agency in turn—hopefully, always hopefully. She would make herself known and remembered, if nothing else! The days were hot and sticky and her feet . . . *O-oooo*, her feet!

No matter. Other girls must have done the same thing many a time—and she made the rounds once again. She'd be such a pest they'd give her a job to get rid of her!

"No fish today?" Clara Booth inquired sympathetically as Sally, coming into her room for a nightly visit some weeks later, sank into a chair.

"No fish. Something's wrong with my bait, I guess." Sally managed a thin grin as she kicked off her pumps. Thank goodness for a friend anyhow.

"Nothing's wrong with your bait. Keep throwing out the line and hang on for dear life if you get a bite!" Clara went on encouragingly. "Everyone has a streak like this sometime or other. I wore out a pair of shoes in the same cause once myself—before I went to Hawaii," and the older girl tact-fully shifted the talk to their mutual acquaintances, to their happy days in Honolulu.

But Clara Booth was troubled by the dark circles under Sally's eyes—the familiar signs of worry and anxiety and growing discouragement.

"Money running low, I bet, and she'd die rather than tell me. *Mm-m-m*—that serving room never has gone well since I put Annie on the cashiering. I've a mind—"

Sally was awakened early next morning by a knock on her door.

"Miss Booth wants to know if you'll come down and help her." One of the cafeteria workers stood in the hall.

"Tell her I'll be down right away!"

Sally flew into her clothes and appeared in the kitchen on the run.

"Take cash for me like a good girl, will you? You know how it goes." Clara, busy overseeing breakfast, motioned toward the dining room.

"I'll be glad to. This the menu? Baked apples with cream, ten cents—ham and one egg—" Sally skimmed down the page. "All right. Set your mind at rest, Ma'am. This is 'duck soup,' as the boys at Manfred used to say," and Sally perched herself at the cash register, glad to lend a hand, thankful to have something to do—anything to keep her busy. And this was right down her alley.

She liked this lunchroom. It was a cheerful, friendly place. Gay curtains lent a homelike air; the glint of nickel on the counters, gleaming shelves—later to be filled with bright salads to catch the eye. Sally sniffed the coffee steam-ing in the shining urns. Not only the girls living in the house ate here but many a woman rooming in the neighborhood found Clara's cafeteria a boon to her slender pocketbook and balm to her lonely soul.

"Orange juice, toast, coffee—*twenty-five cents*"—Sally rang up the first tray and smiled at her customer, a young Italian girl.

After the last breakfast customer had departed, Clara Booth stopped where Sally was counting cash.

"Look, you couldn't manage to do this for me right along for a few weeks, could you?" she asked casually. "I need Annie out back. It will cover your room and meals and a bit more. You'll still have time to fish. It would be a great help to me, if you could?"

Could she! Sally looked up quickly, tears of relief coming to her eyes. "You're a dear!" she said suspiciously.

"No, I mean it."

"So do I!"

And Sally's long lane that seemed never-ending took a turn right there.

Two weeks later had come the note from Dean Ardwell, asking her to report to Miss Kitury, homemaking editor of the *Star*. An assistant who was ill would be away for possibly two months or so. Perhaps Miss Lewis would like to fill in?

And Miss Lewis, hoarding her last few dollars, had whooped for joy.

CHAPTER III

If It Isn't One Thing, It's Another

SALLY hurried up the avenue. The early winter day was clear and snappy and she snuggled down into her coat collar and tucked her hands up her sleeves. How good the fresh air felt! To be stepping off to this Garden Club affair was something pretty special. She wished she were going with someone she knew, but after all this was business and one couldn't expect too much. She would just look and listen and let it go at that.

The Barbarole was new. One of those residence clubs given over largely to college and university women in business or professional life. Sally slid in through the revolving door, checked her coat with the girl at the desk, and looked about her.

The lobby was a-buzz, filled with women wearing hats and an air of the visiting lady. These must be the luncheon guests. Over at the left and down a step or two was the main dining room where the residents of the club and transient guests had their meals. Sally, standing where she could get a good view, watched the room with a (she hoped!) professional eye. Waitresses with loaded trays were coming in through the swinging doors. It was a familiar scene. Whoever was in charge out in the kitchen was hustling around, she could bet on that! Worrying because the cream had not come; proud of the way that new salad had turned out; exasperated with Jenny for not getting those peas on earlier— Oh, she knew the burden of that song by heart!

A plump figure in white came in through the serving-room door. Who was that girl? She looked familiar.

"Lou Davis, as I live!" Sally exclaimed joyfully. "She was two classes ahead of me in college." Sally made her way to the cashier's desk in the dining room. "Would it be possible for me to speak to Miss Davis?" she asked.

"Certainly." The woman at the desk motioned to a waitress. "Kathleen, will you take this lady to Miss Davis's office?"

"This way, please." The waitress beckoned and Sally followed—down the side of the room toward a door at the left. It opened into an alcove off the serving room where were a desk and filing cabinet.

"I'll tell Miss Davis you are waiting." The waitress went on out into the serving room.

"Why, Sally Lewis, what are you doing here?" Lou Davis, appearing in the doorway, held out her hand in cordial greeting.

"I came out to ask you the same thing!" Sally answered eagerly. "I didn't know you were holding forth in this grand place."

"Yes, I came here right after graduation, to substitute during the summer vacation, and stayed on—thanks to a lucky break. But what about you? Having lunch?"

"With this Garden Club, pinch-hitting for my boss-of-the-month, Miss Kitury, of the *Star*."

"Are *you* one of the crowd that's responsible for this morning's madness? We've all but run ourselves ragged getting ready for you! Want to see where you are going to eat? I'll just take a second to show you." Miss Davis, her trim uniform crackling, led the way through to a door opening into a private dining room, done in light gray-green. Mauve and green chintz hung in long folds at the windows, the light softened by delicate rose-tinted net. Tables were set in banquet fashion for thirty or forty guests. The yellow-green of the salad, the soft pink of the china glinted in the clear goblets.

"Lovely!" Sally exclaimed at the pretty picture. "This is better luck than I ever hoped for. Did you have any of this to do?"

"Only to supervise making the salad and the fruit cup. Miss Berry is looking after the party generally. The club's officers arranged the flowers. Aren't the white petunias and lavender lace flowers effective in these low white bowls? Then the candle holders match the bowls, and the tapers are lavender. Pretty, aren't they? And look at this arrangement over here at the side of the room, against this gray-green wall panel. Just pine and rhododendron leaves and red willow branches in this low square dull red pottery container. Aren't the lines graceful? See how this small cigarette box repeats the colors? It would be lovely for a hallway in anyone's home, wouldn't it?"

"This is the third party we've had this week," Lou Davis continued. "Keeps us jumping. Miss Berry has a real flair for parties, though. She has two waitresses who always 'special' for her and a good bit of extra equipment—glassware, table linen, etc. I look after lunch in the main dining room while she's busy in here. And I expect I'd better be getting back there, too. I'm so glad you looked me up. Come and see me. I'm at the Student Club. Have a good time now. Think of me slaving behind the scenes while you eat our food. Hope nothing burned while I've been gone! 'Bye."

Lou Davis slipped back into the kitchen as the waitresses,

finished with serving butter and pouring water, began bringing in the fruit cup. Here again was pale green. Melon cubes and green grapes cut in half, slender orange sections, and, topping all, tiny balls of strawberry sherbet and sprigs of mint. Sally eyed it hungrily. How pretty it looked! Those little very delicate lace paper doilies underneath were something new. Her eye traveled to the salad at the left. Small ring molds of cucumber gelatine, centers filled with cottage cheese and chopped chives and a sprinkle of grated orange peel on top. It looked delicious.

A most efficient-appearing older woman was checking the tables. Must be Miss Berry, Sally decided, watching her competent touch here and there. Satisfied at last, she gave the signal and the doors were opened to admit the guests. Sally handed her ticket to the person in charge, slipped into line and found a place near the end of a table, pleased and with her appetite well sharpened by her lucky preview.

What would come after the fruit cup? As the waitress cleared the first course, Sally made bets with herself. Two to one it would be creamed chicken patties with peas! But she was wrong. Baked shrimp in scallop shells, halves of tomatoes broiled with grated cheese and a speck of onion, broccoli with pimento strips. What an appetizing plate! Melba toast and tiny rolls were passed on a tray. A most delectable lemon torte was the dessert—coffee, of course. Sally resolved to get that torte recipe for the column, *surely*. Her old college pal, Judy Martin out in California, would like it, too. She would write Judy soon and send it on. They still exchanged all bright ideas, and their correspondence throve and flourished.

But hush, the president was speaking and the topic was Herbs—How to use them—Gardens to plant in the spring.

Now that was something straight to the point. Marjoram, sage, and savory, chives and thyme and mint— Her mother used always to have them at home, Sally remembered. So easy to grow, so good to snap up a salad, to dry and use in soups, in dressing, in stew. There was another idea for the notebook, and Sally scribbled quickly. In the discussion that followed the party broke up and she slipped out. At the desk she left a note for Lou—

Lou-lu,
    Your food was a *feast*. Loved your salad! Kindly send recipe for lemon torte to Miss Kitury's Kitchen, *Star* office— and receive honor and acclaim from ye ed, also praise and gratitude from humble sub. Read the *Star!*

                                                    Sally

—and made straight for the office, eager to pass on her tidbits.

But Miss Kitury was not in. Disappointed, Sally wrote up her notes, left them on her chief's desk and settled down to finish the day's work. There were a dozen recipes sent in, with date and name of sender to be typed on cards, as many more helpful hints culled from the morning mail—all these to be filed after Miss Kitury had checked and chosen the best for her radio talks and for the paper. There were ten or more questions. Some Sally knew the answers for, like using iodine to cover scratches on furniture, and salt and vinegar for badly tarnished copper and brass, or rubbing white spots on tables with a little alcohol—very lightly— or with camphorated oil. But some of the answers she did not know. How, pray tell, did you stiffen a rug—hooked or otherwise—that had become limp from cleaning or washing? She had heard of equal parts of shellac and denatured alcohol brushed over the underside, but she was not sure. She would have to save that one for Miss Kitury. But she went through the lot, giving what information she could, digging some out of the files. Then she clipped the letters and left them for approval and further additions. This cleared the decks. If she ever went home leaving one letter unattended to, she was swamped the next day, so she made a desperate effort to cover everything. It was five o'clock. She closed down her typewriter, locked her desk and put on her hat.

Andy, on the copy desk, waved good night as she passed. He and Miss Kitury were friends of long standing. Sally had listened to many a bout of wit and banter between them, her boss often leading, to her delight.

The subway was jammed as usual, and as usual Sally hung to a strap. Mrs. Kaziki's bundles jabbed her on one side, and on the other Guiseppe must have had "mucha garleek" in his noonday "spaghet!" It was a tired crowd going home to supper after a long day in the city's workshops.

"U.S. SPEEDS ALL AID TO BRITAIN. WAR ORDERS MOUNTING" The headlines on her neighbor's paper caught Sally's eye and brought to mind her two major worries of the moment. For Miss Sally was like that. There was always a worry. If it wasn't one thing, it was another—right now it was both! And both boiled down to—Alex. One worry present and immediate, the other loomed ominously ahead. No use borrowing trouble about the one ahead—*Alex might not have to go to war, after all.* And, anyhow, why should she be worrying about whether he did or did not, when it looked from where she stood as if she and Alex were not even *friends.* They hadn't been for weeks! That was the present worry. The ever-present. How could two people who loved one another dearly get into a snarl over *nothing?* The whole thing amounted to just that—*nothing*—thought Sally, as the affair passed again through her mind, for the ninety-ninth time, it seemed. Still vivid. Increasingly trivial.

Alex had driven in to see her. They were coming home from the movies. What *was* it she had said when the police-man gave Alex the ticket for running through the red light? Something pert about his driving. She had only meant it in fun, but he had flared up like a rocket. To be sure, it was no time for her to try to be funny, but he needn't have been so touchy either! And she told him so—to her sorrow—for the sparks flew! And then followed angry words she would have given anything to take back. It all seemed *so* senseless now. Would she never learn to hold her tongue? If tact were the first lesson toward happy homemaking, where did that put her? Pre-school? Lower yet. They had actually quarreled. *She* and *Alex*. He had dropped her out at the Y.W., slammed the door and driven off without a word of good night, and she had gone to bed, resentful and heartsick.

"Well, never mind," she finally comforted herself, "Alex will write in a day or two and say he is sorry." But he did not, and the days went on and on till Miss Sally could stand it no longer. She really was to blame in the beginning she supposed—and finally she wrote and said that if she were, she was sorry. It had not seemed to do any good, though. Perhaps it was that "if." But he could come a little way, too, couldn't he? Her troubled thoughts went round and round. The train lurched on a curve and she came back to the present. Well, maybe she would have a letter tonight, after all.

Anyhow it was pleasanter and safer not to think too far —certainly not to run up and down that blind alley any more. . . . She resolutely scanned the car ads for mental distraction. Here was one: Old Baldy, two straying hairs left on his pate, was giving warning to all—"Use your head. Save your hair. Use Fitch's Shampoo!" Now wasn't that a help! If she had used her head she wouldn't be in the trouble she was in now, that was sure. The world certainly had a way of taking you over the bumps. No doubt for your own good, but who cared about that! If it wasn't one thing it was another that kept *her* ego from ever having any chance to soar. That this was probably her own fault—but why bring that up *again?*

All of which left her right where she was in the beginning —hanging on a strap! But here was her station. She elbowed her way out and up the stairs.

"This Y.W. is a *pretty good* place," Sally thought as she came up the walk. She had stayed on there even after getting her job. She still took cash in the cafeteria at night when the regular girl was off. She sometimes helped Sundays, if Clara needed a lift. It seemed like home because of her friend.

Pausing now in front of the building, she felt again what a real need such an institution filled. Many girls of every kind and creed lived there. They found friendliness and help. Sally never tired of watching them, wondering who they were and where they came from. A girl never need be lonely in a place like this. There were parlors where they gathered. They could and did have fun. There were classes in swimming, in cooking, in homemaking, and much was done for their pleasure. It beat living in a room somewhere all by yourself. No one for company. Meet your friends on the corner? Oh, no, not for Sally! She pushed open the big door and stopped in the lobby for her mail.

"Hi! Just looking for you," Clara hailed her from the dining-room door. "Want to go to the Hotel Men's Show with me tonight? I always try to take it in every year. You pick up ideas. See all the elite of the business."

"Love to." Any evening filled was a boon to Sally these days.

"Good. Let's eat early then. See you at dinner in ten or fifteen minutes?"

"Okay." Sally gathered up her mail (No letter from Alex. She had already seen that from the corner of her eye.) and went up to her room.

Well, if he would be such a goose—didn't *want* to listen —he'd just have to "stay mad 'till he got glad," as the youngsters use to say! Miss Sally's back stiffened but her heart sank.

"Thank goodness I don't have to sit here alone tonight, anyhow." She tossed her head and tried to feel defiant, but it was a poor try. Well, anyhow—

She went on down to the cafeteria, resolved to forget her troubles.

"New dessert?" Sally eyed the dish before her with interest. "Apple crisp? See if I can tell how you did it. Sliced apples baked in a dish with a topping of—m-m—wait now —brown sugar and butter and flour? And cinnamon. How's that?"

"Right on the head," Clara nodded.

They were finishing their dinner at the staff table where Sally, being a friend of the management, had long ago been taken in to the family circle.

"It's delicious." Sally smacked her lips. "Miss Kitury will like this for her housewife's column. Think I must be a sure 'nuff housewife myself. All the things about food and cooking and keeping house give me a real thrill. How to do everything—make a room pleasant, like this, for instance." Sally's eye roamed about with renewed appreciation. Nice to have a friendly homelike place in which to stay—like a *home*—was that always the point?

"Your Alex picked the right gal then, I'd say," Clara responded. "He'll be down this week end, I suppose?" She watched Sally closely, having caught, she thought, a wistful note in her friend's voice, a new worry back of her friend's eyes.

"Guess so," Sally answered quickly. "But Lady Luck's a fickle jade," she added with a shrug.

"Too quick and too nonchalant. Anything wrong there, I wonder?" speculated Clara to herself. Aloud she said, "We had better hustle along, if you're ready. We'll take the sub. Saves time and feet."

The two girls hurried out into the winter night and made for the nearest subway entrance. Like so many gophers scuttling down their holes, Sally always thought, emerging from under ground never out of the same hole twice! Which way was uptown and which was downtown? She never knew 'till she had walked a block or so, always in the wrong direction!

But Clara knew.

"This way." She piloted Sally toward the Garden. "This show is sponsored by the Hotel Men's Association of the city," she explained. "It's commercial, of course. All the big equipment houses, the wholesale firms of all kinds, have exhibits—kitchen gadgets large and small, canned goods, plain and fancy—everything that has to do with eating in a big way. Here we are."

Sally was all eyes. Floor after floor was filled with exhibits

and the girls went from one point of interest to another.

"What have you got there?" Clara, separated from Sally by the crowd, found her finally rooted before a pea sheller that was turning out peas by the bushel.

"Will you look at this, Clara!" she exclaimed. "That's a long jump from my mother with a pan in her lap, shelling peas out on our back porch, isn't it? And look, did you see this little vegetable shredder? You put the vegetables in there—cabbage, carrots—turn that crank and look how they come out! Lovely and feathery. See how pretty raw beets are!"

The white-capped chef who was demonstrating grinned at Sally's enthusiasm. "We use raw vegetables like this for our salad bowls," he explained. Taking up a small wooden bowl beside him, he filled it with a fine lacy mound of cabbage, one of carrots, one of beets.

"The dear public has gone crazy over vitamins now—so —sprinkle a little French dressing over this and—there you have 'em!" He set the bowl on the counter with a flourish.

"It's lovely!" The girls thanked him with smiles and moved on.

"Raw beets! I wouldn't have eaten them on a bet a year ago. But they are really sweet and good—and certainly colorful!" Sally bubbled on as they hurried down the aisle. "One of those gadgets would be grand in anyone's home, too. I'm going to tell Miss Kitury about it, and the raw beets. She *may* be here to see them herself, though she didn't mention coming."

Clara steered her toward the elevator. "Let's go up and see the Cooks' and Bakers' exhibit before we get too tired. That's the high light of the show always." They crowded in and the door shut.

"Fancy seeing you here!" Sally heard a light, familiar voice behind her.

"Hel-lo, Lou! Clara, this is Miss Davis who is at the Barbarole where I had the spiffy lunch the other day. Going where we're going? Good! Come with us."

And the three wormed their way through the crowd to the tables spread with every creation that experts in this ancient art of cookery could form or fashion. There were hams baked to a golden brown, criss-crossed and cloved in geometrical perfection, glazed—Sally couldn't tell how! Gelatin molds—sparkling clear, patterned in elaborate designs with truffles, with artichokes, with—heaven knew what! Spun sugar in fairy castles, all wrought with infinite patience, with skill and loving care. Every work of art—for such they were—bore a card with the chef's name, foreign every one. Italian, French, Viennese. Papini of the Ritz, Antoine of the Belmont—trained through years of apprenticeship and experience to be master craftsmen.

There was bread, there were rolls of every shape and twist, there was brioche—all so beautifully perfect. Here was a birthday cake and a collection of tiny confections for an elegant reception—exquisitely decorated in pink and blue and palest green—proud winner of a blue ribbon! They were the product of a food shop run by a women's exchange that had long been a pathfinder in developing and fostering handicraft among homemakers.

"The head of that institution graduated from my school and helped me get the job I have now," Clara offered. "I worked for her once in bygone days. She's what I call a whiz. A perfectionist, if there ever was one."

"And while you are talking, look at that woman over there," Lou whispered. "The one with the silver fox. She runs a hotel in Washington, D.C. that's a model for the country. One of my classmates is the dietitian there. And look, isn't that Mrs. Perry, head of that big chain of tearooms? The elect are abroad tonight, all right. 'Spose they were ever young and green like us? Great oaks from little acorns do grow, the book says, so keep your eyes on those two and do your best, girls." Lou giggled softly and bowed as before royalty.

Sally had wandered over to a table of elaborately molded desserts and stood lost in admiration before them.

"These people are real artists in their line, aren't they? Wonderfully clever with their fingers and with their brains. Takes both to make anything beautiful, I guess," she decided.

But her attention was caught by an interesting-looking

young woman coming toward them.

"Well, Babs!" she heard Clara's voice. "I haven't seen you in an age. Sally, come and meet Barbara Dutton. She's one of our ilk. State Department of Agriculture, no less. The apple growers and the big butter and egg men are her friends. One of them is usually trailing her, too, I hear. What are you booming now?"

"Trying to give the eggs a break," Barbara answered gaily. "Just finished a pamphlet on them you might like. 'How to Tell a Fresh Egg,' you know."

"Two legged or in the shell?" Lou inquired.

"Both—in this business!" Barbara grinned.

"I tried to tune in on your radio market report a couple of times last week but didn't find you. Aren't you giving them any more?" Clara asked. "I loved your snappy style and used the information, too."

"Oh, I'm on at 6:30 now."

"Not A. M., I hope."

"Certainly A. M."

"Heavenly day! Why so early?"

"Well, I've been doing the markets lately when the trucks come in, getting a line on fresh fruit and vegetable shipments from the South. And I stop at the studio on my way back. Mrs. Homemaker is just up. She listens while she gets the family breakfast."

"You and the early bird! Too ambitious for me, woman," Clara shook her head.

Sally pricked up her ears. "I got a great kick out of going to market the one and only time I did it. I'd love to go again!"

"Come with me some morning, if you can stand getting up way before daylight. I'd be delighted to have company.

How about next week? Call me at this number if you'd like to go. Good-bye, everybody!" And with a wave of her hand Barbara was off, as a well-dressed man appeared, heading toward her.

"My, he's a good-looking fellow! Butter and eggs or not, me for a job like that!" Lou's admiring glance followed the two figures.

"She earns all her fun, don't mistake that. And is she smart, too!" Clara said. "She covers the State, trying to get the farmers to process, pack and grade their produce better so they can sell for higher prices—the truck gardeners, the dairy men, the apple growers. She's the go-between and she *goes*. She tells them, too. And the funny part is they like it. What's more, she writes a weekly food bulletin on what and how and where to buy that's as clever as anything. But time for us to be getting along, Sally. 'Bye, Miss Davis."

"See you again soon, Lou." Sally waved and the girls gathered up their booklets—Jello, Forty Ways to Cook the Ham What Am, Magic Aluminum Cleaner, Fifty-Seven Varieties of this and that—and set out for home.

Those marvelous displays of food rose before Sally's eyes as she was getting ready for bed.

"Three meals a day. That's what it's all about, isn't it? And what a business it is!" she thought. "So often drudgery. And it could be *art* if we just knew how!"

CHAPTER IV

Hurdles

"YOU'VE a cold, haven't you?" Sally spoke with sympathetic concern, as Miss Kitury, looking heavy-eyed, sat down at her desk next morning.

"I have. Isn't it the luck! Struck draughts everywhere I went yesterday. Hot water and soda, and aspirin by the dozen, haven't had much effect to date, either. But no matter. You get over a cold if you're tough—and you'd better be that if you're hitched to this or any other *Star!*" Katherine Kitury wiped her eyes disgustedly. "Thank goodness I can still talk. If I so much as croaked over that radio this P. M., you'd be buried under letters and frantic with telephone calls suggesting honey and alum, hot lemonade, sage tea and the saints know what! But how was the luncheon yesterday?"

"Lovely!" Sally's face brightened with enthusiasm. "I wrote up my notes for you and wangled the dessert recipe. It came in the mail this morning." She handed over the coveted lemon torte. Lou's response had been swift and cordial.

"Good girl." Miss Kitury picked up the sheet in front of her and scanned it quickly.

"Now write it all up for the paper. Pick out the pertinent points. This and this," Miss Kitury's blue pencil went down the page. "Make it short and snappy. You are Mrs. So-and-So, talking to your neighbor over the back fence—or to your afternoon bridge crowd. Talk to 'em. Chatty, easy, alive!" She handed back the paper and turned to the pile of letters on her desk.

"Hope there's something usable in this batch," she thought wearily. "Got to have the goods in black and white this afternoon. No fancy ad libbing with my head the size it is today." She made notes automatically. Had she bothered to glance at her young assistant's face, she would have seen the consternation registered there. But she had not bothered.

Sally was stumped. Writing had not been on her schedule for a good while. "Snappy—alive—" Miss Kitury's words sounded in her ears. She stared at the page in her hand. *"Pine, red willow branches—hallway at home—molded cucumber ring cottage cheese salad—strawberry sherbet on fruit cup—green and pink and yellow—lemon torte— herb garden in spring"*—these were the words the blue pencil had underlined. "How could she make *them* come alive?" Sally thought dolefully. Suddenly she saw herself perched in Clara's room, telling her about everything with gusto. That was it! If she could forget she was putting the words on paper for anyone to *read*—just say them as she would to a friend. That was the idea! Her pencil hurried along.

"Not bad for a first try," Miss Kitury remarked, looking over the story sometime later. "But you've used the word 'grand' three times. I'd change that. How do you spell rhododendron? I think that second vowel should be an *o*, and if you use hallway as one word in the first paragraph, why the hyphen in the second? Either one is all right but be consistent. Best road out of that is to skip the second hall anyway. Say it differently. But the style isn't bad, rather light and informal. That's the spirit. Fix it up a bit now and leave it in my basket." Miss Kitury handed back the page and went on with her work.

"Spelling! I always get hung on it," Sally muttered, her face flaming.

"Don't let that worry you. All a matter of practice. Keep trying. Style is what counts. You might spell perfectly and be dull as dishwater. In which case nobody would read what you wrote or care whether you knew the alphabet, even!" Miss Kitury spoke encouragingly. "Of course the copy reader will catch your mistakes here, but learn to spell, just the same—if you want to be loved in a newspaper office," she added.

"By the way, I'm going to ask you to go to the studio with me this afternoon, if you will." Miss Kitury looked up a minute later. "I'll have some materials there I'd like you to bring back with you, so I can use them tomorrow morning. Think I'll go directly home from the broadcast and see if I can't dose up this cold." She fished a fresh tissue out of her purse. "It's hot lemonade and bed for me after all, I guess."

"I feel it in my bones that something's going wrong today." Sally stood her umbrella in a corner of the office next morning and took off her rubbers. It was cold and storming and the quarters of the *Star* looked dreary and almost deserted. A radiator hissed and a few typewriters clacked. Copy and rewrite men were hunched over their desks, tending strictly to business.

"Bad day for Miss Kitury's cold," Sally thought uneasily as she opened up her desk and began sorting the mail. Buzz went the telephone. A hoarse voice at the other end. Her heart sank.

"I won't be able to get down today," Miss Kitury croaked, "but I'll tell you just what to do. The copy for tomorrow's edition is in the top drawer of my desk. Give it to Andy. You'll have to write a paragraph for the Sunday page (you'll see where I left the blank) so he can have that this afternoon. The rest of it is all ready, but look it over. When Mike sends up the galleys, check the recipes carefully, won't you? Then use your luncheon write-up for the next morning's story. Sign your own name. Don't forget the day's menu. You know how it goes. Choose any four recipes you like but have some of them tie up with the menu. Get your copy in before noon. You can take care of that easily, I know."

"Yes, I'm sure I can," Sally answered. "I'll do my very best. Your cold is terrible, isn't it? Is there anything else I can do for you here?"

"Yes, you'll have to broadcast this afternoon."

"Oh, Miss Kitury, I never did it in my life!" Sally wailed, panic-stricken.

"Get several ideas and questions lined up," Miss Kitury went right on. "There's a batch of notes clipped together in a folder in the second drawer of my desk. Use them. Type them all in order—one, two, three—so you can read them. Get to the studio early and ask Jim Anderson—the announcer you met yesterday—to help you. I'll tell him you're coming. Have a lot of material, then just talk naturally and don't let it bother you a bit. Don't forget that you are talking to friends. Make it helpful and peppy. There's nothing to it. Come by here after you get through and tell me how you made out. You'll be all right now, so don't worry. Good-bye."

"I'll try. Good-bye." Sally hung up.

The Morning Star Presents Miss Kitury's Kitchen

Luscious Lemon Torte Offered, Garden Club Luncheon, Herbs for Spring

SALLY LEWIS BROADCASTS

(Monday through Friday at 1:30 P.M., over Stations LMNO; KLM; and JKL)

It seems early to be thinking about spring gardens, doesn't it? But the Longwood Garden Club is already making suggestions for herb gardens. We attended their luncheon at the Barbarole the other day and savory and thyme and sage were topics of conversation. Do plan to have a pot of chives on your window sill now—also parsley. They will do wonders in pepping up winter foods and then they can be set out in the garden when spring comes.

Jane Berry, who runs the Barbarole served an elegant lemon torte for dessert—with a baked meringue for crust that melted in your mouth. Try it on the family and then spring it on your bridge club. It will take tricks for you and win you praise.

Want something extra special to serve on gingerbread? Try this: Mix a three ounce package of cream cheese with three cups of confectioners sugar, a quarter of a cup of orange juice and one teaspoon of grated orange rind, until smooth. Beat with a fork until fluffy. Spread on gingerbread or spice cake.

Today's Menu

BREAKFAST
Orange Juice
Oat Meal
Bacon, Muffins
Coffee

LUNCH
*Scrambled Eggs
with chives
Hearts of Lettuce with
Roquefort Dressing
*Chocolate Nut Wafers
Tea

DINNER
Roast Lamb
*Orange and Currant Relish
Brown Potatoes
Baked Onions
*Lemon Torte
Coffee

*Recipe given

Speaking of gingerbread, did you know that the new "dromedary gingerbread mix" is made from one of the world's most famous recipes —the 200 year old "receipt" of George Washington's mother?

Another delicious twist for cream cheese is this: Mix chopped preserved ginger with it, plus a little milk or cream and a pinch of salt and make it into balls and fill centers of peach or pear halves for a salad—with French dressing.

LEMON TORTE
(Barbarole Club)

    4 Egg whites, beaten till
        frothy, add: pinch salt and
    ¼ t Cream of Tartar and
    1 C Sugar
Beat until glossy and stiff. Spread in greased tin. Bake one hour at 275 degrees and cool.

FILLING

    4 Egg yolks, beaten light, add
    ½ C of Sugar gradually
    3 T Lemon Juice and ½ T
        grated rind and pinch of salt.
Cook until thick over hot water, stirring all the time—cool.
    1 C Cream, whip and spread half over the crust. Cover with the filling and then a layer of cream. Let stand several hours. Sprinkle chopped toasted almonds on top.

CHOCOLATE NUT WAFERS
(Mrs. Jenks, Dorham, Maine)

    ½ C Shortening
    ½ t Salt
    1 t Vanilla
    1 C Sugar
    2 Eggs well beaten
    3 oz. Chocolate, melted
    ¾ C Sifted Flour
    ¾ C Nuts, chopped
Combine shortening, salt and vanilla. Add sugar gradually and cream well. Add beaten eggs and mix thoroughly. Add melted chocolate and blend. Drop by teaspoon on greased baking sheet. Spread with spoon dipped in hot water. Bake at 325 degrees 12–15 minutes, makes 2½ dozen.

CURRANT JELLY, GRATED ORANGE PEEL, AND CHOPPED FRESH MINT
(For Lamb)

    1 glass Currant Jelly
    1 Orange, Juice, and grated
        rind of half
    2 T Chopped fresh Mint
Break up jelly with a fork, add other ingredients and let stand over night. Good to serve with lamb.

SCRAMBLED EGGS WITH CHIVES

    4 Eggs
    1-3 C Milk
    1 T Chives, cut very fine
    Salt and Pepper
    2 T Butter or Bacon fat
Beat eggs slightly, add milk and seasoning, pour into hot frying pan in which butter or fat has been melted. Stir over low flame until set. May be cooked in double boiler over hot water for a more creamy consistency. Serves 3.

"I'm scared stiff," she said out loud, her mind fluttering helplessly. "I can do the paper work, but talking over the radio!" She stared blankly ahead, her heart in her shoes. She gathered herself together at last.

"What's there to it, anyhow? If I can't do this, I'm not much good, that's sure." A disgusted shake cleared her head a little and bit by bit things began to fall into line. After all, it might be fun. Why not? A slow grin spread over her face and an excited gleam crept into her eye. Her campaign unrolled before her.

She fished Miss Kitury's copy for the evening edition out of the desk and studied the layout carefully before taking it over to Andy. Dozens of times she had read that column without giving a thought to the technique of putting it together. THE MORNING STAR PRESENTS MISS KITURY'S KITCHEN—etc. etc.—head—sub-head—three or four words each—not over. What would Andy use for a lead? This, maybe? Too long. Dead. Andy's headings would catch the eye. She tried again and scratched it out. How about this? She swiftly penciled in a model, just to see how it might look.

Would her part of it pass? Have to. No time to try anything else. Sally found the recipes in the file, copied and numbered the pages in order, typed the menu and clipped everything together. So much for that. Now the bit for the Sunday page—and then those notes for the afternoon broadcast. She needed time for that. Alex's mother might be listening to that radio hour, she suddenly remembered! She must not fail.

How *could* any morning be so short when she was hurrying so fast?

"Am I close enough to the microphone, Mr. Anderson? Can people really hear me if I don't talk any louder than this?" Sally seated herself at the small table in the big bare studio at one-fifteen that afternoon.

"Sure. You're all right. Don't be worried. Nothing to it. Just pretend you're talking to some friend." Jim Anderson carelessly flipped a magazine, one eye on the indicator.

Sally watched the clock. Nearer and nearer came the minute hand. Why that green brocade all around the room?

Thank goodness there were no visitors today as there had been yesterday. Nearer—nearer. The little red light flicked —and they were on the air! Jim Anderson was talking. What *was* it she was going to say first? She swallowed. Her throat was parched— Oh, yes, here it was on the page. Now she remembered, but she couldn't seem to make a sound! Was that *her* voice at last, so thin and funny?

Katherine Kitury propped herself up on her pillow and turned on a bedside radio at her own hour. She didn't know when she had had to miss this before! She listened intently for the familiar signal. There it was!

"This half hour for busy homemakers," the announcer was speaking, "is sponsored by the morning and evening *Star,* and will be conducted for you today by Miss Sally Lewis, graduate of a well-known school of Home Economics in this city. Miss Lewis."

Miss Kitury sat up and held her breath.

"Thank you, Mr. Anderson," came a thin, far-away voice. Miss Kitury leaned nearer and turned up the dial. "You will be sorry, I know, to hear that Miss Kitury is out with a cold. ("Too mild for my feelings!" Kit Kitury groaned.) We are all hoping that she will be back with you on Monday. She asked me to talk to you for her." The voice came more clearly. ("Good girl," Miss Kitury whispered to herself.)

"Miss Berry, who runs the Barbarole dining room, served the most delectable lemon torte for a Garden Club luncheon the other day. We thought you might like to have the recipe, so I begged it for you. This is it:

"For the crust you make a meringue of four egg whites, beaten with a pinch of salt till frothy, then add slowly a quarter of a teaspoon of cream of tartar and one cup of granulated sugar, beating till stiff and glossy. Spread this in a greased pie tin and bake at 275° for one hour and cool. Then for the filling you beat the four egg yolks till light, add a half cup of sugar gradually, three tablespoons of lemon juice, a half teaspoon of grated rind, a pinch of salt, and cook till thick over hot water. Don't forget to stir all the time. When crust and filling are cool, beat one cup of cream. Spread half of it on the crust, then the filling and top with the remaining cream. Let it stand in the refrigerator for six or eight hours. Sprinkle chopped toasted almonds on top. You can make it the day before. It is really delicious. If any of you missed any part of this, you will find it printed in the morning *Star*.

"While we are on the topic of pie, Mrs. Glazier of Wharton sent in a nice variation of crumb crust." There was a pause—("Go on, girl! Suppose she has lost her place? Don't stop!" Katherine Kitury gripped her atomizer hard—then relaxed as the voice went on at last.) "Here it is! Roll four cups of corn flakes fine and mix with four tablespoons of melted butter and four tablespoons of sugar. Pat into pie tin and cool in icebox till set.

"French fried potatoes that stay really crisp seem to be a common problem, judging from many letters. In college we were taught to 'blanch' them first. That is, partially cook in fat not too hot. Drain and later, just before serving, fry again for a minute or two until brown. Drain on absorbent paper. Sprinkle with salt. This is the method followed in first-class tearooms and restaurants. It really works, you see.

"Try cooking beets this way. It beats the old slow method a mile! Peel the beets just as you do potatoes. Slice them thin and cook, tightly covered, with ½ cup water—no more. They will be done in half an hour or less! Serve with butter. We saw this trick tried and proved at the Edison Light Cooking School the other day. It's the discovery of the week! That, and using raw spinach and sliced raw cauliflower in your salad bowl. Have you tried them?

"Miss Kitury would like to know if any of you can send her directions for making Anadama Bread? It is an old New England recipe.

"Also a lady on the Cape wants the recipe for Duchess Soup.

"Send your answers to Miss Kitury's Kitchen, office of the *Star*, or in care of the Beacon Network. Good-bye."

"Good work, Sally Lewis!" Miss Kitury slumped back on her pillow, suddenly limp. "Now that was a hard job for a novice. I came nearer cracking myself the first time I tried," Miss Kitury said to herself. "Thought she was a goner once there, but she carried it off pretty well. At least I couldn't hear her knees knocking together as mine used to do!"

Miss Sally Lewis, young sub and late pinch hitter for her boss, Kit Kitury, homemaking editor of the morning and evening *Star*, rang the latter's doorbell with mingled hope and trepidation. The dreaded broadcast was over—thank heaven for that! But she still had to hear the verdict from the judge and jury. If she hadn't spoiled everything by that fumble! "You *would* do a trick like that," she scolded herself for the umteenth time, as she listened for the click that released the latch. She found Miss Kitury propped up in bed, and her eye spotted the radio at once. It was flanked by an array of medicine bottles on the bedside table. She hoped the verdict wouldn't be too bad.

"Come in, Miss Lewis. Sit over there where you won't catch this bug that has laid me low. I've a dozen questions to ask, but first let me say that I think you did well this afternoon. Your voice was rather faint at first and just once I was afraid you were going to come a cropper, but you recovered yourself and saved the day. Good girl!"

Sally flushed. "Wasn't that awful?" she exclaimed ruefully. "I just looked up from my paper for a quarter of a second and lost my place! Did it seem too terribly long? I've known hours to go by faster than those minutes did!"

"I was worried for a bit because I recognized the signs, but other people probably thought nothing at all of it. You covered the break easily and with poise. That's what does the trick. You can get away with most anything if you only keep from getting fussed or rattled. Next time you won't mind half as much." Miss Kitury reached under her pillow for a handkerchief. "I'll be in Monday, but at the rate I'm going now I'll probably still have this croak, so you had better plan to broadcast again that afternoon. Good practice for you." She smiled. "I'll have to be in shape to speak at a Woman's Club on Thursday and before that Food Managers Conference on Friday.

"Now tomorrow morning you'll have to get the galleys for the evening edition back downstairs to Mike right away. You ran a couple of extra recipes instead of the write-up, didn't you? I often do that for the evening paper—or make a few comments sometimes. Then there's everything to do for Monday—both morning and evening editions. Anything interesting on hand?"

Miss Kitury glanced through the letters that Sally had brought her. "Let's see what your predecessor, Connie Con-

nors, has to say first. She's down in Charleston, South Carolina, according to this postmark." She scanned the page.
"Here, this is just what you need. A recipe for spoon bread
and how to eat it! What could be neater?" She handed over
the letter. "Why don't you go on home now? Have a good
rest. Then tomorrow you can run things off in no time.
Hand me the camphor there before you go, like a good girl.
Thanks a lot for pinch-hitting. See you Monday. Good-bye
—and thanks again."

Sally all but gave a shout of relief as she found herself in
the front hall. Well, the day was over and she was still
alive! Very much so in fact, she suddenly decided, and she
gave her hat a pull over one eye. An hour ago she had been
weak and weary and all in, and now she felt light and airy
and almost gay. All because of a few kind words from the
boss! If she could only talk to Alex now—but—he hadn't
written. Maybe he wouldn't care—maybe— She pushed
the thought away, and headed for home. Perhaps some of
the secretaries would be around and she could inveigle one
or two into going to the theater or the movies with her. She
must do something frivolous after that day of stress and
strain and near disaster.

The Y seemed pretty well deserted when she entered.
Too early yet, probably. "Any of the staff around, Mandy?"
she asked the colored girl at the hall desk.

"No'm. Not much. Mostly they's out. You'se got mail,
Miss Lewis," and she handed out a couple of letters.

"Thank you, Mandy." Sally's quick eye searched anxiously for Alex's familiar scrawl. It was not there. A note
from Judy. The other? No writing she'd ever seen before—
looked like a man's. But it wasn't Alex's and she wasn't interested. She felt suddenly tired, her brief elation gone.

"Might as well see what Judy has to say," and she sat down on the hall settee.

Dear Sally,

Just a line to tell you that a young chap, one **Art Gregory** by name—Greg to all and sundry—will be in or near your city this winter, entering an uncle's business, I believe. Bill and I have known him here in San Francisco very well and like him a lot. He's a wild Westerner. Put himself through college like the rest of us. He's long and lean and lanky, has red hair and a bushel of freckles—but he's fun and has what it takes! We've told him to be sure to look you up. He left a week or so ago. You'll be hearing from him soon, I think. Show him a good time and have one yourself! Bill and I are fine. I do so hope things are going better for you by now.

Love,
Judy

Maybe this was the letter that she held in her hand! Sally tore open the envelope and read:

My dear Miss Lewis,

I promised your friends, the Martins of San Francisco, to get in touch with you when I arrived in the East. I expect to be in the city over the week end. May I call you up when I get in on Friday, around 5:30? Perhaps you would go to dinner or to a show or something.

Sincerely,
Art Gregory

There. Maybe the Lord *was* providing again. He had before, in days gone by. Inscrutable as to the method? Verily, yes. You might occasionally grow tired of waiting on Him, but something worth waiting for usually did turn up at last, she had to admit! Here was this something—with red hair. Sally sat holding the letter, a far-away look in her eyes. Why hadn't Alex written? But she shoved that miserable and persistent fear way down cellar this time and banged the door shut! "He doesn't have to write if he doesn't want to! I can get along." She tossed her head in sudden determination.

"Mandy, I'm expecting a phone call about 5:30. Buzz my bell long and loud and don't forget to wait, will you?" she called from half way down the hall, a note of excitement in her voice.

"Yassum. He'll wait, don' yo' worry." Mandy rolled her eyes and grinned.

"He! How can she tell? Cute darky—if fresh!" And Sally grinned a bit herself as she pushed the elevator button.

CHAPTER V

A Night Out

"MR. GREGORY?" Sally, waiting under the station clock later that evening, stepped forward to greet a tall chap coming toward her. She had offered to meet him there rather than at the Y, knowing he was not familiar with the city. Saved time besides.

"Right. You must be Sally Lewis. Judy said you were pint-size and I spotted the blue feather in the hat you said you'd be wearing. It was mighty nice of you to meet me. I didn't hope for such good luck." His eye flashed an approving glance at her trim outfit as he shook her outstretched hand. "The Martins know how to pick their friends it would seem."

"Yes, so it *would* seem." Sally twinkled up at the pleasant face far above her. "They're old pals of mine. We all went through college together. Did you have a good trip East?"

"Swell, but now let's go somewhere and eat. I'm all for food and the bright lights. Where shall we go? I don't know this town, so you be the guide. None of these calorie-counters nor bite-bars, mind you!"

Sally stole a look from the corner of her eye. There was a sort of gay and insolent cock to his hat, nor had she been mistaken about that glint in his eye. It was there. "He'll do," she said to herself. She was tired of being a forlorn widow— hay, straw or grass! He'd do.

"Like foreign food?" she asked tentatively. "The Russian Bear is right near here somewhere. I'd love to go there. It's quite famous. I understand they have a good balalaika orchestra. How about that?"

"Fine. Try anything once is my motto. Do they eat in Russian, too? We'll starve, unless you know the lingo."

"I don't, but we can point. 'This, that.' The food is really good, I hear. Do you like funny foreign things?"

"Funny queer, or funny ha-ha?"

"I meant queer, but these may be both!"

They set out gaily. Down one street and up another. Where the shops were small and the names long and foreign, they came to a flight of brownstone steps leading up to a lighted doorway, over which hung the flag of old Russia.

"This must be the place." Sally turned Gregory toward the stairs and they started up. A fair-haired young woman in peasant costume opened the door and ushered them to a table in a corner facing the orchestra. Four or five men dressed in silk and satin blouses of red and green sat on a small raised platform in front of them. Bright bands of embroidery on collar, cuffs and belt gave interest and finish to their costumes. Their instruments were like nothing in American orchestras, that was sure—except perhaps the big fiddle. That long-necked, three-cornered, banjo-like affair was the balalaika, Sally knew. And there was an odd-shaped steel guitar and a very long stringed mandolin—as near as she could describe them. Perhaps the musicians were exiles. They seemed very serious and sort of sad. She could wax really sentimental over that leader in the bright blue blouse. And the waiters! Young and silk-shirted all, they lent an air of romance, of foreign mystery to the dimly-lit, smoke-grimed room. Bare tables, bare benches against the walls. Sally gazed with interest at the murals about the room.

Strong colors gleamed in the dull light. Here was the atmosphere, certainly.

"Hope we draw that handsome Cossack with the bright red shirt," she whispered as they sat down. "He could be the prince of the Romanoffs himself. Look!"

"You gals are all alike. Prince! What'll you bet he comes from Podunk?" Gregory grinned. He pulled out Sally's chair and seated her, settled himself and looked over the menu handed them by a waiter. It was not the scarlet prince. He was already busy with other guests.

"Let's have dinner No. 2. I have heard of *some* of those things. I hope you'll like them. Take a chance?" Sally pointed down the card. (If it were only Alex now! He loved everything odd and different.)

"All right, Miss Lewis. Never been stumped by anything yet, except pickled tripe. So tell Johnny there to do his worst. Hope he doesn't operate on any five-year plan. I'm hungry."

The orders placed, they sat back and looked about. The room was filling fast. Well-dressed Americans, if you please. Not a foreign face in the crowd!

"Artists, writers and all that ilk come here a lot, I think. It has sort of a Bohemian air, hasn't it?" Sally offered. Just then the orchestra began to play and everyone stopped eating to listen.

"That was worth the price of admission." Greg clapped heartily. "Funny looking instruments, but I certainly like what they do with them. Balalaika, eh? Bet those fellows are thankful they aren't back in the old country right now, but it must be sort of tough not to be able to stay there if they want to."

Their dinner arrived at this point and interest centered on the food in front of them. Small plates of *hors d'oeuvres* started the procession. There was pink caviar on slices of hard-cooked egg that Greg eyed with a comical grin. There were pickled herring and dressed red cabbage to eat with black bread—moist and dark and sourish tasting. Sort of

good, all of it. It really was. Then there was *borsch*—a red
vegetable soup, made with beets and cabbage and served
with sour cream. Greg went at it manfully and Sally cheered
him on till they were laughing like old friends. Next came
shasklik—cubes of lamb arranged on skewers, dipped in oil,
seasoned and broiled. They were delicious—served with
green onion tops cut in half-inch lengths, and sliced tomatoes. Glasses of hot tea with lemon were filled and refilled
and black bread came and disappeared, amid comments from
Gregory that set Sally off in a gale of giggles. For months
she hadn't laughed like this.

They lingered long over the dessert. The orchestra played
again and again, and finally, after repeated requests, the
prince of the red blouse put down his tray and sang the
Volga Boat Song from the floor. There was quiet and repose
and relaxation—the fragrance of scented cigarettes. Sally
forgot that she had had a hard day. Forgot for the moment
that Alex was not there.

"Well, that was all right for once—far as it went. Makes
you appreciate the kind that Mother makes." Greg took
Sally's arm as they finally meandered up the street. "I sort
of liked it though at that, especially the music. But now let's
go where there's honest-to-John American jazz. I'd like to
dance to a good swing band till the roosters crow for day!
How about it?"

"I could do with a real fling, myself," Sally agreed.

"Okay. Where to?"

"The Rainbow Roof?" Sally had heard the girls talk
about going there and took a flying jump.

"The name has promise. What's holding us back? Let's
go!"

And away they went.

"What are you doing away off here so far from the Golden Gate?" Greg looked over at Sally as they rested between dances, sipping their cool drinks at a table far up over the city's twinkling lights.

"Trying to lead homemakers to the truth by the light of the *Star*," Sally flashed. For a minute she had forgotten what her job was and that morning and work were just around the corner.

"What about you?"

"Starting in my uncle's factory, and if you'll believe it, he makes electrical household equipment. Funny, isn't it? Say, you could tell your ladies the wonders of the Speedy Mixer. That's an idea! 'Cake done in a flash; biscuits made with a dash; hubby parts with the cash'—you know the line. Or 'Wife wins waning love with Speedy Mixer.' How's that?"

"Or Speedy Mixer makes the dough fly?" offered Sally.

"Say, we're good, aren't we?" Greg laughed. "But, come on, let's have one more spin before they lock up here." And he whirled her out onto the floor.

"Don't tell me it's past one o'clock!" Sally exclaimed in dismay, as they passed the big street clock on the way home. "Respectable 'woiking goils' get home before *this* hour." She giggled.

"Do you mind?" Gregory looked down at her quickly. "Not me."

"Atta-girl. What about tomorrow night then—tonight it is now. Let's go to a show. What do you say? Is it a date?"

"It's a date."

What was that? Not the alarm surely? Where was she? The Rainbow—? No, these were her feet in her narrow bed at the Y. Oo-o-o. It was Saturday morning—Miss Kitury was out sick—she'd be alone at the office—she had such a lot to do— Sally stretched and rubbed her eyes. Gay night life was wonderful. She *had* had a good time! But getting up next morning was something else again. And Miss Sally groaned as she swung her feet to the floor.

Walking to the office in the chill morning air, however, brought her fully awake. She was still pleasurably excited over her night out. Getting in at such an hour! She grinned to herself as she sat down before her desk at the office, as she hitched a heel over the round of her chair and prepared to settle down to business.

"Read proof for Sunday's page; call Andy; recipes and 'story' for Monday—" She mentally checked the morning's duties. "You know it's going to be sort of fun being responsible for the whole show—pulling the strings for this and that," she thought to herself.

Anyhow, the worst was surely over by now. At least she had jumped that radio hurdle without barking her shins *too* badly, she remembered. Nothing could scare her much more than that had. But now the next thing was to see whether she could really swing a job like this, all by herself, if she had to.

Miss Kitury had caught and held the interest of women throughout the country. She had established a real spirit of friendly co-operation, of mutual helpfulness among home-makers who read her column and listened to her programs. Could she, Sally, be of such service to them? Could she stir up such enthusiasm for their endless round of three meals a day? For darning, dusting and doing dishes, for cleaning house and cooking for company? For mending Junior's trousers and putting on and taking off Sister's coat and rubbers—world without end? Could she make them see *why* it was worth while? Her mother had done these things for many years, all to make a home for her family. That was the answer! To make a *home*. Not just to get the meals. Not just to keep the house, but to make a *home*.

Part of an old familiar verse ran through her mind:

> One rubber plant can never make a home
> One day did not suffice for building Rome.
> One gas log and a cat
> Can't civilize a flat,
> No! Something more is needed for a home.

And so it was. That "something more" should be the province of this column. It should shine in this realm of the "plus values," the *fine* points of homemaking. Wheels could be greased to turn more smoothly. Meals helped to be made gay as well as good—variety and vitamins and color and taste. And what about the setting of the stage? Furniture, curtains, carpets to be assembled into charm and comfort for all? *There* was a real task, calling for fine judgment and skill, for cleverness and ingenuity if your budget were small —and whose wasn't? These were the spots where a home-makers' column should give real help.

"And heaven will need to help *me*, I can see that!" Miss Sally concluded as she sorted the morning mail.

Culling items of interest for her "story," she laid the letters out in front of her. Materials finally assembled, she wrote busily, picking here and there:

"Miss Constance Connors, whom you know through this column, writes from Charleston, South Carolina, where she is recovering her health and incidentally gathering data on Southern cookery, that she hopes you will all have fried ham with cream gravy and spoon bread soon. It is a real

Southern treat. She sent the recipe, which we pass on to you. Do try it.*

"While in Virginia she also discovered that George Washington's favorite breakfast dish was a thick mush of corn meal, water, salt and butter, dropped in little thin cakes on a hot griddle. If he had hot maple syrup and fresh country sausage to eat with it, no wonder he liked it!

"Someone wants to know how to freshen cocoanut that has grown dry and tasteless. We tried pouring a little hot water over it with excellent results.

"A good friend from Hilton passes on these ideas, picked up at the Grange last week:

1. The scheme of having a basket for all cleaning materials—ammonia, furniture polish, soap, detergent, dust and cleaning cloths, iodine for scratches on furniture, etc. Saves many trips to the kitchen if all these articles are kept together and carried about, from place to place. Good idea, isn't it?

2. Equal parts of turpentine, linseed oil and vinegar make a good cleanser and polish for varnished surfaces.

"Fresh pineapple will soon be in season. Do you know the easiest way to prepare it? This is the way it is done in Honolulu, where it grows biggest and best." And Sally, seeing again in her mind the old loved kitchen at Haiilani School, proceeded to give careful directions for fixing pineapple as she had seen her Chinese servants do it times without number.

"Chilled, cubed fresh pineapple, with date icebox cookies like the ones made from the recipe sent in by Mrs. Hope,† is a tophole dessert for summer. Add chopped fresh mint

---

* See SALLY'S NOTEBOOK, page 253.
† Look in the back of the book! Page 253.

from your garden and you have a delicious cocktail!

"Miss Kitury asked me to thank the good ladies who sent the recipe for Duchess Soup and for Anadama Bread. Here they are:

"This is the Duchess Soup. Miss Frances Little says she cooks two tablespoons of instant tapioca in four cups of milk with a teaspoon of grated onion until the tapioca is clear. Then she adds a couple of tablespoons of butter and a half cup of grated cheese. She stirs in a couple of spoons of chopped parsley. It's really delicious. I tried it.

"Here is the Anadama Bread. I will copy it as sent. Hope you will clip it out for your scrapbooks, because it sounds quite unusual.

Anadama Bread (An old New England recipe)

½ c Corn Meal (Yellow)
½ c Boiling Water
2 Tablespoons Melted Shortening
½ c Warm Water

½ c Molasses
1 Tablespoon Salt
2 Yeast Cakes
2½–3 Quarts Flour

Stir corn meal into boiling water, cook for a minute and cool, add shortening, molasses, salt and yeast cakes dissolved in the warm water. Stir in the flour to make a stiff dough. Let rise to double in bulk. Form into loaves. Let rise again to twice the original size and bake in moderate oven. 3 loaves.

"The story goes that a certain henpecked Down-Easter used always to refer to his wife as 'Anna, damn'er.' She made this kind of bread. It still bears her pet name, Ana-dama!"

So much for Monday's column. It was almost eleven, only an hour left for all those letters stacked on the desk! Sally wanted so much to get away early, as she tried always to do on Saturday afternoons. But she would have to fly if she were to leave the office at the usual time today. And fly she did. Wasn't she stepping forth again that night with the gay Lochinvar from the West?

For Miss Sally was sitting in solitude no more.

CHAPTER VI

A Home Missionary

MISS KITURY was back in the office on Monday, feeling shaky and none too fit.

"I don't know when I've gone under like this, just for what seemed like an ordinary cold. I'm disgusted, to say the least," she complained to Sally as she opened her desk. "The doctor says I can stay only a few hours any morning this week and no speech making before Friday, which means that I've got to call Mrs. Baxter of that Woman's Club in Allton and cancel my engagement for Thursday." She reached for the telephone, gave the number, and told her story.

"Oh, I *am* sorry," came the voice at the other end. Katherine Kitury could feel the disappointment, could see consternation register itself on Mrs. Baxter's face.

"I can't think just what I can do," came the worried voice. "The notices have all gone out—you haven't anyone there you could possibly send in your place, have you?"

Kate Kitury took a running jump. "My assistant here, Miss Sally Lewis, could do it, if that would help you. She's a capable young woman. You'll like her, I think. You'll meet her at the station, you say? Very well, she'll be there. I'm very sorry to disappoint you, but you'll be pleased with Miss Lewis. Good-bye."

Sally, wide-eyed and flabbergasted, swung around in her chair.

"Why, Miss Kitury, I couldn't take your place! The only

time in my life I ever made a speech I nearly had heart failure and forgot everything I planned to say! I—I—" she stammered.

"Now I'll help you. You can't learn younger. I've never talked before this particular club but I am sure there's nothing formal about it. They'll probably want to know about any new housekeeping tricks that have come to light. Ideas that will give them a little inspiration. They may want to know about this kind of Home Economics work as a possible profession for their daughters and so on. You know plenty about all that. Use your own experience. Use mine. Feel that you are there to help them and forget about yourself. Also, remember that you are helping me—a lot. I'll jot down a few points that may give you a start."

Sally shook her head in futile protest.

"Now let's see how you can organize this thing." Miss Kitury's pencil hovered over the paper. "First you could give them a little pep talk on the very great importance of their jobs. The home really is the foundation of the whole country. That's been said hundreds of times, to be sure, but they still don't realize it. That's where everyone starts, rich or poor or in-between. If the start is good, the climb is half over. If poor—and money hasn't everything to do with it by any means—that handicap has to be overcome before any real beginning can be made. All right. Now what can they do to make sure their homes are *good* starting points?

"Number one: Everybody's house can be clean and orderly. Soap and water are cheap. Even the simplest place will be attractive if it *looks* clean. Shining windows. Polished floors. That's bed rock.

"Then I'd talk to them about becoming kitchen conscious. Are their kitchens drab and dull, or bright and

cheery? Are they small, compact and convenient—streamlined—or rambling, unorganized, time and energy wasting?
Have they fresh pretty curtains or just dingy shades? Are
their kitchens hard to keep clean? Don't forget that Valspar
idea that somebody sent in, for their shelves and tables—
three or four coats. Then tell them about tacking pretty
oilcloth onto their old shade rollers and having plain ruffled
curtains to go with them. Encourage them to paint their
old dark woodwork. Where there's a will, there's a way.
A pretty kitchen will do wonders for the whole family. So
much for that. You could talk for an hour on that topic
alone.

"Then, of course, you come to the subject of food. Anybody can become a good cook if she just makes up her mind to do it. Cook books never were so attractive, so good, nor so easy to follow. Nothing is much more important than well-cooked food, no matter how simple. Give them names of a few of the best new cook books, and then give them some of your pet recipes. They'll be thrilled with them.

"That one of the lemon pie where the filling is made with condensed milk is a good one.

"One day, a week or so ago, when I was talking somewhere, I gave the ladies that recipe for Russian Sauce and it made a wonderful hit. I can scribble it down here for you from memory:

> 3 egg yolks—beat till lemon colored
> Add 1⅔ cup sugar and beat again
> Add ⅓ cup orange juice
> 2 t grated orange rind.

Cook over hot water, stirring constantly. It will be fairly thick, like heavy cream. Set it in the icebox till cold. Beat ½ pint cream stiff and then beat in the orange mixture. If your women are lucky enough to have electric mixers—well, they are lucky indeed, that's all!" ("Here's where Greg's Speedy Mixer makes a bow," thought Sally.)

"This elegant 'goo' served over wedges of angel or sponge cake and sprinkled with moist shredded cocoanut or with toasted, shredded almonds, is really something.

"You'll have a lot of your own recipes just as good, I know. Then, if you have time, tell them some short cuts for doing familiar things—or some bright ideas, like using orange shells, after squeezing out the juice for breakfast, to serve jello or cornstarch pudding or fruit cup in—and so on.

"But, mercy, I don't need to be telling you all this. You can think of a dozen just as good. These may help you to get under way. So much for that.

"And now we must see about our work here. You concoct your radio script for this afternoon so I can check it over for you and I'll do tomorrow's story before I leave," and Miss Kitury opened up her machine.

Thursday came, as days have a way of doing, particularly the ones you least want to see. Sally had hoped that Miss Kitury would surely be able to do the broadcast by that afternoon, but no luck. So she had that job to do again, still a real worry, even after several trials.

"It takes *so* much material to keep going for a half hour," she wailed, remembering how near she had come to panic the day before when she had run out of everything five minutes ahead of time. Not able to think of one word to say, she had motioned frantically to Jim Anderson to take over the mike. "I'm *done!*" She shaped the words with her lips, dismay and entreaty in her eyes. With a comical cock of his eye at the clock and back at her, he came to the rescue: "What about that pumpkin pie recipe, Miss Lewis, that you promised you'd bring for my wife? What was it that made it extra good, did you say?" He pulled Sally back to the mike. "Tell them," he motioned. She caught the life line thankfully. The audience might think this all part of the act but they had another guess coming this time!

"Oh, that *is* a nice variation of pumpkin pie. You'll like it, too. You put bits of preserved ginger into whipped cream and serve it on top. I'll bring you the full recipe tomorrow, if you'd like it. Good-bye, now," and Sally, winding up with a flourish, slumped back in her chair as the light flicked off!

"Thank you a hundred times for saving my life, Mr. Anderson!" she had exclaimed gratefully. "I was scared and I couldn't think of a thing to say. Wouldn't I have been in a jam if you hadn't helped!"

"Think nothing of it." He waved her appreciation aside with a grin. "Bigger and older ones than you get stuck every once in a while. Don't take it so seriously. Loosen up a little. Have a good time, then you won't get scared. If you run out of dope, you can ad lib a little—sounds more natural. People like it. Miss Kitury still sick? Well, take it easy tomorrow. You'll get there all right," and he was off.

"The good scout!" Sally recalled gratefully now, as she piled letters in front of her from which to pick her material. "Bet I'll have enough 'fillers' this time or know why!" She bent over her job, going at top speed. "It would be just my luck to run *overtime* today with all this. Get cut off in the middle of a sentence. That would help things along, wouldn't it!" she thought as she gathered up her notes, numbered the pages carefully, and laid them in a folder.

She had worn her best afternoon dress and her newest shoes that morning, knowing there would be no opportunity to change, before she went to Allton. She made a swift foray now to freshen up and tidy her hair. Lunch at the corner drugstore would leave fifteen minutes or so to rest and quiet down before she must hunt Jerry's taxi that would be waiting near the side door of the *Star* building at 1:10. He had been driving Miss Kitury for years.

"Okay, Miss. Right on time today, I see." He touched his cap as Sally came round the corner. "Miss Kitury still out?" he inquired as he shut the car door.

"She'll be back tomorrow or next day I think, thank you," Sally answered. "I *hope!*" she added to herself as she leaned back.

But the broadcast went much better this time. She had planned carefully. She felt much more self-confident than on any afternoon so far, as she seated herself before the microphone. Being thoroughly prepared, she could take things more calmly—keep an eye on the clock and still not lose the thread—and she came out to the minute!

"There. See what I told you?" Jim Anderson said as the little red light winked out on the tick of two o'clock. "Nothing to it if you just take it easy. The *important* thing is to have something *worth saying*. The rest is A B C. Nothing to it."

But Sally was already half way across the room. She turned at the door of the studio, waved good-bye with a grin and was gone. She rushed to hail a passing cab that would take her to the train for Allton, fortunately a nearby suburb. High gear and fifty miles an hour was the only speed for a day like this, if you expected to make all connections. If she mixed her radio notes with her speech to the club women it would be small wonder, but she hoped and trusted the ladies had all been too busy to listen to any radio program that afternoon so would not know the difference. She hustled through the station gates just in time.

"Heavens, that was a close shave!" she panted, as she made for a seat on the train. "I don't know if I'm all in one piece or not." She relaxed into a corner, thankful for a few minutes to rest and collect her wits. She took out her speech and read over the headings, trying to visualize the points under each, and before she knew it, hers was the next station. Well, here was where she tried herself out on a new and different trick, apparently one that had to be mastered early, if you were to go far as a public figure in the food business. In fact, a good course in public speaking would have been elegant preparation for this present crisis, Sally realized now. It would have saved a lot of grief—besides affording her pleasure all her life long and unending opportunities for community service, as she was to learn in years to come.

She gathered up her bag and belongings, stepped off the train, and looked about. Cars, taxis and station wagons lined up at the curb gathered in their passengers and departed.

Sally eyed each person but nobody looked very likely. Had she made a mistake in the time? Three o'clock the notice said.

"Oh, here comes somebody." A car swung round the circle and a woman got out hurriedly and looked about in worried fashion. Spying Sally, she came hopefully toward her.

"Are you Miss Lewis, I wonder?"

"Yes, I am. You must be Mrs. Baxter."

"I'm *so* relieved. I was late and so afraid you might think I wasn't coming or something. We had unexpected guests for lunch—relatives of my husband from up in Vermont. I'd have been delighted to see them any other time, but they *would* have to come today! Both my youngsters have bad colds, too, just to add a finishing touch. Some days are like that, though, aren't they? You wouldn't know, of course," she smiled at Sally's young face, "but you will. Get in, my dear." She held open the car door.

Sally hopped in, thinking to herself, "Here I've been dreading and stewing about this afternoon, and this good lady has been tearing around, all upset and worried over it on this end of the line. Silly, isn't it?"

"I know just how you feel," she said aloud, trying to put Mrs. Baxter at ease, "but don't be troubled on my account. It doesn't matter a bit. Why don't you go on back to your family as soon as you drop me where I'm to go? Too bad to spoil their visit when they have come so far."

"Well, I've invited them to go to the meeting. They'll enjoy it, then we can visit after we get back." Mrs. Baxter's face lightened and the worried look gradually faded out. But Sally wondered how *she* would have managed. To make perhaps touchy in-laws feel welcome without upsetting everyone's plans would take real tact, graciousness and presence of mind. Mercy, yes! "To be sure, I wouldn't know, but there again *maybe* I will!" thought she. "Though from the way things look at present writing, maybe I *won't*."

Now this was a situation that neither the cook books nor Miss Kitury's Kitchen had said anything about. Social ease and poise—what was that word—aplomb, was that the one? —seem never to be taught anywhere, Sally mused as they drove along. You have it by intuition maybe, or you get it any way you can—or not at all! And how you do need it, she thought wistfully.

Listening to Mrs. Baxter's troubles, Sally almost forgot about her own and by the time they reached the house where the meeting was to be held she was surprised at her ease of mind. But her respite was not for long! One look at the parlor as she entered showed it filled with women— many as old as her own mother, well-dressed, well-educated all. Elegant and sophisticated they seemed to simple Sally. "Two maids apiece and two cars in every garage, I'll bet!" she thought. Her heart sank as Mrs. Baxter introduced her to the hostess and hurried away.

They would think she had colossal nerve! She, a mere slip—no older than their own daughters—coming out here, presuming to give advice from her bottom rung of the ladder to any such gathering of the town's elect! That patter in her speech about the importance of the home! Her cheeks burned at the thought. She'd have to skip that, but how? So busy was she trying to rearrange things that she listened with only half an ear to her hostess. What she herself answered she hadn't the faintest idea!

But Madam President was calling the meeting to order and Sally was being presented. Her knees felt weak as water in spite of all her efforts at self-control. She knew that she looked young and inexperienced and very unimportant. Her voice sounded scared as she acknowledged the introduction. She *was* scared. She knew right then that she would have to go through with her speech word for word as planned or she would be utterly lost. Nabobs or not, they would just have to listen and like it! Anyhow, they all had kitchens, she guessed. They all had to eat—moreover, most of them looked as if they *had*. Plenty! She would just have to forget about Mrs. High-Hat on her right and the Oxford glasses on her left and talk to that young woman with the tired face. She didn't look as if she had two maids or that taking care of a home was any such picnic! Perhaps after all she, Sally, did have something to give that some of them might want—ideas that other women had found helpful, and gradually she forgot about herself and the words came more easily. She even remembered—believe it or not—to say a word for her new friend, the Speedy Mixer! Such a useful gadget for the home!

There were a *few* questions at the end to break the chilly spell. Sally welcomed any show of interest but shook in her shoes for fear she wouldn't know the answers. Nor did she.

Had Miss Lewis found casein paint satisfactory, and what did she think about that new glass cloth for draperies? Miss Lewis hadn't the remotest idea! They were very interesting materials, weren't they? Had any of the ladies tried them out, she countered, skating swiftly over the thin ice (so very thin), hoping by much enthusiasm to cover much ignorance! Glass cloth and casein paint! And just *what* were they, pray tell?

When tea was served the lady with the tired face did come up to thank her.

"You know my kitchen is a doleful dump. It annoys me every day. I've a mind to go home and see what I can do. What was the name of that paint?" The wistful look in her eyes changed to the light of battle. Sally could have hugged her. Perhaps she had made *one* hit, after all. She should worry about those frosty dowagers! And Miss Lewis chalked up *two* scores for her afternoon—a long one to experience, a very little one to service.

But she heaved a sigh of relief when she was at last on board the train for home. If she had helped Miss Kitury, she was certainly glad. If she had hauled kind Mrs. Baxter out of a hole, she was glad for that, too—and for any small lift to the tired lady. But as for the rest, "Anybody can be a home missionary to the elect that wants to—and welcome!" And Miss Sally crumpled into her seat, tuckered out!

CHAPTER VII

The Spinning Wheel and the Speedy Mixer

"LOU, you wouldn't by any wild chance be off tonight, would you?" Sally was sitting at the office telephone, some days later. She flirted the leaves of her desk calendar as she talked. ("Mercy, I didn't realize Christmas was so near!" She noted the date with a start.)

"You *are* off? Hooray! Look, go with me to the Old Spinning Wheel for supper, will you? Sort of a busman's holiday, I know, but Miss Kitury asked me to report on it for her. She wants some data for the radio. She suggested that I ask a friend. It's on the house! I hear that it's a darling place. We can go to the movies afterward. There's a good picture on at the new theatre, I noticed. How about it? Slick. Meet me at the tearoom at six, then? See you later. 'Bye!"

That was good luck for short-order planning, Sally congratulated herself. She copied the last recipe card—How to Make Meringue Shells, Three Steps to Success—filed it in the cabinet behind the desk and grabbed her hat and coat. She was leaving the office early in order to get back to her room before going out to supper.

"A man tel-foned yo' two times, Miss Lewis. He say he gwine try once mo'," Mandy called as Sally passed the desk. "This he now, mebby." She took up the telephone as the bell rang. "Miss Lewis? Yassir, wait a minit, please." She motioned toward Sally.

Alex? Sally reached hopefully for the receiver, her heart

74

waiting to beat.

"Hi, Sally. I'm in town unexpectedly. Doing anything tonight?" But it was Greg's voice and not Alex's. Her heart beat slowly again but from down—way down.

"Oh, I'm sorry. I've just asked a friend to go out to dinner with me, to a place my boss wants to know about. But why don't you come with *us?* Do! This Lou Davis, who is going with me, is a jolly girl. You'll like her. Come on! Meet us at the end of Plymouth Street, off Sutton Place at 6:00. Be seeing you." Sally hung up. "Thank you, Mandy." She walked slowly toward the elevator. It would be fun, no doubt— Of course it would be fun! She jerked herself up quickly and pushed the bell with determination.

"Now, this is what I call neat." Lou and Sally were standing in front of a lighted, glass-enclosed frame, a small diorama showing a scene of an early colonial kitchen. The figure of a young woman seated at an old spinning wheel occupied the foreground, a waiting supper table behind her. The frame stood in the grass plot in front of a quaint old house wedged in between modern apartments, a relic of departed days.

"Clever way of advertising their business, isn't it?" Lou spoke admiringly. "I love those cute cooking pots in front of that old fireplace. Somebody had real imagination." She turned at the sound of footsteps. "Would this be the boy friend, perchance?" she whispered to Sally as a man's figure swung into view.

"It would. Good evening, Greg! You were smart to find this out-of-the-way spot right on time. Lou, may I present Arthur Gregory, late of the big open spaces, now chief sponsor for the Speedy Mixer!" Sally introduced her friends.

"I've no more idea than you have what sort of a place this is, but come on. I can't remember when I had lunch—if ever!" And she ushered her party up the walk.

Inside were most interesting rooms, one on either side of two central brick fireplaces built back to back. The firelight shone on immense old copper kettles used for kindling and on low ladder-back chairs on either side of the hearth. Ears of corn braided together and strings of red peppers hung over the mantels. The hostess, dressed in an old-fashioned costume of Quaker gray with full white apron and Priscilla cap, showed them to their table.

"Will you leave your wraps and then take your plates and be served at the buffet, please?"

Sally's quick eye took in the scrubbed table tops, the tallow candles for light in old-fashioned brass candlesticks, the bare studded walls rubbed smooth. White starched ruffled curtains were looped back at the windows, and geraniums blossomed gaily on the sills. So very simple, yet somehow so very real. Sally glanced down at the old colonial plate in her hand. "Aunty used to have dishes like these, when I was little!" she exclaimed.

Progress toward the buffet was altogether too slow for their young appetites, but what food greeted them when they finally arrived! A long, narrow table, scrubbed white like the others, was spread with the most delectable-looking dishes Sally had ever seen. There were platters of fried chicken, there was beautiful baked Virginia ham that a white-haired old darky carved to a paper thinness with loving skill. Amber globes of candied sweet potatoes, and golden corn pudding wreathed with tiny sausages also tempted their appetites.

"How can I eat both spoon bread and corn sticks that I

love and everything else?" wailed Sally.

"Look at my plate, will you? I'm a disgrace!" Lou giggled.

"How are you doing, Greg?" Sally looked around at her new friend.

"Swell! Plate's too small, that's all!"

The waitresses served coffee at the table and brought lovely tiny hot rolls that Sally waved regretfully away. "I couldn't," she groaned. "And I'm sorry, I want to tell you! They do look so good. I'd like to come here again and start backward and try all the things I had to miss this time!"

"Woman, on occasions like this you talk too much!" Greg was addressing himself strictly to the mound in front of him, and Lou, cheeks flushed, her brown eyes sparkling, laughed delightedly. "Aren't we the pigs!"

"Dessert? Yes, indeedy! I cast an eye on that table when we came past. Everything looked wonderful!" Sally leaned back in her chair. "There was apple betty with whipped cream sprinkled with grated yellow cheese that I'd love to try. I saw that much as we passed on the fly."

"Pumpkin pie with ginger meringue is our 'special' to-night," a little waitress stopped at their table to announce.

"Ha! That saved my life and reputation one day this week. I'll eat a sliver for remembrance!" and Sally bounced up to follow the others toward the dessert table.

"I hate to pass up apple pandowdy or Indian pudding with ice cream. Two of my favorites. Oh, but here's float-ing island, my childhood delight!" and Lou bore it off in triumph.

"Nothing so airy-fairy for me." Greg was in his glory. "I'm having that big apple dumpling with the hard sauce and you can all just wait till I finish it. Come on." They trooped back to their table.

"People do love good food, don't they? No wonder this place is crowded. Simple, homely, old-fashioned. All you can eat and more and dee-licious. No style, but look at the class of people who come here! It's the food that does the trick, must be," Sally observed as she finished her pie.

"Miss Kitury told me to talk to the woman who runs this place, a Miss Keen, she said. Will you wait for me while I see if I can find her?" Sally beckoned to the hostess. "May I see Miss Keen for a minute? Will you tell her that Miss Kitury of the *Star* has a message for her?"

"This way, please."

At a desk, in a storeroom just beyond the kitchen door, sat a young woman busily adding a column of figures. She glanced up as they approached and to Sally's astonishment the hostess said, "This is Miss Keen." ("Why she's not much older than I am!" thought Sally.)

"We have just had such a delicious dinner," Sally introduced herself, her eye taking in the familiar scene. "Miss Kitury asked me to say that she would be glad to feature your tearoom on her radio hour, but will you tell us a bit about how you began? It's such an attractive place! I want to know about it myself." Sally was all ears. "The spinning wheel—where did you get it?"

Miss Keen rose. "It was my grandmother's. I fished it out of our attic. An artist friend made the sign for me. You see, when I graduated from college (naming a well-known technical school) I came here as an assistant. Two years later Miss Sawyer, who ran the place, died very suddenly and I had to carry on as best I could. When, after a year or so, her family offered to sell out at a real bargain in order to settle the estate, I took the plunge and borrowed money to buy the equipment and the good will. I changed the name but otherwise it is much the same. That was three years ago, and—well, I'm *still* here." She smiled. There were faint lines in her young face, wrought by weariness and worry Sally could see, but there was also determination and never-say-die. "That's what it takes," thought Sally. She wished she had time to hear the story covered by that simple, "I'm *still* here," but Lou and Greg would have been wondering what on earth was keeping her long ere this, no doubt. She mustn't take any more time.

"I think your place is lovely! I shall tell Miss Kitury all about it. Thank you so much for seeing me. I'd like to come again. Good-bye." And Sally hurried back to her friends.

She found Greg leaning across the table, talking earnestly, and Lou's usually merry face was for once intent. So engrossed were they in one another that they hadn't even missed her, apparently! Sally eyed them for a minute speculatively. "Now see what I've done!" she said to herself. "Speedy Mixer!" She laughed softly. Announcing her arrival, she asked, "Well, where do we go from here? Movies? If it isn't too far, let's walk. Do us good after such a dinner." And they filed out.

"Let's swing over onto the avenue and window-shop." Sally proposed. "I love the shops at night and I never have time enough to look at them as much as I'd like." She was already three jumps ahead up the street but not too far to note over her shoulder how completely her one-time knight had gone down before the charms of Miss Davis!

"West meets East—and look what happens!" She giggled. "These lovely windows—beach clothes for Southern wear —might just as well belong to a junk shop for all they see."

But the beautiful picture was fading for her, too. She was remembering that she and Alex had walked along these same streets and seen nothing but each other only a year ago—and the wave of loneliness that she had fought back for so long rolled clear over! "It's a good thing those two are blind or they might think I was jealous or something." She disgustedly blinked away the tears and moved on to the next block. Ah, a furniture store. She was standing entranced before the display as the others came up.

"Look, Lou, at this darling kitchen set up here in this window, with the little breakfast nook on one side!" Like Judy's maybe, she thought. But that was the wrong thing! Another wave, bigger than the first, was coming,—and Sally flew up the street to safety.

CHAPTER VIII

MyOMy

"DO you know, Miss Sally Lewis, that there is little more
than a week left before the winners of that cooky
contest have to be announced? A week from Sunday, to
be exact. Heavens, I didn't realize the time was so short!
And here I've made appointments for nearly every day next
week!" Miss Kitury, seated at her desk one morning, suddenly stopped writing and anxiously turned the leaves of
her calendar, dismay on her face.

"I certainly slipped up on that item. We'll have to do
some hustling, you and I!" Kate Kitury's quick mind covered the week's work in one leap—the regular routine, the
two "stories" every day, the two sets of recipes and the
daily broadcast that *must* be ready, signed and delivered
on time, come fire or flood; plus the files of the daily letters
that clamored for attention; plus innumerable telephone
calls—Mrs. Brown wanting to know how many pounds of
cod to buy for escalloped fish for the church supper;—
"This is Mrs. Jones speaking, can you tell me how to take
fruit stains out of silk?"—Mrs Dootson offering a remedy
to keep cake frosting from peeling off, and so on and on;
plus emergencies, plus—plus.

"We'll just have to concentrate and speed up, that's all,
I guess. How many entries did you say we had? Forty! That
ought to be enough—certainly! They are all typed in dupli-
cate, aren't they, with name and address of sender? Good.
Have you looked them over? Are they all usable? Let me

see the lot, for a minute." Miss Kitury reached for the folder Sally handed her from the file.

"Some are duplicates. There are three or four Chocolate Crunch," Sally offered. "And there are one or two where they left out the baking powder and one, I noticed, skipped the sugar. I put a question mark on them." She waited while Miss Kitury ran through several pages.

"Let's see—that's out, and that. This is too ordinary, and— Well, here are thirty. Check these over again, then mail them by special delivery to Miss Lally of Deever Brothers. She is at the head of their home economics laboratories. She and I are co-operating on this. She agreed to test out the recipes in their kitchens, provided they could have them to use for their advertising of MyOMy shortening—also provided I would speak a good word for it on the radio. Fair enough."

"Deever Brothers? I thought they made soap," Sally said, surprised.

"So they do. This MyOMy shortening is a new by-product that they have just put on the market and it is booming, I understand. Now, we'll have to rush things along here every day, for as soon as Miss Lally starts on this job you'll have to trip over there every afternoon until the tests are finished. You and the staff will have to decide on the winners—first and second prize and honorable mention. Get those entries into the mail as soon as you can now and I'll rush ahead on these 'stories,'" and Miss Kitury turned to her typewriter.

"*Me* to help decide on the winners? Me? Think of that now, Miss Lewis," Sally said to herself. How many times had she made cookies? Not very many, she admitted, and her repertoire was decidedly slim, but here was a chance to learn and nobody need be the wiser—maybe. She went over the recipes carefully, trying to visualize each one, also making sure she had copied correctly. She must get them into the afternoon mail.

Three busy days passed. Sally worked early and late, getting her regular jobs caught up and ahead as far as possible. She wrote Mrs. This about taking grease spots off her parlor wallpaper with starch mixed with a cleaning fluid; to Mrs. That, thanking her for the special hooked rug pattern that someone had asked for, to Mrs. Newly-Wed, telling her to put an apple in with her brown sugar to keep it from getting hard. She sent two sets of suggested menus to the ladies of the Eastern Star for their annual supper, with recipes for one hundred eaters to go with them. These were but samples of a few of the requests and each mail steadily brought more.

Don't think for a minute that Miss Sally knew all these things! Few of them, to tell the truth, and often vaguely when at all. She looked in the quantity cook books and the household management texts on their reference shelf, she scratched through the files, or asked Miss Kitury as a last resort. It all took *so* much time!—and her typewriter seemed never still.

"Miss Lally just telephoned that they would have ten varieties of cookies baked by this afternoon, ready for inspection and judging," Miss Kitury announced about 10:30 on Wednesday morning. "Be there at two o'clock. Their kitchens are on the top floor of the new building across the river. The subway goes right near. And by the way, theirs is a very interesting setup over there. Take time to look around and get someone to explain their organization to you, if you can. Miss Lally belongs to my day. She has had an interesting career. When she first came out of college, years ago, she got herself a job by marching right into the office of the president of a big milling company out West and suggesting that he could sell a lot more flour if he had on his staff a woman trained in home economics who could make up recipes using his product; that homemakers would be only too delighted to have them and would beat a pathway to his door if he could show them how to do better baking. 'If eventually, why not now?' was the slogan of that firm, if I remember. Anyhow, it worked for Genevieve Lally. Now here she is at the head of this big new organization, telling the world about MyOMy shortening. But I must be off! Keep an eye out for ideas. See you in the morning."

And Miss Kitury flew to keep an appointment. The Morten Dairy was putting out a new line of fancy cheeses. If she could only land the contract to advertise them daily on her radio hour, it would mean dollars in her pocketbook, not to speak of helping her own homemakers to keep abreast of the times and, incidentally, be it confessed, spreading the fame of one Kit Kitury. Oh, yes. Business was business—though she was always very sure of the merit of a product before she recommended it.

Sally clipped through the forenoon on the wing. If that telephone wouldn't ring so often! Who wanted to know what now?

"Yes, Mrs. Smith. Have you tried putting a little vinegar in the water when you cook your fish? That will help to keep it from going to pieces so badly. You're welcome."

Thank goodness, that was an easy one. She had seen her mother try that trick more than once.

Well, so much for this morning's work. Sally shut down her desk, put on her hat and coat, grabbed the galleys for the morning paper, the story for the evening following, and skipped down the back stairs to her old friend, Mike. If anyone wanted to know anything else, she could just look it up herself in *The Book of Wonders* or *Who's Who,* for all of Sally Lewis! She was *out.*

"Think of working in a *grand* place like this!" Sally stepped in through the door of Deever Brothers' new office building and gazed about the lobby in wonder and amazement. Beautiful murals adorned the walls to the ceiling dome—away up. There were that new blond mahogany, much gleaming bronze and beautiful appointments throughout. Sally moved a cautious toe on the polished marble floor. All this grandeur out of soap! She felt small. She was conscious of her simple clothes. She felt—could the word be *green?* Well, the shade was very similar, certainly!

A perfectly-groomed young woman greeted her at the information desk, back by the elevators. She, Sally, had negotiated that stretch of shining floor—like going into the presence of royalty.

"I will call someone to take you to Miss Lally. Your name, please? James, show Miss Lewis to the home economics laboratory."

A liveried chap bowed her into the elevator and they floated to the top floor.

"This way, please." Down the hall and through a door into a beautifully light room filled with girls and women busy at desks and typewriters. "Miss Lally's assistant is in the office at the left there." A well-dressed young woman rose as they approached.

"Miss Goring, this is Miss Lewis." Her guide bowed, and Sally found herself being cordially greeted by a very attractive person indeed.

"Miss Lally will not be at liberty for five or ten minutes. Will you sit down and wait, or perhaps you would like to look about?"

"Oh, I would very much." Sally was all eyes. Through a glass partition she could see girls in white busy in a wonderful looking kitchen.

"That is our cooking laboratory," Miss Goring explained. "This morning those girls baked the cookies that we are going to sample very soon. We'll go in and look around."

"What a lovely place!" Sally exclaimed. Streamlined was the word indeed. Monel metal and stainless steel. The newest gadget. The latest in planned efficiency. Sheer ruffled curtains framed the windows that looked out over the river. Cupboards concealed all that might detract, revealed all that could add.

"All our research work is done in here. Recipes are tested again and again, and yet again, and the results written up. Last week we worked on devil's food cake—how to make it dark or how to make it red. How to have it moist and soft. Whether it makes any difference if eggs are beaten in whole or the whites beaten stiff and folded in last, and so on. These girls are all home economics graduates who specialized in chemistry of foods and laboratory technique."

"Not for me!" thought Miss Sally. "I'd be ready to fly out the window if I had to be so very accurate and do things over and over. And, besides, when I cook I want somebody to eat it, and say it's good, what's more!" But, everyone to his own taste, she supposed. Someone had to do the careful, painstaking experimenting after all—or there would be

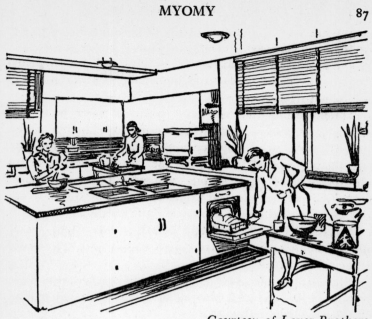

Courtesy of Lever Brothers

no fool-proof recipes for *her* to scurry through. *Um—m,*
maybe so.

"Are all those people in that room out there part of your
organization, too?" Sally asked interestedly.

"Indeed, yes. That's the editorial department. Miss Morris, a graduate of a western university who came to us from
one of the household magazines, heads that work," Miss
Goring explained. "This is their latest recipe book for pies,
cakes—everything where our shortening can be used. Take
one."

"Oh, thank you! What do you do with these? I mean,
where do you send them?"

"We hope every homemaker in the country will get one

eventually, through buying MyOMy at the retail grocers or by mail. 'A can in every cupboard' is our motto, you know. We have a radio hour, too. You may have listened to it. Wednesdays, 'Helps for Homemakers,' Fridays, 'News for Newlyweds.'

"Then besides that we have twenty-five or more field workers. Demonstrators," Miss Goring explained at Sally's puzzled look, "who conduct cooking schools or do exhibition baking using MyOMy, for the big grocery stores, for clubs and civic organizations. Sometimes they co-operate with the gas and electric companies. Miss Morris works out their printed recipe sheets, and all instructions."

"MyOMy!" Sally laughed. "I had no idea there was so much behind a can of shortening. I shall look at it with new respect hereafter."

"Be sure you buy ours." Miss Goring laughed, too. "Our rival's causes headache, heartache and remorse, remember! But here is Miss Lally."

Sally turned quickly. A gracious person, hair graying, poised, alert, so quick to put one at ease, this was Miss Lally. Everyone seemed so *very* courteous here, thought Sally. *So* anxious to please. Part of their stock in trade? Perhaps. But wasn't it grand stock to own!

"Will you call Miss Morris, please, Miss Goring? She needs a breathing spell, and we'll see about these cookies now." Miss Lally led the way toward a little serving table, where ten trays of cookies had been laid out, each one tagged stating the variety. And there was tea. Wasn't this fun!

"I'm glad you girls made these cookies small, since we have to taste every one." Miss Lally smiled at the girl who served the tea. They all tasted and sampled busily, from one tray to the next.

"Have you all chosen your favorite?" Miss Lally asked at last, looking about inquiringly. "Write the name on a slip of paper, and fold it over. Mary, you gather them up and read them off. Ready? Three votes for this one, you say? (Sally almost gave a bounce. That was her choice. Icebox cookies they were, with nuts and raisins.) One for these? And two for those over there? All right. That settles the first prize for today then. We'll keep these three best ones and see what we draw tomorrow." Miss Lally rose. "Fix up a box of them, Mary, and Miss Lewis can take them to Miss Kitury. See you tomorrow afternoon, then? So good of you to come. Good-bye."

And Miss Sally took her cooky box and herself down the elevator, across the grand lobby and out the front door. She waved a salute to the wonderful building.

MyOMy! A side line of soap. And what a line. Make a mint of money and do a real service to mankind, besides. Something about a better mouse trap flitted through her mind. What was it? But she was pretty tired and she sank into the corner of the subway seat, her cookies in her lap.

A very interesting day—a real eye-opener. Sally had no idea there were so many phases of her own profession. Four or five right there in that one business, too! She leaned her head against the back of the seat. Where was her little recipe book? Oh, yes, in her pocket. One to every home-maker in the country? No homemakers, no soap. No side line of soap. Remember that flight of eloquence on the importance of the home in her speech before that women's club? (She could laugh if it hadn't seemed so tough at the

time!) Must be really true. MyOMy! Next year, when or if
she was a homemaker herself—her eyes twinkled happily
for the merest instant and then clouded.

The next afternoon was similar to the first and the third
was like unto that. Each day Sally and the three heads of
Deever Brothers' department of home economics sampled
cookies and drank tea and picked the winners. And then
came the decision between the three tops for first place.
Miss Lally lined the cookies up side by side and they nib-
bled and discussed and balloted, and Sally's pet came out
"honorable mention!" Not bad for a novice. She was satisfied. Flattered, in fact, to be in the running at all.*

She hustled back to the office, the proud bearer of *two*
cooky boxes this time, one belonging to Miss Sally Lewis.
She typed the three winning recipes, with name and address
of sender, in the space Miss Kitury had saved on the Sunday page and laid the material on Andy's desk fifteen minutes before the dead line!

"A close shave for you, young lady!" he grinned.

"Have a cooky, Mr. Andy? I've a whole box of them—
prize winners, too. They're what made me late. Take three
or four. Good, aren't they?"

"Tops. I vote for this one. Say, what about a pie contest,
too? Next week, eh?"

" 'Deed not! Don't mention it on your life. I'm all be-
frazzled over this one." Sally laughed as she shut the box.

"I'm going home right this minute, too. Night!" She
skipped back to her desk. "I'll just save some cookies for
Mike," she said to herself, "and take the rest home to Clara

* (Would anyone like to know Sally's pet cooky recipe and the ones
that received first and second prizes? Look in the back of the book!)

and the girls. And in case anybody cares to know, which they won't, I'm glad *this* week is over!"

Miss Lewis sighed in relief as she fished out her rubbers and put them on.

It was a satisfied sigh, though. That was something. She had learned a lot—about home economics in business—and in a *new* place this time besides. She had been not only most impressed with the painstaking research, the infinite care in making a high quality commercial food product, with the cleverness and ingenuity used to make it appeal to the home-makers whose cupboard shelves were its ultimate goal, but also with the fact, now growing quite clear, that the home-makers were the ultimate goal of much—so very much—of the world's effort. Why nearly every food product put on the market was designed to please Mrs. John Smith so that she would buy and buy again! And so many other things—curtains and carpets and furniture, linens and household equipment, electric irons and Speedy Mixers, all made to catch the eye and enhance the home of this same Mrs. S.

And now was she, Sally, sold to MyOMy? Of course! She hoped to use it herself some day soon. It would bring up pleasant memories of a handsome building built with soap, of a wonderful cooking laboratory and department presided over by three clever, ambitious and charmingly competent women who had all started from scratch. The whole setup was really *educational* in a way. Certainly it was. Designed primarily to bring shekels into the coffers of Deever Brothers, to be sure, but nevertheless there was real service in making something truly superior and in edu-cating homemakers to buy it. MyOMy, yes!

Miss Sally went on home with her cookies. She was really tired. If only Alex were coming to see her on Saturday, as he used to do, she wouldn't be tired at all! Wasn't it funny how something pleasant to look forward to could take all the weariness away or at least keep you from caring whether you were tired or not? That is—well it used to be so. But to have nothing nice ever happen, not that night nor the next nor the next after that—*Ooo!* What a doleful way to live! Surely that wasn't going to happen to her. Christmas was coming. Surely Alex would write or—or something.

CHAPTER IX

"As Though It Had Never Been"

SALLY was seated at her typewriter one Friday afternoon a week or so later. Office hours were over and her day's work was done, but she thought she would just stay a while and write a note to Judy. "It's easier on the typewriter for me—and for her certainly, since I write like a hen!" said she. Adjusting the paper she wrote:

At the Office

December -------------

Mrs. Judy—

Many thanks for that last recipe. Your name is already in the annals of the *Star* and Miss Kitury has sung your praises on the air. My two months are up but nothing seems to be happening. The girl whose place I am taking hasn't returned from the South yet, so here I still am—hardly knowing what to do next. I hate to leave, I do really. This is a *very* interesting job. However, I suppose I'll have to be hunting for something else soon—but—well, till you hear differently, keep tuned to this station!

Remember me to Bill.

Love,

Sally

She pulled the paper from her machine, folded it, and addressed the envelope, looking up as a Western Union boy breezed in through the door. He fished in his cap— "Miss Sally Lewis? Sign here." Sally signed—in panic— and he was gone. Alex? Her mother? She waited a minute for courage, then tore open the yellow message, with fumbling fingers:

Chelton, Mass.
Alex not well. Can you come Saturday? Wire train.

                              Helen Merrill

"I knew it. I knew it!" The message blurred before Sally's eyes. Alex was sick! In the hospital maybe. Perhaps he was going to die! Mrs. Merrill had only said "not well," but probably she was afraid of frightening her and was just letting her down easy. Sally seemed rooted to the spot, but she finally shook herself awake.

She mustn't stand there like a bump on a log. She must find out about trains and wire an answer. She called the ticket office—a train at 12:00?—another at 3:00 P. M.? Too late. Miss Kitury would excuse her if she left a little early so she could make the twelve o'clock. She would explain why she had to go. *How* did you send a telegram? She couldn't seem to remember. Something about 'Not over ten words.' She scribbled tentatively:

Arriving Saturday afternoon, four o'clock
                              —Sally

Five words. Safe. Now what? You telephoned the message to Western Union. Of course, stupid. Where were her brains—if any? She sent the message—forty cents—she would pay Miss Kitury.

All the way home on the subway she upbraided herself for her lack of faith in Alex. "I might have known it was something like this. The *poor* dear. Of course he was all tired out— His father at death's door for months—extra work

at school—the old Doctor wasn't too well himself and depended more and more on Alex— Who wouldn't get sick?
Especially if the girl he was actually engaged to was such a
—well, make your own choice! Stubborn donkey—obsti-
nate little goose," were the names Sally called herself. But
all the same, why hadn't Alex written her and explained?
He certainly could have! Maybe he was tired of her, after
all— Maybe he didn't care any more—maybe— And so
on and on, through supper; through the evening till bedtime and she fell asleep at last; running as an undercur-
rent all through the morning at the office; all the way out to
Chelton, as the train wheels turned over and over.

"Alex, dear, will you drive down to the station and meet
the four o'clock train for me, please? I've a friend coming
out for over Sunday. She's small and wears blue usually.
She'll know you, I'm sure. You'll need to hurry, dear. It's
nearly time now." And Mrs. Merrill bustled toward the
kitchen, giving no chance for questions, lingering at the
door only long enough to note from the corner of her eye
that Alex rose obligingly—if listless and thoroughly indif-
ferent.

"I don't know what's come over him, but something
surely has," she thought worriedly to herself as she put her
husband's beef broth to heat on the kitchen stove. "Not a
letter from Sally have I seen on the hall table in weeks and
I can't remember when I've heard Alex going out to the mail
box on the corner as he used to do every night. I may be
an old meddler but they might just as well have it out right
here and get it over with! I've been so concerned with getting Father started back on the upgrade that I just haven't
paid any attention to Alex until lately and when I did I was

shocked at him. He's *thin* and tired looking. Not to be wondered at, the dear knows. But on top of that he's *so* quiet and sort of morose, and he doesn't eat—and that's away off for Alex! Well—we'll see. I can't let anything silly spoil things for them, if I can help it. That cute little Sally, so quick and smart—and so genuine. Well, we'll see." And Mrs. Merrill sat down at the kitchen table.

"Everything's all set for supper, isn't it, Hilma? Miss Sally is coming out. She likes those baked apples with the dates and nuts in them. They look nice over there," nodding toward the pan on the drain board.

Hilma's rosy face brightened.

"Ja, Miss Sally, I like." She beamed. "Summer time she vork, good."

"We're having fried eggplant, aren't we? Mr. Alex's favorite,—and you won't forget the roquefort dressing for the orange and onion salad, will you? The grocery man sent the big Bermudas, I hope. I'll fix Mr. Merrill's tray early, so you won't have to think about that. I'll just take his cup of broth up now." And, lifting the saucepan from the stove, she carefully filled the delicate eggshell cup—part of her wedding china, she remembered. It would be Alex's some day—and Sally's, she hoped!

"Chelton, next," the conductor called. The train was slowing down for the station. Sally tucked her purse under her arm and picked up her overnight bag. She stepped down onto the platform as the train stopped, and looked about. It was a gray afternoon. The air was colder than in town. She shivered slightly. There would be taxis, surely. Why, that was Alex coming toward her! Her heart did a complete handspring. He wasn't sick. That carefully rehearsed scene at the hospital bedside—*pouff!*

"Hi, Sally, I didn't know you were coming."

"Why, Alex—why—y, Alex! I thought you were sick—your mother—" Sally floundered.

"Me? Nothing the matter with me. I'll take your bag." And he led the way toward the car. No smile. No happy light in his eye. She could be the scrubwoman for all he cared! Sally followed miserably, wishing heartily she had not come.

"How is your father?" she asked perfunctorily as they drove up the street.

"Better," Alex answered briefly, his eyes on the car ahead. Sally stole a quick glance at him. He seemed so different —so down, sort of—and unhappy. Her heart misgave her.

"Alex, you *have* been sick, haven't you? You're—so *thin*. I—I'm sorry," she faltered.

No answer. They were now on a quiet street.

"Stop here at the curb, please, where we can talk." Sally decided to take matters in hand right then and there. It would have to be done. She might just as well dive in head first, now as later.

"What *is* the matter, Alex?" She looked up anxiously. "We seem to be in an awful jam and I don't for the life of me know of anything sillier. Truly, I don't. I guess it was my fault in the beginning. You thought I meant something when I didn't at all. I guess you just didn't believe me when I said I was sorry, did you? Why didn't you write? I waited and waited. *Why* didn't you, Alex?" Sally touched his hand on the wheel.

"I was afraid maybe you were tired of waiting for me—that maybe you didn't care as much as you thought you did after all, I guess. That you just wrote because you wanted to be kind." Alex was still looking straight ahead, his face glum.

"What!" Sally swung around, incredulous. All those days —day after day after day—when she had waited for word from him! They rose before her now, and the nights— dozens—when she would have cried herself to sleep if she had ever had any practise. Tears of exasperation came to her eyes.

"Why Alexander Merrill, you big goose! How *could* you have been so dumb?" She shook the tears off her cheeks, her eyes snapping. All those weeks of grief for nothing? Slowly Alex turned and looked at the fiery bit beside him. Slowly the old light came back to his eyes, the old grin to the corners of his mouth. One arm drew her toward him. One hand lifted the wet face—

"You *do* care, Banty?" he asked gently, at last.

"Oh, Alex, you are *so* dumb. So *dumb*, and so—so very dear!" she sobbed, the pent-up floods coming down now in earnest.

"There, dear, there," he comforted her. "I was dumb. I *am* dumb. I'm *sorry*, sweet." He brushed away the tears and held her closer against him. "I've had a terrible fall, Banty," he said at last, his cheek against her hair.

"You and me, both!" And Sally, her arm around his neck, relaxed with a sigh—in happy safety once more, her lonely days and nights as though they had never been.

"Alex, dear, it must be getting late! Where in the world is my hat? We had better be going on home. Your mother will be worried!" Sally sat up at last. "The neighbors! What *will* they think?"

"A hoot for the neighbors, but what time is it? Five-thirty! Mum's probably been pacing the deck for an hour!

Fish your bonnet off the gear shift there, girl, so we can get out of here. But take a look at yourself in the mirror first!" Alex grinned.

Sally craned her neck to see—tear stains, straggling hair. "I *am* a sweet picture, am I not?" She giggled as she tucked in the straying curls and hunted in her purse for her compact.

"That's what *I* think." Alex kissed her ear in passing as he bent to release the brake.

When they swung into the driveway of Alex's home, Sally's eye swept over it with new appreciation. There was an air about it of permanence, of solidity, of graciousness and hospitality. Alex's grandfather had built the house, white with green blinds, New England style. It had seen a lot of living. Alex's grandfather had planted the maple trees in the front yard, huge now, and the old graceful elms beside the garage where once the stable had stood. They had been there a long time. It took time to grow things of lasting beauty and permanence, didn't it? Trees or homes.

"One day did not suffice for building Rome," Sally quoted to herself. "It makes one feel safe, sort of," she thought.

Alex stopped the car by the kitchen door, in front of the garage. His mother was already on the back steps, waiting. Sally hopped out and ran up the walk. She threw her arms around the older woman, impulsively. "I'm *so* glad to see you!" she cried.

Mrs. Merrill took Sally's face between her two hands in the old familiar gesture, scanning it closely. This time she saw shine and sparkle and happiness there and she kissed the girl, thankfully.

"And I to see you, my dear. You're all right? Happy,

aren't you?" she asked.

"Grand! And happy, so happy! Thanks to you," Sally whispered the last in Mrs. Merrill's ear. "Is Mr. Merrill well enough for me to see him?"

"Yes, indeed. He's expecting you. Run on up—but don't stay too long, will you?"

Sally was already through the kitchen door. She stopped to greet her old pal. "Hi, Hilma! How are you?"

"I good. You come, I glad." Hilma beamed.

"What are we having for supper that smells so good?" Sally sniffed the air. "Stuffed chops? Hooray! I could eat bones and all right now! I'll be back." Sally waved as she ran up the stairs.

"Everything all right again, son?" Mrs. Merrill stopped Alex as he came in from putting up the car.

"Swell, Mom! You're a brick, do you know that?" He swung his mother off her feet. "Swell!" he repeated. "Hi, Hilma, have supper right away, eh?" he wheedled. "I could eat the side of a house this minute!" He was off to clean up.

"It does pay to lend the Lord a helping hand sometimes," Mrs. Merrill thought happily as she watched Alex take the stairs two steps at a time. He was back in his old stride once more. "Listen to him!" She stood, her hand on the newel post—

There's no cloud up in the sky—
Sunny weath-er
Since me and my gal am together
Shinin' all the whi—ile

Her son sang lustily, suiting the words to the occasion. She smiled. "Father won't mind the noise. He'll be so glad to have that spell of gloom broken." And Alexander's mother smiled her relief.

It was such a happy week end. Sally was curled up in the
sunny window seat of the living room next morning. It
was Sunday. She had wiped the dishes for Hilma, and
chatted a long time with Mrs. Merrill while they made the
beds together. Why did it always seem easier to talk to

people if you were working with them? And now she was just resting. Letting the peace and quiet and comfort of this old home flow over her, washing all the worry, the uncertainty, the loneliness of the last six months clear away. Whatever happened in the months ahead, she wouldn't mind now. She and Alex were happy together once more. If her job petered out, all right, she'd get another! She couldn't be bothered with it today. She relaxed in the sun.

What was it made this such a comfortable, peaceful sort of a home to be in? Sally's eye roamed idly round the room. It was spacious and light. There was old mahogany furniture—a fireplace where a fire burned. There were comfortable chairs, worn and well used, and soft shaded lamps. Not elegant but everything in good taste. There was harmony. That must be what she felt. Nothing jarred. It became a part of you and you forgot all about it. That wasn't all. The whole household seemed to run smoothly, as if by itself. Meals were bountiful and good and on time, with little fuss made about them. There was leisure and time to talk. Could all this have just happened? Sally was too smart for that. She knew good and well that someone must know *how* to keep the house, how to plan and cook the meals, how to order the food, how to manage a maid—if you were lucky enough to have one! Perhaps Mrs. Merrill was just *born* to it. Perhaps her mother had taught her. Surely every girl should learn it somewhere. But that wasn't all, either. There was something more—sort of underneath and all around. Something that held everything together and made you feel happy. Was it the love and sympathy and understanding of which she had seen so many evidences? Was that the "something more" that was needed for a home? Perhaps so.

Sally sat up suddenly, sniffing—listening. Roast beef—

m-mm. Was that Hilma's egg-beater? She made a spring toward the kitchen. There was going to be Yorkshire pudding for dinner and Miss Sally must be there for the making. "I've always wanted to taste it and see it made. How do you do it, Hilma?"

"One cups milk, half cups flour, two eggs, salt. I beating very hard. Finish, pour in roast pan. Fat come down. Joos come down. Taste good. You like, I think." Hilma deftly poured the thin and bubbly batter into the pan around the roast.

"Only twenty minutes for this to cook? I'd better hurry." And Sally flew to change and freshen up for dinner.

CHAPTER X

After Christmas

" 'CHRISTMAS comes but once a year'—thank heaven!" Lou Davis's weary but fervent gratitude ascended as she all but staggered into the dressing room after serving the last Christmas diner at the restaurant of the Barbarole. She had been off last year. This time it was her turn on. Such a *crowd.* So much extra work. So much preparation beforehand. She had been worried to death for fear she wouldn't have turkey enough. My, how the waitresses had lined up at the steam table! Everyone had worked frantically, but the service had seemed *slow* in spite of everything she could do.

Well, it was over. If she could only get home to bed.

"And tomorrow," she groaned—"tomorrow people will have to eat just the same!" Things must go on as usual. And you weren't expected to *act* tired next day either, no matter how dead you felt. You were in business. Were you numb all over from weariness? No matter, you smiled and went on—or at least you went on. You were in business. A smiling front—if your back were broken!

" 'Tis the season to be jolly!—Maybe. At least so the song says, but I'm here to tell you it's the hardest one of the year in this business," thought Miss Keen of The Spinning Wheel, as she said good night to her last helper at the end of Christmas day, snapped off the kitchen lights and wondered if she could possibly manage the stairs to her apartment above.

104

What a *mob!* Run, run. More of this. Hurry the salads. Encourage and help the vegetable cook who was frantic. "Another duck, Tilly. How about that roast beef? Keep the broilers coming. They are going fast." Would the crowd never stop? "I made money yesterday and today, too, I know, even if I did give the help an extra day's pay, but oh, I'd rather have less and not have to work quite so hard. Well, here goes for the stairs." Tomorrow—heavens, tomorrow! People would eat again just the same! "Well this is *your* tearoom, you know, sister. You didn't have to choose this business. Take the bitter with the sweet. Business has to go on, however you feel," she reminded herself as she fell into bed. Yes, it was *her* business. The day was saved by that fact. The steady grind, day after day after day, was saved by that. And Miss Keen knew that she would carry on and that her Spinning Wheel would continue to spin.

At the Y.W. on Harvard Street, too, Christmas day came to an end at last.

"Thank goodness, that's over. What a week!" Clara Booth wearily locked the cafeteria at closing time and dragged her lagging steps toward the elevator. That big party for the girls Tuesday night. The tree to get ready. So much decorating everywhere beforehand. Refreshments. Gifts for everyone who couldn't get home or hadn't one to go to.

"I don't know how I could have managed if Sally hadn't helped," she thought. "And that Gregory chap—Speedy, they called him—was a sport to play Santa Claus. And then today—special dinner—and—and—I *must* get to bed. I don't know *when* I've been so tired. And tomorrow—" she groaned, "tomorrow everybody will eat just the same! Well, if you *will* pick a cafeteria to run!" Clara told herself, as she leaned against the elevator.

Yes, she had picked a cafeteria, that was true, and picked it, what's more, because she liked it. She wouldn't have chosen any other job for the world, but there were times —peaks, as she or anyone else in that field would have to admit, when every ounce of effort you could muster didn't seem enough to take you over the top except in tatters. But what career didn't have peaks and who was there working for a living who escaped being tattered and torn at times? They weren't in the food business, that was sure, Clara decided, as the elevator stopped at her floor and she made thankfully for her room and bed.

Only *one* day off at Christmas. "That's the shortest vacation I ever had in my life at *this* time of year!" Sally grumbled as she finally came awake enough to get out of bed on the morning after. "What did you expect, girl? You're in business now," she reminded herself. "Newspapers go to press every day of the year but one. Be thankful you had that one, even if you did work like mad beforehand so you *could* have it. Clara didn't have *any* and I'll wager Lou didn't either. I can imagine what *her* day must have been like in that restaurant. Whew! You've been spoiled with your school vacations. You're in business now." Very well, so she was.

Well, never mind. She had had a lovely Christmas day just the same. At Chelton? Of course! ("Suppose she and Alex hadn't made up?" Her heart sank at the thought. Well, she would have helped Clara and worked like fury all day so she couldn't think. *But—they had made up* and the world

sang a different song for Sally. It would be dreadful *not* to be happy at Christmas time, wouldn't it? She had been saved that fate just in the nick of time!)

Trains ran more frequently during holiday week and by working overtime for days she had been able to get away at two o'clock the afternoon before Christmas, arriving at Alex's home just in time for supper. Oyster stew with hot buttered toast! The Merrills always had it for Christmas Eve. And Waldorf salad. And roquefort cheese.

There had been a small tree to decorate and put on a table in the corner of the father's room where they all gathered. He was improving slowly. They piled their gifts around the tree, lighted it and then sat in the dark while the village carolers sang outside. It was very nice.

Later Sally and Alex went to hear the Christmas music at the white church with the slim spire that stood at the end of the village green. A feeling of wonder and reverence. That was fitting always for Christmas Eve, wasn't it? There was snow, white and sparkling and squeaky. The evergreens on the square were loaded. Just like a Christmas card. Sally skipped a step or two beside Alex on their way home, her hand tucked under his arm, her eyes sparkling. Next year, they'd be in their own home!

They sat in front of the living room fire and talked for a long time. Could they be married in June? Maybe. If Alex's father continued to improve. "I have to stay with Miss Kitury till Connie Connors gets back—anyhow—April perhaps, or May," Sally decided. So—well, what were four or five months? The time would be gone before they knew it.

"That's what you think," Alex observed as they went upstairs at last.

Next morning there was breakfast for all in Mr. Merrill's room, a tray for each. Sally and Alex helped Hilma carry them up. Big grapefruit, tree ripened, little sausages with scrambled eggs, buttered toast, so good—and lots of coffee.

Then came the gifts! A ten-cent one for each with

rhymes—

Sally's, tied to a set of measuring spoons, read:

> This set of spoons for Sally is
> To guide her in her future biz.
> To make the cakes and biscuits riz
> So friends will think that she's a whiz
> She needs must use this gift, as is.
>
> From Santa Claus

She suspected Mr. Merrill Senior's fine hand in that effort!
Alex's was a pocket comb—with this:

> Your hair stands straight up on your dome?
> Lick it down with this handy comb.
> You will vie with Hollywood
> All the girls will think you're good.
> You will never be alone
> While you use this magic comb!
>
> Merry Christmas!

And so on. There were lovely gifts besides. Sally found
among hers a soft quilted housecoat in dainty flowered silk
that pleased her mightily. And Alex's gift, everything for
her dresser in that new material with gold inlay, thrilled her
to the toes. How she did need them, too! Nobody knew
how much. Her old brush and mirror from college days
still doing duty could at last be retired. They hadn't been
displayed to the light of day for years as it was!

She had hoarded her pennies like a miser to buy Alex
the desk set he had admired once in a shop window. She
watched from the corner of her eye as he opened the box,
content and repaid by the pleased look that came over his
face. Wasn't it fun! Then away with the wrappings, the
ribbons, and the rubbish—and the room was tidy again.
Sally and Alex took a basket to neighbor children and to

old Jake who lived alone, getting back hungry for dinner. Sally helped Hilma finish setting the table. Red candles in old silver candlesticks and red carnations in a crystal bowl—

There was roast goose for dinner. She had never eaten it before. It looked so brown and beautiful, with quarters of red apples baked in the pan for garnish.

Two teachers from Alex's school—Ralph Adams, whose wife had been called to her mother's home by illness and —what was that chap's name—fair hair—Marshall somebody—were the guests. Jolly.

Mr. and Mrs. Merrill had their dinner quietly together upstairs, while Alex did the honors below—and Sally queened it with three men to her heart's content. A hilarious game finished the afternoon and train time came all too soon.

And now it was the day after—and who wanted to work? "But you'd better snap into it, young lady," Sally prodded herself. Mail would be piled high at the office. There had been a deluge of Christmas ideas for weeks before. Sally had saved dozens for herself. How many "best" ways of making dressing had come in? She had lost count. With egg or without, wet or dry, with sausage, with oysters, with peanuts, or savory-browned crumbs or soft. And plum pudding and fruit cake and Christmas cookies world without end.

There was a new wrinkle for cranberry relish that sounded extra special, now safe for future use in Sally's private notebook. So simple. Just a quart of cranberries (raw!) and an orange, peel and all (minus the seeds) put through the food chopper together, mixed with a cup of sugar and set away for a day or two. Anything easier? And good, too, she could tell by the sound of it.

Weren't women kind to take time from these specially

busy days to send in their recipes and clever ideas, hoping
they might be a help to someone else? To be sure, Miss
Kitury would see to it that they were thanked and *praised*
publicly. Was that the *real* reason? *One* reason, no doubt,
they being of earth and not yet of heaven! And why not?
Everybody liked being praised, if they had done something
smart. And the house top wasn't a bad spot for said praise
either! No use hiding the light under a bushel basket, after
all. So, in vague fashion, ran Miss Sally's thoughts, as she
neared the *Star* building, trying to get herself back into
line. Seemed like more than *one* day since she had left. The
office was almost empty. Andy and one or two others. Sally
skipped over to see if he had had a nice Christmas. Somehow
she had an idea that he had not—very. He looked sort of
lonely. Probably she imagined it.

" 'Morning, Mr. Andy!"

" 'Morning, Miss Small Fry."

"Have a nice holiday, Mr. Andy?"

"Very." (Not much enthusiasm registered, but—) "Tell
me about yours," he parried.

"Oh, grand!" And Sally was off full speed ahead, to be
brought up short only when the office boy dumped her desk
top *full* of mail.

"Look at that, will you?" she groaned. "I fly to the help
of the homemakers. Here's hoping they only want to tell
me something, not ask it. The brains, so called, are still on
vacation. 'Bye!" She waved in comic dismay as she surveyed
the job in front of her. *What a pile!* Certainly nothing on
this job slowed up just because yesterday was Christmas.
The presses turned and Miss Kitury's Kitchen must appear
on page ten of the morning and evening *Star* three hundred
and sixty-four times more before it could skip again. Every

day and every day and every day.

But so it was for anyone who had a job, she guessed. Mrs. Everybody in every one of the letters in front of her, no doubt, had to get up that very morning and get breakfast for the family. And the house—walking away from yesterday! Mrs. Everybody was tired. The children would be cross from too much candy and excitement. She must put away most of their toys—give a lot to that family on Winter Street. It was a shame to let Christmas wear you out so, but —*she was* tired. There were beds to make, the house to clean up, and not to much avail either, for Billie and Junior would be riding their tricycles up and down and running their trains all over the place. Meals to get. Bread and milk for the children, after yesterday—and she guessed there was plenty for dinner—cold chicken and vegetables left. She'd see pretty soon. She'd just read over some of their cards—

"My, I haven't heard from Bertha since last Christmas. Cute picture of the baby, isn't it? And here are Sam's folks an'— My soul, it's nearly ten and here I sit—with everything still to do!"

"And here I sit with all *this* to do!" Miss Sally jerked herself back to her job, grabbed her paper knife and settled down to the morning mail.

The first letter read: "We spent so much more for Christmas than we planned. What dishes can you suggest that are cheap?" January would be devoted to the simple life, she could see that!

But if Christmas Eve and Christmas Day for all who dispensed food for a living were times of super extra effort— something to dread if the truth were told—and the day after was one of bottomless depression and weariness, New Year's Eve was the all-out signal for fun and frolic.

The big hotels, the fashionable restaurants and the night clubs carried the load this time and the managers of the humbler establishments turned a trickling business over to their subordinates and took the night off. There was let-down and gaiety in the air.

Even Miss Kitury seemed to be pushing everything with extra speed that afternoon as though she, too, wanted to get away.

"Going to see the old year out tonight, Miss Kitury?" Sally asked, as the former closed her desk early.

"Yes, even *I*. We may give you young things a run for your money tonight. Don't get caught for speeding or anything. See you in the morning, I *trust*. Good night."

"I wonder if she's going out with a *man*," Sally thought as her eyes followed her boss to the door. She would have been all agog if she had heard Andy in the hall outside say, "I'll call for you at seven, Kit. All right?" And her eyes would have popped clear out had she seen the stunning couple they made at the St. George Roof. But Miss Sally was hustling herself. She wasn't ten minutes behind her boss in making the sidewalk. Oh, yes, she was stepping out. Really stepping, tonight. "*Dinning* and Dancing," as a road sign said. Alex was coming in. Clara and a friend were going with them.

"Hasn't she been the sly puss, keeping that good-looking man hidden all this time," Sally smiled as she made for the subway. "She says he's a *cousin*. Far removed, I hope!"

They were meeting Lou and the "Speedy Greg." Destination? Some place way out. The orchestra was "swell" there and no cover charge. Alex knew about it. The food? Who cared tonight! They'd eat and dance and then come in to the "midnite show," if they could get through the jam.

"A tough night on silver slippers," Sally thought happily, as she dropped the filmy blue net evening dress over her blonde head and pinned the silver ornaments in place— "from the Five and Dime, but they look nice, don't they? There's my buzzer! That's Alex." She gathered up her party purse, her evening wrap (still good, praise be, from more affluent days) and *ran*.

"My, we had a good time, didn't we?" Sally remarked as she and Clara leaned, woozy with weariness, against the elevator as it carried them to their rooms, hours later. They had dropped Lou and Speedy off at the Student Club and said good night to the boys in the lobby. Confetti fell from their hair as their heads drooped. Each clutched a tooter with streamers. Oh, they had hooted and squawked with the best and the worst. They had been pushed and shoved by the crowd and had laughed and shoved in return. Ham and eggs at Joe's diner had finished the fun. The hour? Why ask? Early, of course. "My slippers are a wreck and my feet— But we don't care. It was fun! Good night and good morning, Miss Booth—and Happy New Year!" Sally waved her tooter shakily from her door.

Would her own New Year be a happy one, she wondered sleepily as she tumbled into bed? "Should be, unless—" But she was already asleep.

CHAPTER XI

Off Agin, On Agin

TIME flew by and Sally's sojourn with the *Star* stretched out day after day. Connie had finally written: "The doctor thinks that if I stay here in this mild climate for another month or so that I'll be all right." Tough for Connie Connors maybe, but not bad news for Sally Lewis! Two months more before she had to begin worrying? Elegant! She took "heart of grace," as Prexy used to say, and settled into her job with a will.

She was learning a lot about a very specialized and interesting phase of the food business—in, but not on the production line. Sort of a correspondence course, as it were. You wrote about food, talked about food. You listened and observed and learned and passed on what you heard and saw to encourage the doers. She had also learned a little about the advertising of food products on the radio, a little of newspaper work, and much of the world of homemakers. Their letters were a revelation. Sally was convinced that, next to a determination to do a good job, the two most necessary attributes for happy housekeeping were imagination and a sense of humor. With these handmaidens, dishes three times a day, even doing the family washing, could be part of the adventure of living. Without them, it was all just *work*—too often dreary and drab and dull.

Miss Kitury's Kitchen tried daily to fan the feeble flame wherever found and to supply the vision where lacking; to provide the lift of a little gilt here and there, a bit of glam-

our; to praise the aspiring and cheer on the weary. It was really quite a satisfying job—this reaching out to so many homes. Advice about this, a pat on the head for that. The personal touch—Miss Kitury *insisted* upon it. These homemakers were all her friends. Was that why she was successful—increasingly so, as Sally saw by the daily growing piles of letters?

They, she and her "boss," chatted once in a while about

the profession in general, to Sally's delight. Miss Kitury's own success, if seemingly assured now, had come only after much traveling over a hard and devious road, and her tales were many.

"How did I land in this column?" she echoed Sally's query on one such occasion as they were winding up the afternoon's work.

"Well, I was shoved suddenly from the job of a woman reporter on the *Star* (in those days not too welcome!) into that of a feature editor, so called, and asked to develop a household department—sink or swim. And whether I was to hold any job at all on the paper thereafter depended on whether I could or could not do it, I knew that," she told Sally as she slid the next day's "story" into a folder. "I had never been specially trained in home economics, as anyone starting this type of work now would certainly need to be," she went on, "but I had always been greatly interested in people, in women particularly—their homes, their problems, what they most enjoy and what they hate worst—so I began with an informal chat and whatever recipes I could beg from my friends. Luckily the time was ripe and the column caught on. Women were beginning to be home-conscious. They wanted help. They wrote begging for more and more, and I had to find it. When I finally hit on our present plan of an exchange of ideas, I had to have help myself. So I asked for an assistant, stipulating that she should be a home economics graduate with ability to write, and that she have some commercial experience in food production—tearoom, restaurant or lunchroom management, and that she be someone I could like personally and depend on. Connie Connors was the result, thanks to your Dean Ardwell, and she has certainly been a lifesaver. Your school has a reputation for turning out good girls." She smiled over at Sally.

"Now, having delivered myself of all this, I'll let you go on home. I've one last job to do still," and Miss Kitury turned back to her desk. But whatever that job was, it didn't seem to be getting done very fast. Kate Kitury's hands were idle on the keys and her thoughts were far away. That little talk with Sally had started her off again on a plan she had considered many times of late.

"This department has grown so these past few years. We get more and more letters every day—well over a hundred last week. I need a regular stenographer right this minute. And also I wish we had a cooking laboratory where I could test these recipes. We have hundreds of them on file. Why not a cook book of our own? That's an idea! And this radio hour—I could do much more commercial food advertising if I were free to go out after all the business myself. That's where the money is. But I'll need more help, that's certain. Federal regulations for commercial 'continuities' are so fussy. So much paper work to do—copies of everything to this one and that one. Supposing I ran my own radio hour? Bought the time, then solicited the business to fill it? I could earn twice what I do—and feel much more independent. More independent—that's really what appeals to me. When Connie gets back, I think I'll turn over a lot more of this work on the paper to her. She can do it as well as I can. And then I'll—" Her eyes narrowed, as she looked forward into the future.

"Why are you here so late, Kit?" Andy, of the copy desk, stopped for a minute on his way home.

"Crystal gazing, Andy." She looked up at him. His hair was getting quite gray, she noticed.

He swung a long leg over the corner of her desk. "I suppose it would be too much to ever hope that you might see
a fellow looking like me anywhere in your crystal ball?"
There were tired lines around his keen eyes. She hadn't
seen them there before, she thought with a pang.

"Oh, Andy, we can't go into all that again." Kate Kitury's
voice held genuine regret. "You've been such a grand friend
always—my best. Let's go on as we've always done." She
laid a capable hand over his. "I don't think I'll ever marry
—but you're a real dear," she said gratefully. "Good night."

And so the winter moved along. January and February
were always dead level, especially January. There were the
birthdays, George's and Abraham's, to lift February a bit.
Requests for Lady Washington and Dolly Madison cake
recipes had come in to Miss Kitury's Kitchen and suggestions for parties. (Cherry tarts, for instance, made from the
fresh frosted cherries so easy to get now in most of the
good stores. You baked the tart shells over the backs of
muffin tins or patty pans. Cooked the cherries with a little
minute tapioca for thickening, added sugar and a dab of
butter and filled the shells. Served them with whipped
cream, decorated with a cherry cut in slim petals to make
a flower.)

But mostly this whole stretch was sort of dull. You just
stuck to your job—shivery mornings and snow and slush.
You prayed that you wouldn't get a cold because you
couldn't afford to be out. You plugged along—wished for
spring. That is, you would if your job weren't going to fold
up then. The time *was* getting short and Connie Connor's
return nearer and nearer.

That was the only trouble about spring, thought Miss Sally,

as she stamped the letter to Mrs. Brown of Belmont, telling her to use a crumpled paper napkin to clear the fat from the top of her chicken soup or to strain it through cheese-cloth wrung out of cold water. That had been an easy answer. It took only half her mind. The other half was worrying about her job. How she did wish it might hold out till June—May at least. But that wouldn't happen and there was no use hoping. She might just as well get busy and start hunting again. "How I do hate to think of it!" She shoved the thought ahead of her. One week more and then she'd begin—

"Well, Dale O'Hara! I haven't seen you in months," Kit Kitury leaned across her table at André's to greet a modishly dressed woman who had just come into view in the line that was waiting to be seated. It was the peak of the luncheon hour and André's was very busy. Too busy of late, thought Miss Kitury, but the food was good and the atmosphere quiet and restful usually, so she continued to come.

Dale O'Hara was a member of the staff of *Your Home*, a woman's magazine, daily growing more popular. She and Miss Kitury had often collaborated in days gone by—swapping ideas and discussing trends. Kit Kitury's finger was always on the pulse through the stream of letters that crossed her desk and she had generously passed information along. But of late she had been *so* on the fly scouting for business. There was little time to chat or she hadn't seen her friend.

"Hello, Kit! This *is* a surprise. Do you come here often?"

"Quite. It's convenient and I feel at home. Why don't you take this chair here at my table?" She beckoned to her waiter. "A friend, Tony. Will you serve her, please?"

"What luck for me!" Miss O'Hara slid gratefully into the

chair the waiter held for her and unbuttoned her fur coat.
"That line looked endless. I had visions of wasting far too
much time on my two feet to suit me. What's good for
lunch? Let's see— Mushrooms on toast with bacon and
broiled tomatoes? Couldn't be better." She smiled at the
waiter as she handed back the menu.

Miss Kitury's quick eye swept the figure in front of her
meantime. "Style! I never have time to hunt for clothes
like those," she thought with a touch of envy. "Though if
I really cared enough, I suppose I'd probably take time, so
that's the answer to that, I guess." Aloud she said, as Miss
O'Hara settled back to wait for her order, "Well, what's
new at *Your Home?* Circulation going up by leaps and
bounds, I hear."

"Yes, it is going ahead at last, thank heaven. I thought a
year or so ago that it would never start. We seemed bogged
down for good and all."

"What did the trick finally?" Katherine Kitury leaned
forward with interest.

"I don't know. Eternal vigilance, I guess. Everlastingly
keeping two jumps ahead. Finding out—by whatever (leg
work mostly!)—what women want before they know it
themselves and dishing it up with color and snap and style.
Usable ideas. Practical, pertinent, pretty. Cheap, neat, and
tasty. Color photography has done more than any other
one thing, I'd say. Mrs. Doe likes to *see* how a dinner party
table can look and what's wrong with brown for a bedroom. You know—eye appeal. Next to that, the new
streamlined kitchen has been about the most revolutionary
thing that's hit the home in many a day. The idea didn't
originate with us, I'm sorry to say, but it has given us all
a grand boost and a steady job at remodeling. 'Before' on

this page, 'After' on that, you know. And then we've made a real effort to cover the country more generally. Is the idea good in Palm Beach and Peoria and Portland, Oregon? And after that, will it strike the *average* woman? We've made a real bid for her. Tried to find out what her home is like. What it *might* look like, given a few dollars, an idea and a little determination. But mercy, Kit, I shouldn't be telling *you* all this. You know as well as I do what it takes. It just takes and takes, and that's the answer for all of us, I guess. Any special news from the Kitchen?" She turned the conversation toward her friend. "I read your sprightly bit every day, along with the headlines. You have *style*, Kit. I always get a lift and a push ahead and I've borrowed many an idea from you, I confess."

Miss Kitury bowed. "Help yourself. I got them from somebody else and nobody knows where *they* got them —from the lady next door, likely. You know," she leaned forward, "I've a yen to sort of branch out a bit." She spoke tentatively.

Dale O'Hara looked up inquiringly and Miss Kitury went on. "Well, in the first place I might publish a cook book. I've a wagon load of good recipes. And then I've thought quite a lot about a cooking laboratory for testing, and my own radio hour rather than time paid for by the *Star*. What would you say?"

"We-l-l, the cook book idea I can see. By all means. Particularly if you can give it an original slant or an unusually attractive form, and of course you're the best judge of whether you could swing your own radio time. I don't doubt for a minute but what you could. But I'd go slow on that laboratory. Would it bring you business enough to pay? They are expensive things to set up and run and I wonder how much you, in your particular circumstances, need one. Try the other things first, why don't you? But if you do decide later on that you need a kitchen, come down and look over ours. I could probably wangle the figures for it out of old Clark if you want them."

"You're probably right. I won't be doing anything for several months anyhow—not until my regular assistant gets back and is established again."

"Oh, that reminds me, Kit. One of our best girls has asked for her vacation in a few weeks, plus additional leave in order to take her mother away for a rest. The magazine suggested Mexico, offering expenses for several articles on Mexican cookery, housekeeping, and so forth. Everybody's eyes seem turned south of the border these days. So that's where she's headed. But to get to the point, I've got to rustle a girl to fill in. Jo Daniels will step up but that leaves her place to fill farther down. Ordinarily, we'd double up and get along, but we've two or three extra projects already in the pot that have to go on. It's always hard to get good people—no matter how many need jobs, isn't it?" Miss O'Hara gave a sigh of vexation.

"Wait a minute!" Miss Kitury's teacup stopped in mid-air. "When did you say you needed someone? My Sally Lewis will be free and looking for work about then. The fifteenth you say? Miss it by a week. I've a mind to write Connie and ask her if she can't manage to get back a little earlier. My girl needs a job for a few months—she's getting married in June, she tells me. You'll like her. Sorry I can't keep her myself, but I need a regular stenographer most right now and I can't afford both—yet. She's a little piece but intelligent and quick on the trigger. Has good background and training. Interested in and enthusiastic about everything and doesn't mind working overtime. How's that?"

"Too good to be true." Miss O'Hara sat back in relief. "It pays to get around and see your friends, doesn't it? 'Leg work and divination,' as I often said. Well, I've got to get back. Send your girl around to see me when you can spare her. Thanks loads, Kit. Best of luck on your ventures. Good-bye." And Miss O'Hara swung out through the revolving doors.

"A profitable and pleasant lunch hour," Katherine Kitury reflected as she gathered up her wraps. "I'm relieved to find a place for my Sally—a stroke of luck all around. Furthermore, I'm glad she's getting married. Business will be losing a smart girl, which it can't afford, to be sure, but if there's anything the country needs it's more women with home economics training and ability and understanding for this job of homemaking. That's a career that can stand developing or my name's not K. Kitury!"

"Well, what did you think of *Your Home?*" Miss Kitury asked as she appeared in the office the morning after Sally's interview with Miss O'Hara.

"Oh, it's a very interesting place, isn't it?" Sally brightened. "They've the cutest kitchen there and a lovely model dining room and such nice offices everywhere. It seems quite an elegant place to work in, but—" she hesitated. "I *hate* to leave here," she blurted out. "I love this dingy old place. You've been so good to me. I've learned such a lot. I had no idea this could be such an interesting job. It's quite a different world from any I'd ever been in before. I'm sorry to be going, really."

"And I'm sorry I can't afford to keep you—very. But

you'll like the place where you're going. You *are* going there, aren't you?"

"Miss O'Hara *said* to come in next Monday," Sally answered.

"Good, I was sure she would."

"It was so nice of you to tell her about me," Sally said gratefully.

"Nonsense, why shouldn't I, pray tell? It works out well for both of you—and for me. I'd certainly hate to turn you adrift at this time of the year." Miss Kitury looked kindly at her young pinch hitter. "You do get fond of these girls. That's the trouble," she said to herself.

"It will not only be a help to Miss O'Hara to have someone step in who has just been doing similar work," Miss Kitury went on. "But you should learn a lot that will be of real benefit to you personally. It will be home territory for you, I'd say. So it's not such an ill wind after all." Miss Kitury sat down at her desk. "Got anything real snappy for my 'story' today? My ideas are few and skimpy this morning."

"Here's one in this letter about putting a little minced onion and chopped pimento into canned string beans to sort of take the curse off them, and another about garnishing cauliflower with minced cooked carrot or a row of slices around the dish and there—"

"Enough! Hand them over. I'll just whip up a little something on pepping up the menus at this tag-end of winter." Miss Kitury's typewriter was already clicking.

Sally worked early and late that week. She did so want to leave the decks clear for Connie Connors. But the letters poured in by the dozens. Before the week was over she wished Mrs. So-and-So and Mrs. Everybody Else in Jeri-

cho. She didn't care if grated orange peel beaten up with
cream cheese and powdered sugar *did* make a good frosting for gingerbread or that a pinch of soda in cream puff
batter made them rise big and high. They could rise to
glory for all of her! She was just getting *so* tired. Hereto-
fore bright ideas and cheap had been more to be desired
than gold, than much fine gold, but enough was enough.
Out the window with the lot! Click-clickety-clack went
her typewriter. There. That was done and that and that.

"Time for you to be getting home, young lady." Andy
stopped at her desk at five-thirty on Friday night. "What's
this I hear about your skipping out on us? What's the
idea?"

"Well, as the old darky woman said when someone asked
if her dead husband had been resigned to dying, 'Resigned?
He was 'bleeged ter!' That's me! I'm 'bleeged ter. I was
only pinch hitting for Miss Connors, you know, and she's
coming back Monday."

"Oh. I thought maybe you were getting married, or
something. Tell me the truth now," he probed as Sally colored and laughed a bit.

"Well, not before June." And Miss Sally made a big
wish right there, remembering the year before.

"That's just about what I thought. Some men have all
the luck." Andy grinned down at her. "Well, come and see
us once in a while and don't forget your old friends tied
to the *Star*. Good luck. Get yourself home now. Good
night."

"Good night, Mr. Andy. You've been very kind to me.
I'll think about you every time I read the *Star*. 'Bye." Sally
waved to her lean friend going out the door, and shut her
desk down with the next move. She couldn't do *one thing
more*.

"Connie's in town. She called me last night. I wouldn't be surprised to see her here this morning," Miss Kitury told Sally as she hung her hat on the rack next day.

Sally was cleaning out the desk drawers. She still had a lot to do to catch up but the task didn't look quite so hopeless, now that she was rested. She took the galleys down to Mike for the last time and said good-bye.

"Just about the time we get to liking somebody real well and looking for them every day, they fly up and leave," the old foreman grumbled, taking his pipe from his mouth. "Well, good-bye. Be a good girl."

"Good-bye, Mike," Sally answered from the stairs. Good smoking tobacco would remind her always of the lower regions of the *Star* and her old friend Mike.

Upstairs she found Miss Kitury talking eagerly with a young woman, perhaps six or eight years older than Sally— tall, slender, with very curly ash-blonde hair. She looked up as Sally approached.

"Connie, this is Sally Lewis who has been helping while you were away," Miss Kitury introduced them.

So this was Connie Connors. No wonder Miss Kitury thought she was a whiz. Sally's eyes took her in from head to foot.

"I'm so glad to meet you," she said. "I've heard so much about you since I've been here."

"Think it's safer for me not to inquire *what* you've heard, but I'm glad to meet you, too, and I do want to thank you for leaving my affairs in such good shape. Oh, I can tell just by the looks of things," she said in answer to Sally's look of surprise.

"There are these letters that came this morning, though. I'll try to finish them all. But there may be a few for seed, at that," Sally answered worriedly.

"Don't give them a thought. Label the ones you don't have time for and leave them in the drawer. See you Monday morning, Miss Kitury. Good-bye, Miss Lewis," and she was gone.

"My, I'm relieved to see Connie looking so well," Miss Kitury remarked, watching the departing figure.

Was there a twinge of envy—jealousy maybe—in Sally's heart? Perhaps, just a speck, but she answered, "She's very attractive, isn't she?" and swung to her endless letters.

"Mercy, I forgot that I have an appointment at 11:30. I'll have to fly." Miss Kitury looked at the clock and put on her wraps. "Good-bye, my dear. Thank you *so* much for all your hard work. I do hope you'll like *Your Home*. Drop in and see me so I can keep track of you. Be *sure* to see me before you leave town for good. Good-bye." Miss Kitury shook Sally's hand warmly.

"Thank you so much for everything." Sally rose. "I'll always read your column with very special interest. Good-bye." And she slid again into her chair and turned once more to her letters. There. Just one more left. It was way after twelve but she must finish. She spread the letter out in front of her and read:

Dorham, Maine
March 19—

Miss Kitury's Kitchen
    Morning Star
Dear Madam—
    Will you kindly send directions for making a Mexican charm string by return mail? Thank you.
                    Very truly yours,
                    (Mrs.) Jenny Williams

What next? Sally slumped down in her chair. A Mexican charm string. She didn't know any more about making one than the man in the moon! And she wouldn't know any more if she sat there till supper time. "Jenny, you would!" she said in disgust as she clipped a card to the letter. "For seed. Sorry. Answer unknown. S. L." and stuck it in the drawer. "Just for you, Jen, I go down to defeat within a yard of the goal post. That for you," she muttered wearily as she put on her wraps. She did stop to scribble a card to Judy:

> To My New Job—
> Off agin, on agin, gone agin.
> Me agin, Sally

And slid it down the chute in the hall.

Out on the street newsboys were already calling *"Star. Evening Star. Star,* lady?"

"Here you are, young man."

She would always read the *Star*—with pleasure and with pride. It would remind her of many new experiences, of many kindnesses, of many, many new things learned in Miss Kitury's Kitchen.

CHAPTER XII

Your Home

SALLY made her way uptown at eight-thirty on Monday morning. She was due at nine, but she wanted to make sure of being there early. She dreaded the day—getting started on a new job again. It took all the courage she could muster. It did seem as if there had been an awful lot of this "stop and go" business since she had been graduated from college. "But I didn't know I was going to get married when I left Hawaii to take that institutional management course. Nor when I accepted the lunchroom job at Manfred," she sought to justify herself, "and I certainly didn't know when I gave it up that I *wasn't* getting married, after all! This year will look like a first-class dish of hash, I'll say. But, never mind, I always did like hash. It has interest and variety, to say the least!" She drew up her shoulders. But these reflections weren't going to save her from a hard day, that she knew, and she stopped a minute to gather herself together before pushing open the brass-studded door of the tall office building that stood on one of the city's swankiest streets.

"Floor, please?" the operator asked as Sally stepped into the elevator.

"Twelve," and before she had scarcely caught her breath, here it was!

The offices and establishment of the magazine, *Your Home,* spread over the entire floor. It was an intriguing place to come into. Framed paintings—the original designs of many of the magazine's covers hung in the halls—water colors and drawings in black and white. The unusual floor covering and hall bench prepared one a bit for the charming reception room. Where had she seen that old-looking, softly colored maple furniture before? The Sugar Maple Tea Room in the Berkshires! She and Alex—Columbus Day. The happy memory flicked through her mind—and out. So much had happened since then— Her eyes swept over the room again with growing appreciation. If she didn't do one other thing for herself in the next month or so but keep her head above water and absorb these clever ideas the time would be well spent, she thought. A real yearning came over her. She would *so* like to know *how* to put a room like this together herself. It didn't look *expensive* (Maybe she didn't know!)—not elegant, but just—just charming—that was the word. Where did you look for old copper lamps with rough—was it silk or linen—shades? And that chintz with the interesting pattern, and the graceful pieces of pottery? None of the furniture stores she had ever been in carried old tables like this one—the color of a little stand her mother had at home, cherry wood she remembered it was. Antique shops? Must be. But how did you know what you were getting? One could be gypped, as the boys said, gypped plenty in such a place. But maybe, if she kept her eyes and ears open every minute she was here, she might learn. But what, pray tell, could *she* give in return? She hoped there was something, or she'd lose her job, but right that minute she couldn't think of a thing!

Sally crossed the room, toward the reception desk. A girl (Miss Day, the sign said)—dark, thin-featured, evidently just arrived—looked up from stowing her pocketbook into the desk drawer as Sally approached and asked for Miss O'Hara.

"Are you Miss Lewis?"

"Yes, I am," Sally answered in surprise.

"Miss O'Hara told me you'd be in today and to show you the ropes till she came. I'll take you to the dressing room." And she led Sally out and down the hall. "You can hang your things in this locker, and here's your key."

Sally felt the girl's sharp eyes on her as she took off her coat and hat and tucked in a straying curl. She was glad she had put on her most becoming dress—a tailored turquoise wool crepe with white turn-over collar—some kind of a classic, the salesgirl had called it. Good with her hair, if she did say so.

"These rooms along this side of the hall are the offices mostly," Miss Day pointed out as they started forth. "The editor, Mr. Drake, is here; advertising manager next—Mr. Scott his name is; circulation in here, and so on. Mrs. Andrews and Miss O'Hara, Foods and Home Furnishing editors, have these rooms. You must have come here before, didn't you?"

"Just for a few minutes."

"Did you see the kitchen?"

"Only a glimpse."

They crossed to a door leading off the reception room.

"It's a darling place, isn't it?" Sally exclaimed again.

"Yes, if you like kitchens. You'll probably have one of these desks here." The sweep of Miss Day's arm took in an alcove separated from the kitchen by cupboards about waist-high. The woodwork, small desks and all, were done in pale gray with blue accessories to match the kitchen. Chromium chairs with blue leather seats, blue blotters,

Clouded dark blue and gray linoleum covered the floors. Ruffled organdie curtains—gray Venetian blinds with blue banding at the kitchen window over the sink. Gray enameled steel cupboards around the kitchen, blue linoleum with chromium banding on the working surfaces. Blue and yellow pottery on small corner shelves. Not so grand as the kitchen of MyOMy, but so attractive—so compact. Six steps from side to side. "Handy as a pocket in a shirt, as Aunty used to say," thought Sally delightedly.

"Who cooks here?" asked Sally.

"You, probably. And Jo Daniels. She can make swell biscuits."

A small dining room opened from the kitchen—beige with peach—very modern in design.

"There's a living room and bedroom beyond that get changed around every so often with much commotion. But I think Miss O'Hara is in by now, so I'll take you back. There goes my buzzer this minute."

Sally crossed the reception room, quick eyes darting from right to left again. Beautifully bound books in a bookcase always gave an air to a room, didn't they? They stepped across the hall with the tiled floor to Miss O'Hara's office. The latter was busy at her desk but looked up as Sally entered.

"Good morning, Miss Lewis. Sit down. You use a typewriter, don't you? Good." Miss O'Hara swung round abruptly. "Take that pile of letters there in the basket, will you, and answer each one with just a line thanking the writer for her information—or whatever—saying we will pay a dollar in due time if any idea or recipe proves usable. Then copy the recipes on one sheet, suggestions or what-have-yous on another, with date and name and address of sender. Number them in order. That will keep you busy till lunch time and give you a chance to get oriented a bit while I get this proof back to the printer. There's a machine in the next room you can use. After lunch I'll outline your duties, but I've got to get this job finished first."

Well, this was familiar business, thought Sally in relief. She could shut her eyes and think she was back at the old *Star!* She gathered up the letters, found paper, and prepared to write.

But these letters had rather a different tone from the ones that poured into Miss Kitury's Kitchen. A little more formal, evidence of perhaps better education? First families? Well, second or third, maybe. Anyhow, a little more sophisticated—or something, Sally felt. The recipes sounded more expensive and elaborate as she clicked off one or two. But, now, listen to this: "Did you know that a pinch of salt in the vinegar bottle will keep 'mother' from forming?" "Not me!" thought Sally. "That's a good idea anybody can use—the governor's lady or—who was the other one? Judy somebody or other," her thoughts clicked along with the keys. It was certainly better to be doing something she knew about this first morning than stumbling along through—well, she didn't know what. Perhaps it was just this "not knowing what" that made any first day hard; the fear that you wouldn't be able to do what was expected of you. She guessed so. But whatever it was, she didn't like it much, anyhow, and she was glad for the forenoon's respite.

At eleven-thirty she gathered up her letters and carried them in to Miss O'Hara's desk for signing.

"All finished?" Miss O'Hara picked up the top letter and read it through. "Sounds as if you had done this sort of

thing before," she said. "Sign my name to the lot, if you
will, and drop them into the mail chute as you go out for
your lunch hour. Put the list of recipes into this folder
marked "untested" and the suggestions into the one for
"ideas." When you come back you might look over the supplies in the kitchen. Check the cupboards so you know
where things are and the dining room for silver and linen.
I'll be in shortly after one to talk with you and lay out
the week's program."

Sally hurried toward the dressing room, donned her
wraps, and made for the elevator.

"Is there any good place around here for lunch?" she
asked Miss Day at the desk.

"What do you mean 'good'? Good with style that you
pay for, or good and cheap?"

Sally grinned. "Good and cheap, if there are such."

"Try the Blue Bowl. One block up the street, turn right,
and three down."

Sally thanked her and went down onto the pavement.
"One block up, turn right and three down"—she counted.
There was the sign and there was the blue bowl in the window. Two steps below the level of the sidewalk. Yellow
curtains—heavy cotton in basket weave—hung at the windows. Tearoom? Attractive, whatever it was. Dark blue
tables, yellow chairs, blue and yellow wall brackets with
pots of ivy. Self-service, Sally discovered at once. You paid
for food and not to be waited on. All right with her. She
swept the counter with practiced eye. Fried apple rings
with tiny link sausages, clover-leaf rolls, a fruit cooky, and
a glass of milk—thirty cents. Cheap enough. The cookies
just out of the oven. That was smart. The two young
women behind the counter looked like college girls. "If

they didn't graduate in home economics, I don't know the signs," Sally thought to herself. There was that cole slaw with sour-cream dressing. "Somebody in that kitchen took quantity cookery under Miss Lawrence, I'll bet a cent." Some day when she had time she'd investigate the Blue Bowl, but this wasn't the day! She swallowed her lunch. Oh, yes, it was good. Sausage links and apple rings were a very tasty combination, but this was no time to think about them. Three blocks up the street and one around the corner—and here she was at the brass-studded door again. Funny how a city could change from homely to handsome, from simple to sumptuous, in four short blocks, wasn't it?

Sally knew she was back early, but she had noticed copies of *Your Home* on the little desk by the kitchen and she wanted to look them over.

She settled into one of the blue and chromium chairs and turned the pages with interest. To be sure she had seen this magazine before but never really—*really* looked at it till now. Here was the Homemaking section—the departments of House Furnishings and Decoration and of Foods. See these pictures of a whole house done in color! Living room, bedroom—this one was darling! White furniture with wild-rose pink knobs on the dresser, pink ruffles on the dressing table—um—m! It made her ache inside and she turned the page wistfully. Look at this ducky kitchen with a little dining room on one end—red and blue and yellow and— A picture of the old kitchen on the farm flitted through her mind. Immense, cheerful, pleasant and home-like, to be sure, but a long shot from this little gay-colored square of super efficiency! Sally turned on. Here were meals, menus, recipes, food—and terra firma. That is, a little "firma"—but only a little!

This food was *so* elegant looking. Here was a colored page—an Easter breakfast—lovely! And then pages of photographs, one for every recipe given, showing just how the food should look when ready to serve. Wonderful dishes they were! How in the world was she, Sally Lewis, going to fit into all this? She felt again the old scared feeling creeping over her—so familiar, so hard to control. She jumped up and started opening cupboards and poking into drawers. See this shelf done like a terrace—bleachers—to hold spices so you could always see every tin! Wasn't that smart? And here was a clever gadget for holding kitchen knives on the inside of the cupboard door. Electric stove, electric icebox, electric dishwasher, electric beater. (It wasn't the Speedy Mixer. She must tell Greg!) Everything to take the work out of housework certainly, to use Miss Kitury's phrase. It shouldn't ever be anything but a pleasure to work in a kitchen like this. Everything unsightly was out of sight. Step-saving, time-saving, nerve-saving—slick!

She was so busy investigating the dining room buffet where the silver and linens were kept that she did not hear Miss O'Hara come in until a blue hat appeared around the kitchen door-frame.

"Oh, here you are! How do you like our layout?" Miss O'Hara asked.

"Lovely!" Sally's fervent tone bespoke her admiration.

"We think it is. And, what is more to the point, so far, I'm happy to say, it has proved convenient and adequate— The final test of any workshop."

"Did you plan it, Miss O'Hara?" Sally asked in wonder.

"No, one of the kitchen equipment houses did that, but we each made suggestions, adding a bit here and taking out there, so that we almost think we did it all! Now, if you'll come into my office, I'll try to explain what is ahead for you. Bring a couple of those magazines there on the desk. They may help to illustrate."

Sally followed Miss O'Hara across the hall. My, she was good-looking in that gray Persian coat with the blue flower toque—stunning with her black hair and blue eyes.

"Sit here." Miss O'Hara slipped off her coat and sat down at the desk, indicating a chair for Sally. "Now. The April number will be off the press in a day or two, in the mail, and on the newsstands by the twenty-fifth, or the twenty-seventh at the latest. My part of the May number is practically finished, with the exception of the final touches on the write-up for our Mother's Day celebration —all the old-fashioned dishes that everyone's mother made at home—and maybe a few fillers, and so on. The central theme—idea to be developed—for June has been decided on, the recipes chosen and tested, and color scheme worked out, but the pictures haven't been taken yet—and there's a lot of writing to be done for that. Every month we try to feature something that's timely and seasonable—holidays and such. For instance, for June we are having a wedding breakfast, the bridesmaids' luncheon done in color, and suggestions for a graduation party.

"Now, what would come to your mind at once for July?"

"The Sunday School picnic on the Fourth," Sally answered before she thought.

A quizzical look from Miss O'Hara. "You must have grown up in the country. What did you have to eat at your picnic?"

Sally colored a bit. "Fried chicken always and delicious

lemon pie. Every neighbor brought something different, you see—homemade Parker House rolls, I remember—and Aunty always brought the first strawberry shortcake of the season, baked in a big dripping pan, with a pitcher of cream to pour on it. Sometimes someone brought a freezer of homemade ice cream, and there was always lemonade in a barrel for everyone."

Miss O'Hara smiled. "That was good country style." Her eyes narrowed. "It wouldn't make a bad opening paragraph, at that. Then contrast the newer and more up-to-date ideas—for a family dinner at home, a supper party out on the terrace, maybe. Not bad." She made a note on her memorandum pad. "Then, of course, cool drinks should be featured for July. And salads and summer vegetables," she went on. "We must begin on all these ideas very soon, too."

"You mean you begin work on the July number *now?*" Sally asked in astonishment. It was only the middle of March—involuntarily her eye caught the snow still piled up in the shaded corners across the street.

"Yes, indeed, and we must have ideas for August and September right away, too, so we can find appropriate linen, dishes and accessories, and so on. The firms of the city are glad to lend anything for the advertising, but we have to run the things to earth first, and that takes time. Miss Daniels is out today making the rounds of the markets, the specialty shops for household equipment, the fancy food stores, and so on, and shopping for the bridesmaids' luncheon table, and for Mrs. Andrews' summer curtains and slip covers. Hunting for new ideas. 'Leg work' to the trade. She'll work with you this week in the kitchen and get you started. Then she will help Mrs. Andrews on house furnishings, except for advice on party table decorations, if we need any. She's very clever and original at them. You can cook, I hope?"

"I have more or less, but I haven't done any fancy cooking since I left school," Sally answered honestly.

"I guess you can follow a recipe. Miss Daniels will help you at first. I'm hoping you can get the things for the wedding breakfast and the luncheon made and photographed this week and what other recipes were chosen as the winners in this month's entries. Usually there are seven or eight. You might look up the folder for June, see what is planned, check your groceries, make a list of anything you think may be needed. Miss Daniels will know what to do in the morning. I'll see you then."

Sally went into the adjoining room to look in the files for the material, took it into the little sanctum beside the kitchen, and settled down to study the job ahead. She opened the folder. Here were typed sheets clipped together —wedding breakfast—bridesmaids' luncheon—a wistful thought strayed clear away to Alex and Chelton. Nonsense! She wouldn't be having a wedding breakfast nor be giving a luncheon for her bridesmaids either. Too far away from home. Too poor—well, no matter—she was marrying Alex, and no other girl was *that* lucky, bridesmaids or no bridesmaids! "But let's see what I might have if I were a debutante." She bent over the sheets.

Bridesmaids' luncheon: Whole strawberries with the hulls on, mound of powdered sugar—and a penciled note. (Flat stemmed crystal dishes—look in R. H. Stacy's.) Chicken custard (toast circle), fresh asparagus Hollandaise, tomato and cucumber slices, tiny rolls, heart-shaped ice cream, pastel shades, small cakes, iced and decorated like a bouquet. (Look for paper frills at florist up the street.) Coffee. "*Hm-m.* Sounds complicated if you read it fast, but take it slowly and it's not too bad.

"Chicken custard? I'll bet it's made with milk and eggs and cubes of cold chicken—white meat, baked in custard cups and turned out. Let's see how near I came to it." She looked at the accompanying recipe. "Almost on the head! Chicken stock and top milk, half and half, of course. That would give it more of the chicken flavor. You're getting good, Sally L. You didn't study a thousand and one recipes under Miss Kitury for nothing, did you?" She was holding pleasant conversation with herself—an old trick. Pencil in hand, she jotted down the market order.

At the foot of the page were notes: "Color scheme. Try

for pastel-colored damask cloth—ice blue—or embroidered organdy in pale pink or green. Flowers: delphinium, pale yellow African daisies, pink sweet peas. Look for unusual container. Go to Carroni's. Spode china, white with flowered center, or try pale-colored glass or crystal. See Orrington's."

"Why, you could spend hours—days—chasing from one end of the town to the other after those things and then maybe not find them!" Sally exclaimed. "Wonder if I'll ever have to do it?"

Now for the wedding breakfast. She read along with interest. This was a buffet affair. Molded salad, chicken, elaborate garnish, little cream cheese molds with tomato jelly tops, many fancy sandwiches, open-faced and filled. Note: Silver platters. Arrange in rows. Garnish. Make Picture. Silver coffee-tea service. Punch bowl. See Max for flowers. Yellow Roses? Bride's cake. See file under cakes (Takes a whole forenoon to make!).

That assignment was a tough one! Sally's heart sank and her courage waned. It was five o'clock and her head was spinning. Everyone was going home, so she put the folder in the desk drawer, found her way to the dressing room, followed the stream to the elevator, and went home to the Y.

"If I don't learn a heap on this job, it will be because I just haven't got what it takes!" she told Clara that night as they stopped to chat. "The chef of the Ritz will have nothing on me come June!"

CHAPTER XIII

Getting Under Way

NEXT morning Miss Sally appeared at the quarters of *Your Home* bright and early. She was carrying an overnight bag in which reposed a freshly laundered blue smock. Courage and confidence had returned with a night's sleep. She guessed maybe she could make chicken custard if she set her mind to it. If she couldn't, it was because she hadn't any mind to set!

Miss Day was in the dressing room, making up before the mirror, when Sally entered.

"Good morning. You don't know whether Miss Daniels is in yet or not, do you?" Sally asked as she hung up her wraps.

"Yes. Saw her a minute ago." Miss Day plied her lipstick assiduously. "Gosh, I'm a wreck this morning." She turned from the mirror. "That band at the Roof is certainly smooth. The boyfriend's nuts about dancing. I'm dead, standing up. Hope every dame in town won't come trailing into that reception room today. 'May we just look around? We've heard so much—' They've heard *too* much, if you ask me. Why people rave over cooking and kitchens, hanging up curtains and painting woodwork, is beyond me!"

"Well, I guess you just do or you don't, that's all. I'm one that does, luckily for me," Sally answered as she whisked out the door, her smock under her arm. "Cheerful crab, that," she commented as she made her way down the

143

hall. "But I suppose it's a good thing we aren't all made alike, at that. The world might be deadly dull, and so far I've been spared that fate, I'm pleased to state!"

She found Miss Daniels already in the kitchen, checking the contents of the icebox. She was taller than Sally by several inches, older by a year or two, dark hair, thin, clever-looking face. A certain drive and nervous energy showed in every move. She turned as Sally appeared.

"Good morning, Miss Lewis. I'm Jo Daniels. Miss O'Hara asked me to show you the ropes this week before I take over my own new job with Mrs. Andrews on home decoration." She shut the refrigerator door, her hand (such long fingers, Sally noticed) still on the latch, as she paused to greet her helper.

"Oh," said Sally, "you've always worked in this department then?"

"Two years. I'm only transferring while Anne Dixon is away. It just happens that Mrs. Andrews' work is extra heavy right now. She's doing a new set of bulletins on home interiors—many in color, besides one on rugs, another on furniture, one on making curtains, and so on. And then she has to redecorate the demonstration rooms for summer and stage a show for some textile firm, and goodness knows what all else. I've helped her a few times before, so she and Miss O'Hara thought it easier to find someone to fill in here. I'll be glad for a little change, too," she added.

"Haven't you liked this work?" Sally asked, a bit anxiously.

"Yes, I've liked it. One side of it especially. I love putting foods together to make them look pretty—lovely color combinations, nice shapes, arranging a table in some unusual and attractive style. To tell you the truth, I'm afraid

I'm a lot more interested in the looks of food than I am in the taste. That's a dreadful confession for me to be making to you, isn't it? Miss O'Hara would be shocked beyond words if she ever heard me! But right now the whole business seems so sort of—well, perhaps not futile exactly—but— I guess I'm just tired of spending hours cooking and then having the food eaten in fifteen minutes with nothing but a stack of dirty dishes left to tell the tale! Whereas if you create a lovely room you have really accomplished something that stays put—for a while, anyhow. You can sit in a room and enjoy it—if you have time to sit! But maybe after I've struggled with French plaits and slip covers and chased all over town for some special lamp shade to match something else that I can't find either, I'll be glad to come back to an egg-beater and a paring knife! There's one thing about our profession—if you get tired of one angle there are a dozen others to slide over into. A lot of them are right here in this organization, too."

"These all have something to do with homemaking, don't they?" Sally asked.

"Oh, definitely. That's the why of this magazine, of course. It's run for homemakers—and by them too, more than anyone would guess, I might add. Our material in this department of foods, for instance, would run mighty thin if our readers didn't send in scores of recipes and suggestions and questions to answer. Mr. Towne, the home building editor, would have been stuck long ago, too. But I guess nobody worries about running out. We're so swamped we don't ever catch up!"

("Where have I heard that groan before!" thought Sally. "Only at Miss Kitury's we talked with the women every day instead of once a month! But a magazine is more elaborate than a daily newspaper column, of course, something lovely to look at, to keep, and refer to. Maybe not so intimate, though, or so—so responsive?" She'd soon find out.)

"We are really a woman's exchange—like the back-yard fence," Jo Daniels concluded. "And anyone would think we were two biddies hanging over one right now, with nothing to do but gossip! We've a stiff week ahead, if I remember correctly. Do you know where to look for the June folder in the file?"

"It's here in the desk. I was studying it last night." Sally opened the drawer. *The folder was not there.* Her face fell. Was it the other desk? They were just alike. She whirled to look, but that drawer, too, was empty. Her heart sank, then raced with fright.

"Why—why I put it right here in this drawer, thinking we would be using it the first thing this morning! What could have happened to it?" she stammered, her eyes big with growing apprehension.

"Look in the file. Maybe Miss O'Hara saw it and put it away. She's very particular about that." Miss Daniels' tone was quite casual. Sally flew through the reception room and across the hall to the outer office and opened the filing cabinet. C—D—F—Foods—May—June! Yes, here it was. What a relief! She hurried back with the folder.

"Find it?" asked Miss Daniels over her shoulder.

"Oh, yes, thank goodness! My, I was frightened! I would have perished if anything had happened to it."

"I pulled a worse boner than that when I first came. I put a folder back in the *wrong* file once and we couldn't find it for *two* days. Meantime, I had to just about reconstruct the whole layout from memory. I was a wreck."

"This will do for me, thank you," muttered Sally, her

face as red as it had felt pale before.

"Well, now, let's see." Jo Daniels' slender finger ran down the page. "We have seven dishes to make for the black and white pictures—the one that got first prize for the month's entries and the six runners-up. Some are on the timely topic of things that come in spring, tra-la—Fresh Rhubarb Pie, for instance. And there's Asparagus, Country Style," Miss Daniels went on. (That was a childhood favorite on the farm, Sally remembered. Why her father wouldn't touch asparagus unless it was cooked just that way—cut in inch pieces, boiled quickly in a little salted water, and then real cream poured right in with it. They had it on toast for breakfast and as a main dish for supper —always with cream, every day while there was a stalk left in the garden. Dee-lish!)

"Fresh Beet Greens," Miss Daniels' finger traveled down the page. "The little beets will be cooked right with the greens and served in a row around the dish for a garnish," she explained.

"We used to cook a little salt pork with beet greens in the country and eat them with vinegar." Sally offered. "Good, too, aren't they?"

"Well, if you like 'em. Anyhow they're heading the list these days for vitamins q, d or x. Then there's a spring salad bowl—chicory and escarole, romaine, radishes, chives, Roquefort cheese or slivers of Swiss, tossed together with French dressing. Nothing hard about any of those when we get the materials rounded up," Jo Daniels was running on. "But now we come to Fresh Strawberry Puff that isn't so simple. It takes a vanilla wafer crumb crust and a meringue baked on top of that. The crushed berries go on when it's cold and whipped cream over all. Whole berries for garnish. Not hard to do really, and it looks lovely. That drew the prize, it says here on the margin. I'd forgotten, so that will head the list.

"Then there's a Red Raspberry Bavarian Cream—lemon jello, orange and pineapple juice, crushed berries, and whipped cream. And a Blueberry Nut Bread that I think the judging committee said was delicious. Looked nice when it came out of the oven, I remember."

"Who are the judges?" Sally asked.

"Oh, Miss O'Hara and Mrs. Andrews, always. Mr. Drake, the editor, likes to be asked. He's no mean cook himself. And Miss Cory, one of the secretaries. She's rare. An old-timer here, and she can spot a flop as quick as the next one and tell what's wrong besides—and *does*, to the queen's taste! But, mercy, we've got to get our supplies in or we won't even get started by noon! Here, I'll make a list—berries, rhubarb—we have eggs and butter in the ice-box and milk and cream came this morning, and chicory. There, that's all for that lot, I guess. Let's see. We'll need chicken for that custard tomorrow. We've a can on hand—that will do. All right. Now, could you run down street and leave this order, and perhaps bring back the berries and rhubarb if you can. Then we won't have to wait for de-livery to get started. There's a little fruit and vegetable store—Cazetti's—turn left, down two blocks, and around the corner. I'll order that fancy ice cream and check the things for those wedding affairs tomorrow and next day."

"Cazetti's. Turn left, down two blocks and around the corner—" Sally was already headed for her wraps, the list in her hand. A sharp March wind was blowing and she grabbed her hat as she made the street corner on the fly. Caz—here was the place. How nice the fruit and vegetable

stores were in the big cities now, she thought. Everything
from everywhere—California and Texas and Florida and
Puerto Rico, the market gardens in Jersey, new potatoes
from Bermuda.

"Any beet greens?" Sally asked the Italian who came to
wait on her.

"Plenty. Verra tender. Look." He showed a big basket of
small, smooth, uniform leaves. Hothouse.

"No, no. Garden kind. Little beets, like this?" Sally pan-
tomimed swiftly.

"Naw, Mees. Too earla. Mebby four, fi week more."
He smiled, regretfully.

Now what to do? Sally glanced swiftly at his shelves.
Here were small cans. She had a thought. "You got canned
beets, very small, very red?"

"Thees kind, Mees?" He fished down a can. Ha! The
day was saved. They could cook the little leaves and put
the canned beets around the border and who would know
the difference in a picture! Anyhow, she'd take a chance.

"You can put everything in one big bag, please. I'll take
it along," Sally said. They might not get things till afternoon if she left them to be delivered. She had had that happen too often. Rhubarb—escarole—chicory—radishes—
berries— Whew, what a load! Maybe she wasn't as smart
as she thought she was.

"You go two, tree block—upstairs? I tink too beeg.
Tony," the vegetable man called, "come." A young, black-
eyed, olive-cheeked lad appeared from the rear. Jabber—
jabber—jabber—or so it sounded to Sally.

"He take. Back way."

"Oh, thank you, very much." That was better. The back
way? Of course there must be one! Wouldn't she have

looked sweet tugging a big bag of vegetables in through
that august front door and up those stylish elevators! She
suddenly saw the picture and blushed. That would have
been a *faux pas* for sure! Well, she'd tag Tony up that back
way certainly and find out where it was. She might need
to know again some time.

At their kitchen door she gave the grinning Tony a quarter. (Cheap—for saving her face!)

"Everything here so soon?" Jo Daniels looked surprised
as Sally and her satellite appeared. "Good for you. That's
a help. Did you have good luck?"

"I don't know what you'll think about the beet greens."
Sally told her tale and waited.

"Humph," Miss Daniels commented. "I guess maybe
you'll get along."

Miss Daniels already had the fruit and vegetables out
of the bag when Sally returned from the dressing room.
"Now, we'll have to think through our line-up and see
what should be done first," she said. "Would you like to
make the rhubarb pie?" she asked Sally. "The flour is here
and the shortening, the board pulls out there, and you'll
find the pie tin in the cupboard next to where you're
standing. I'll stir up this jello business and set it to cool
for the Bavarian and then wash the greens and the asparagus and get the salad things ready for the hydrator."

Sally put on her smock and assembled her materials. The
flour and—MyOMy, her old friend! That electric stove—
she'd never used one. "Oven burner," she read. "Turn right.
Set regulator." Simple enough. She washed the rhubarb
and cut it into small pieces. So often she had watched her
mother do this. Always *her* rhubarb pies were criss-crossed
and always there were bits of dried lemon peel to sprinkle

in before the sugar and flour went over the rhubarb. So crisp and tangy it was, straight from the lush row that grew in their garden out back. Daughter would follow her teaching.

Sally loved to make pie since she had learned the secret of flaky crust. Chopping the shortening into the flour, leaving it very coarse, like peas, and then stirring in a very, very little cold water—barely enough to hold it together. It was fun to roll and cut and fit and turn out a professional job—if you could!

Quiet reigned in the little kitchen as the two girls bent to their work.

There! Sally stuck the last cross strip on with a little water, as she had done the others, patted the edges down all around, presented her pie for approval, and slid it into the oven—hot at first, and then moderated. That stove was so slick to use! No wood, no coal, no ashes, not even gas or matches! Just turn a button. Seemed like magic! She cleaned up her board and stacked up her dishes.

"Now, will you whip the cream for the Bavarian in the beater—" Jo Daniels directed. "It goes like this." She noticed Sally's hesitation. "Set it in second so you won't get spattered, turn the little switch, and you're off. When the cream gets stiff, add that gelatine mixture that's beginning to thicken in the icebox, and then these crushed raspberries. When it will stand in peaks, pile it in those tall stemmed sherbets in the cupboard, and decorate to please yourself. Want me to do one for you the way we did them when we tried out the recipe first? Like this. You probably have better ideas yourself. There."

Sally watched the quick, clever fingers. The girl certainly had the eye! Lovely! No wonder she wanted her creations to last longer than the space of a swallow! "Now watch *me*," thought Sally, as she took over. But— "Well, there—" She caught her lower lip between her teeth in an old childish habit, as she surveyed her handiwork. "Not up to teacher's, maybe, but not so bad at that!" she thought, in pleased surprise.

Meanwhile, the prize puff was taking shape for Miss Daniels. She had rolled the vanilla wafer crumbs, mixed them with melted butter, and patted them over the bottom of a layer-cake tin. (Suddenly Sally saw herself in the studio of the Beacon Network the afternoon of her first broadcast. She was saying, "Here's a nice version of a crumb

crust" when she lost her place! Those crumbs were corn
flakes. Remember? The miserable things!) Miss Daniels
spread the meringue over her crust and put it in the oven
to bake slowly along with the rhubarb pie. Sally had kept
an ear cocked for the telltale sizzle that meant juice running over onto the oven, but so far she was safe!

With the pie and the puff finally done and the oven
turned off, the girls paused to check progress.

"Now we'll cook the asparagus and the greens, make the
salad, and I'll put the top on this strawberry puff when we
come back from lunch. Then we must get everything lined
up and ready for Demmy to shoot the pictures—about
three 'clock. Never mind the dishes," Miss Daniels said as
Sally began rolling up her sleeves. "Kitty will do those for
us. Our maid," she explained.

Hooray! Sally cheered silently, for the sink was full.
"That's a real help, isn't it?" she said aloud.

"Indeed, yes. You'll give thanks for her more than once.
So much for this. See you at one o'clock." She waved to
Sally from the hall and Miss Lewis hung her smock in the
little broom closet and made for her coat and hat. She was
hungry and she certainly wouldn't mind sitting down for
a change!

"My word! Do you know what we didn't do this morning?" Jo Daniels exclaimed as she and Sally started in after
their lunch hour was over. "That Blueberry Nut Bread!
Turn on the oven. We'll have to fly to and switch that
together in a hurry. You want to pick over the berries and
then cut up the nuts? They're in that can there. And I'll
put the other things together in the beater." She grabbed up

Note: Any reader who has not received her copy of *Your Home* will
find these recipes in Sally's Notebook at the end of the book!

the recipe for a quick look and then assembled her materials—eggs, sugar, flour, baking powder, and melted shortening.

Sally hustled with the nuts but before she knew it Jo was waiting for her. That little beater was certainly a whiz!

"That's fine. Thanks." Jo grabbed the nuts and dumped them in—the berries had gone in before—and gave the beater a whirl. Removed the bowl, poured the batter into a greased loaf pan and whisked it into the oven. "It will have time to bake and cool a little before three, I guess," she said as she put the bowl and beater to soak.

"Now for the vegetables. Use those small, heavy aluminum tight-lidded pots and you won't have to put any water on the greens at all, and very little on the asparagus, and they cook very quickly. On they go. Now, while they cook we can think about how we'll have these things photographed. That's the object of all our labors today, so here's where any imagination you happen to be blessed with and any artistic ideas, need to come to the fore. In that further cupboard are all sorts of dishes, plates, platters, and so forth, that we sometimes use for this job, and in the drawers down below are doilies, squares of linen, lunch cloths, and so on. Now, let's go over what we have. The Strawberry Puff being the prize winner draws a bigger space and more elaborate setting. Let's see." Miss Daniels' eyes narrowed. "It would do to serve at a dessert bridge, wouldn't it? That's an idea!" Her face brightened. "Mrs. Neighborhood Nabob would use her best cloth to impress Mrs. Down Street—here's a lovely Venetian one," as she fished in the drawer, "and here are little napkins to match." She laid them on the shelf. "We'll use these china plates and our best sterling forks. So much for that setup. But, mercy, I haven't even finished making the thing yet, have I?" She took up the puff shell from the rack, slid it out of the tin onto a plate, spread crushed berries over it, and whipped cream on top of that. Sally watched the deft, sure fingers.

"Now we'll put a row of berries around the edge, make a petaled flower of small ones cut in half for the center, like this, and that's the end of that."

"You do it so quickly and *so* beautifully." Sally sighed, in envy.

"Don't forget I've been practising every week for two years."

"Um-m. I know, but—" Sally looked at the lovely dish before her, wondering how she— "But now you just wait, Sally Lewis," she sternly admonished herself. "You may be surprised at what you can do when you try." She would be surprised, no doubt!

Jo Daniels was hunting in the linen drawer again. "I'm looking for a lace doily. Here it is. Put it on that round silver tray and set three of your Red Raspberry Bavarians in the stemmed glasses on it. All right?" She squinted at the effect. "These next six pictures will be smaller so the background won't show much, but we have to have some. Here's a peasant style tray cloth to go under the dish of beet greens and we'll serve the Blueberry Nut Bread—it came out nicely, didn't it?—on this board with the design around the edge. Here's a plate and the knife."

"But where are these pictures going to be taken? Here?" Sally asked, wonderingly.

"Oh, in the studio down the hall. Did nobody show you that little glory hole? We have to take all these things down there, too, and we might as well begin our travels."

So they loaded their silver, their dishes, the linen and the food onto trays and started out, through the dining room and down the hall. "I heard Miss O'Hara make a date with Demmy for us, so I hope he'll show up on time. He's temperamental and life's a bore to him a lot of the time, but he's clever—when he wants to be. You have to sort of handle him," Miss Daniels said over her shoulder as she opened a door into a long narrow room.

"Glory hole is good," thought Sally as she set down her tray on a box. Properties of all sorts stood about—screens, backdrops, this and that and everything else! A photographer's camera stood at one end of the room and a young chap was arranging the lights.

"Hi, Demmy. Miss Lewis, this is Mr. Demming, our photographer." Jo Daniels made the introductions as she found a spot to set down her load.

Sally's eyes traveled swiftly to the lanky figure by the camera as she acknowledged his brief nod in her direction. "Not much to look at certainly," she thought. Straight, nondescript hair. "A lot younger than I expected. Looks as if a square meal wouldn't hurt him," she commented to herself.

"Anything good to eat today?" He eyed Sally's tray. "What's this? *Greens?* Ugh! What's the idea?"

"They're good for all that ails you, Demmy," Jo spoke up. "You should eat plenty. Ever try them?" she asked wickedly.

"Not when I was conscious. Pop-Eye stuff for kids! But let's get going. What's up first?"

"This elegant number." Jo whisked the Venetian cloth over a small table and set the Strawberry Puff on it, arranged plates and silver beside it. "Do your best, Demmy.

This gets the prize."

"Okay. Push her over to the right farther, then."

"Would you run down and see if Miss O'Hara is in her office? She always passes on these, if she's around." Jo spoke to Sally, who was watching proceedings with interest. But Miss O'Hara appeared in the door just as Sally turned.

"How are things going, girls?" Her quick eye swept the scene, Sally included.

"Do you think this arrangement is all right?" Jo asked anxiously, as she set the last fork in place.

"Very good, Miss Daniels. Would it help any to cut a piece out of your—whatever—and show it on one of the plates, so that readers can see just what it is like inside? Let's try. Got a sharp knife?" Sally flew back to the kitchen for one.

"Thank you, Miss Lewis. But we'll let Jo do the cutting. She knows the anatomy better than I."

They were all very still and tense while Jo cut regretfully into her creation, and landed the piece safely on the plate!

"Good! Set it over here now and re-arrange your forks. There. How's that, Demmy?" Miss O'Hara stood back to get the effect. "All right, go ahead," she directed. The camera clicked and the Strawberry Puff, its hour of glory over, was retired to oblivion by Miss Sally Lewis.

She ran from studio to kitchen and kitchen to studio many times in the busy hour that followed—for extra silver, for a different plate, a gay bordered tray cloth—as Miss O'Hara's sure eye saw need of this and that for the picture she wanted to create. And Sally, trying valiantly to miss no important point or telling move, found herself going—"like a pinwheel!" she said.

"The latticework on that rhubarb pie is perfect, Miss Daniels," she heard Miss O'Hara say on one return trip. Ah! Her feet weren't nearly so tired now!

"Not guilty. Miss Lewis made that."

Sally blushed as Miss O'Hara turned in her direction, and said, "If it tastes as good as it looks, we'll give you A, Miss Lewis."

"I hope it does then," Sally answered, as she gathered up dishes and linen for another journey.

"I'll take a piece of that Strawberry Puff—and one for Mrs. Andrews, if you'll cut it for me. Put the plates on that tray, with a couple of forks," Miss O'Hara directed. "Why don't you three finish it up? That will give you a chance to catch your breath." She took the tray Jo handed her and went out the door.

"Isn't she nice!" Sally exclaimed.

"Very," Jo answered, "and *smart*." She was dishing out the dessert with a practised hand. "Here you are, Demmy," she called over her shoulder. Sally handed the plate across to him.

"What, no greens?" He tossed his hair back off his face and eyed her impudently.

"This is a reward of merit," Jo explained. "You were very nice today, Demmy."

"Well, after all," he shrugged. "I'm not *dumb*, I hope." He slumped carelessly against the table, eyed his plate critically, and picked up his fork.

"Not dumb, no. Too smart—and much too fresh!" was Sally's mental comment.

"*What* do we do with all this food?" Sally asked wonder-

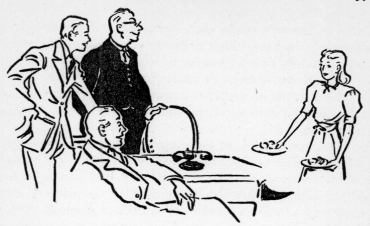

ingly when everything was re-assembled in the kitchen once more.

"That's always a problem. Give it away—to Kitty usually, if they are things she can use," Jo answered. "Why don't you peddle these Raspberry Bavarians down the hall? Miss Cory has girls under her who are always good bets— or try the men," she grinned.

Sally wiped her hands, put a surreptitious dab of powder on her nose from the compact in her pocket, and started forth. She wasn't especially interested in the stenographers but she was dying to see the editor-in-chief of a magazine. Would she dare? She went down the hall. The door was open. A small, kindly-looking gray-haired man sat behind the desk—but *two* other men were standing about the room. Sally would have gladly ducked, but it was too late. They had seen her.

"Come in," Mr. Drake called.

"Miss Daniels thought perhaps you might like these," Sally faltered. *Why* did she always have to blush just when she minded it most! Were those looks of pleasure on the men's faces or just amusement?

"Ah, 'the pause that refreshes,' gentlemen. Thank you very much. Put them right here on the desk. Our compliments to the kitchen." He bowed.

Sally, covered with confusion, did manage an answering smile, but lost no time getting out of there!

"You asked for it, Sally Lewis!" she reminded herself as she flew down the hall.

The three men watched her through the doorway.

"They come smaller and cuter with spring, it seems," Mr. Drake commented, a twinkle in his eye.

CHAPTER XIV

That Wedding Breakfast!

"THIS is our big day, isn't it?" Sally remarked as she appeared in the little kitchen next morning. Jo Daniels, still in hat and coat, was depositing various packages and parcels on the shelf.

"It's one of them, certainly," she answered. "Wait till I get rid of my wraps and we'll see just what's what. You might read through the folder again to check up."

Sally was deep in page two when Jo returned. The high lights of June—the wedding breakfast, the bridesmaids' luncheon, and the party of the sweet girl graduate were the assignments still to be covered. If they got out of all this alive, surely any other day would seem tame!

"Let's get ourselves organized." Jo looked over Sally's shoulder. "Miss O'Hara decided last night just after you left not to show the luncheon plate for the bridesmaids, after all, but just the first course with the strawberries—I got a box on my way up—and the last one. All we have to do for that is bake and decorate the little cakes. The paper frills from the florist's are there in one of those packages. I ordered the ice cream hearts yesterday, you remember."

"Then we don't make chicken custard, after all?" Sally asked in mock disappointment.

"No chicken custard. The recipe will appear and a description of the plate, but no color photo. The layout seemed better without it."

"Hooray for us! No?" Sally exclaimed.

"My, yes. But don't think those cakes aren't headache enough for one morning. I don't know about you but I'm not so wonderful with a pastry bag."

Sally's heart sank. She was worse! Her mind raced ahead. "What about this three-decker bride's cake the sheet calls for? How will we *ever* do that?"

"Heavens, girl, if we had to make that we'd never get finished in this world. It would be *very* expensive, besides. Miss O'Hara is borrowing a dummy from a caterer. She saw it in a display window one day. In exchange we just advertise his shop. 'Bride's cake from So-and-So.' Easy as that. So, after all, our day shakes down to this: making the little cakes, the salad molds, and the fancy sandwiches, decorating the platters of each, and then setting up the tables. We'll be *busy*—don't mistake that—but not *sunk*, I hope."

"It's all in the 'know-how,' I guess," Sally decided. "See how quickly things can be simplified and worked out when somebody takes hold who knows the short cuts and the quick tricks!"

"If you'll make the cakes, I'll get the frosting ready," Jo offered. "There's a little recipe file in that drawer there. Look for Cup Cakes No. 1. It's quick and easy and sure-fire. While you are at it, hand me the card on ornamental frosting, will you? We've small jars of vegetable coloring to use. But we're getting way ahead of ourselves here. Those gelatin molds must be done first. We use chicken aspic. Comes in tins. Melt it gently over hot water, add this canned chicken cut in nice even pieces, plus celery and pimento, pour it into the mold, rinsed in cold water so it won't stick —we hope. If we make a circle or two of sliced stuffed olives in the bottom of the mold it will look well when it is turned out. It sets quickly. The little cheese and tomato affairs are easy, too. Just tomato juice cocktail, heated, with gelatin added. (Two tablespoons to a quart—Sally remembered.) Pour a layer into these tiny molds and then when it sets pack cream or cottage cheese in on top. They are very pretty."

The girls flew about from cupboard, to sink, to stove. They stirred and cut and folded, and the little mixer whirred.

Sally watched her cakes with anxious eye. She hoped they wouldn't run over, that they wouldn't hump up in the middle, that they wouldn't burn on the bottom, that they wouldn't stick, that— Silly! The recipe was right and she had guarded against all these calamities. Of course they wouldn't happen. And no more did they! She turned the cakes out on the rack with care and heaved a sigh of relief. So far so good. While they were cooking, she washed the dishes and cleaned up the shelf. She couldn't stand a clutter, maid or no maid. There, that was better.

Meantime Jo had small bowls of colored frosting, and two pastry bags rinsed and ready. "Here we go," she said. "The idea is to make the top of each cake look like an old-fashioned nosegay—flower petals, pink and yellow and lavender, with green leaves around the edges." She picked up her tools and began. Sally groaned inwardly. She had better practise a little first on a piece of paper. How in the world did you make the thing work? She watched Jo from the corner of her eye. A quick twist—like that? Not so bad. Not—so bad— "There now, see what I told you, Miss Lewis," she said to herself. "You can do it as well as the next one if you just think you can. You're such a fraid-cat so often!"

Around the cakes and around—green and pink and lavender and yellow—"Why they're lovely, aren't they!"

Sally exclaimed delightedly as she blew the hair out of her eyes and surveyed their efforts. "They are!"

"Now the little frills go on. Cut out the center and slip them up like this," Jo demonstrated. "They *do* look nice—for us. Anne would have done them with half the agony, but *she's* really good at these things. Now we make a border of them around the rim of this large flat glass plate and the little ice cream hearts go in the smaller dish in the center. We have a pale green embroidered organdy cloth for the table. If Demmy gets the colors well it will make a nice page, won't it?" She leaned against the cupboard. *Why* should she feel so weary already?

"You look terribly tired," Sally said to her. She wasn't always pale like that, was she?

"I *am* tired, for some reason or other. Let's sit down for a minute and think what comes next. There's Cazetti right now with the watercress for the platters, and the radishes and parsley. Did you bring the sandwich bread from the bakery next door, as you promised, Tony?" she called.

"Oh, sure. I get fi' cen' from baker for bringing."

"Good boy. Thank you. 'Bye."

"I'll take care of the things. You rest a minute," Sally said, opening up the bags. "Radish roses? I can do those." She found a sharp knife, perched on a stool and began. She had done these many times before.

"We had better make a few celery curls, too, for extra garnish. I can do them. I feel better now." Jo rose and got the celery from the icebox. Sally stole a look to see if there would be some new wrinkle to it that she didn't know about. Sure enough. Jo cut her celery in *short* lengths, about an inch and a half long, and then very carefully and evenly slit one end down nearly to the other. "When these stand in ice water for a while and curl back they look almost like a flower," she explained. "They are good for fillers."

"Now we could cream the butter and fix the sandwich filling—cream cheese with olive and pimento. Not original at all but it shows up well in a picture. And then right after lunch we'll fix up our platters and get ready for the big show. There's a round silver tray for the salad mold and two oval ones for the sandwiches and the little tomato cheese molds that we made."

"How do we arrange them on the platters? Could you give me an idea, then I can help more. You be the boss, I'll be the coolie. Here, draw me a picture on the memo pad."

"I never know exactly what I *am* going to do till the time comes," Jo took the pad and pencil—"but I had an idea something like this—watercress and chicory around the edge —a row of sandwiches set, cut edge up, in a semicircle across each half of the platter—like rainbows back to back, sort of. Then the little tomato molds inside the crescent at either end. Olives, radishes, celery curls, parsley, through the middle of the tray. Clear as mud, isn't it?"

Sally hung over the drawing. "It will be lovely, I'll bet. Let's go to lunch, I'm starved. Hope you feel better." She washed her hands and took off her smock and hurried toward the dressing room.

Sally was back early. Fresh air and something to eat had given her a new lease on life, aided by the fact that she had a reasonably clear picture of what was ahead for the afternoon, so she thought. Anyhow she could make the sandwiches. Nothing much to that. Sally loved to cut bread if the knife were sharp. She tested the edge on a cautious thumb. Good. Slice after slice, thin and even, fell under her hand. This was a *very* familiar process. Missed a slice!

"Too cocky, Miss Lewis."

Off went the crusts. She lined the slices up on the board, buttered and filled the sandwiches, patted them together and cut through the middle. Now for the dark bread. Pack in pan, cover with waxpaper and a damp cloth. Crusts into the dry bread can for crumbs. She was in the middle of things when Jo returned and sat down at the desk. "The caterer hasn't sent that wedding cake yet, has he?" she called to Sally.

"Not yet."

"I'll call him." Sally heard her give the number, then silence. "*What?* Not before *four?* Oh, but that's way too late. It's a rush day? It is for us, too. Well, all right if you can't, you can't. I'm sorry. Good-bye." Jo slumped back in her chair. "Isn't that the luck! The caterer can't send the cake till four and maybe not then. Miss O'Hara will be wild. She has been called out of town for the afternoon, but she left very careful directions for everything and said for us to be sure to get these pictures taken today so Demmy can finish them for the art editor on Friday. Now what? My head aches so—" She looked utterly fagged.

"Where is this place?" Sally asked.

"Down on Seventh Avenue—about eight blocks or so, I guess."

"Why can't I go after it? The thing won't be heavy, will it? I'll taxi back if I have to."

"Well, if you will. I'll set the tables up and—" But Sally was already gone.

She clipped down the street, dodging right and left. The traffic would be so thick and the lights against her at every corner! Here was Seventh Avenue. Now where was this— this, what was the name? She fished in her purse. Carter, the

Caterer—726 Seventh. Across the street. It would be, of course! She dodged a truck, landed safely and sped along. Here was a window and the three-decked contraption right

in the middle of it, bride and groom standing on top! She
went in and told her story. They'd have to see the boss.
Sally waited on one foot and then the other. Finally the
girl came back. The boss was out but they guessed it would
be all right.

"Will you wrap it good then please, with lots of string?"
Sally asked. She would have liked to add, "And for mercy
sake, move!" but this was a favor. One must be polite re-
gardless of strain! But at last her ungainly parcel was ready
and she departed, the bride and groom clutched tightly in
one hand, her—parrot cage it looked like!—in the other.
She certainly couldn't dodge traffic with that thing. If any
one bumped into it she might just as well resign right there.
So she hailed a cab and carefully eased herself in—and out
—and into the elevator. The operator looked at her but she
couldn't be bothered with *him*. She was staging a wedding
breakfast!

Sally made straight for the studio thinking to avoid un-
necessary doors with her pet. Her eye took in the scene at a
glance. The tables were only partially ready and Jo was
not there. She unwrapped her dummy, folded the paper
and chucked it behind a box, tossed her hat and coat in the
same direction, and went down the hall toward the kitchen
on the fly. Mrs. Andrews was waiting for her in the doorway.

"Miss Daniels fainted while you were out and I sent her
home with one of the stenographers. She said you knew
what to do. Kitty is here. Can I help you any?"

Sally's heart struck bottom—quick. "Oh!" she exclaimed
in dismay. But already her mind was racing ahead. She
would do this and this—and this. She could.

"Thank you, I think I can manage," she answered. She'd

have to. Kitty could help her carry things. She was already in the kitchen. She must take a second to get her bearings and see what was to be done, so she wouldn't get panicky. The bridesmaids' luncheon—strawberries, unhulled, around powdered sugar in tall stemmed flat glass dish, Spode china plate. Ah, there it was ready. Thank heaven for that. "A knife and fork, two spoons and a goblet go with that, Kitty —and that napkin. Put those on a tray with the little cakes. Where's the ice cream?" Kitty's face looked blank. "Don't tell me it hasn't come!" Sally held herself very still.

"I heard someone outside before you arrived. Wait." Kitty went out and came back with a small cardboard container. "Would this be it, do you think?"

"Maybe. It would be packed in dry ice. Open it up." Sally watched anxiously. That was it. A box inside with three hearts of ice cream, pink and green and yellow.

"Thank goodness," Sally breathed. So much for the brides-maids. Now for that breakfast: The jellied chicken mold. She took it out of the icebox and poked it hopefully. Solid, praise be. Heart leaves of lettuce and parsley for the tray and then she set the mold in luke-warm water just for a second and loosened gently with a spatula. She prayed that it would come out whole. Oo-o, it nearly went on the shelf —but there it was at last—beautiful, really! Tuck the gar-nish around. Mayonnaise in glass dish. Forks. Plates. Nap-kins.

Trays of sandwiches next. She had the blueprint for those!

"Bring me the little cheese molds in the icebox, Kitty, please, and the celery curls and the radishes and the olives," she directed. Things were clicking so far! Watercress and chicory and parsley, the sandwich rainbows—those streaks of filling *were* pretty. Now the baby molds. Warm water, a paring knife—e-asy—and there they were—little white mounds with red tops, cute as anything! A little more parsley here, celery curls there—

"They look lovely, Miss Lewis. Why, they're beautiful! Miss O'Hara will be thrilled." Kitty looked on admiringly.

"Thank you, Kitty. This is my top flight to date. Now let's begin to march. You take the strawberries and I'll take the cakes and ice cream and we'll get Mr. "Demmy" started. He has probably been champing at the bit and tearing his hair for—"

"For an hour, just about!"

Sally whirled at the voice. There he stood in the doorway, registering impatience and bored disgust.

"Oh, I'm sorry," Sally said. "We *are* late I know. Miss Daniels was taken ill. We are about ready now, though, and it won't take long." She smiled at him a bit, hoping to mollify his nibs. "Would you mind carrying this down for us?" She handed him a tray with a naughty grin.

"I would, but I will since you're stuck." He reached out a languid hand.

"Who's stuck? Not yet we aren't!" Sally rose in her own defense. "But here we go. Forward march."

Fortunately Jo had made a start. It was the work of a minute to set up for the two single courses of the luncheon. First the berries. "Does that look right, Mr. Demming?" Sally asked, as she placed the goblet at the end of the knife, drew the bowl of roses that Jo had arranged into view and set delicate pink and blue figurine salts and peppers near by. That embroidered organdy cloth over white was a new idea and really lovely!

"Push the flowers back. Hold it. Okay."

Then that dessert—the ring of frilled cakes and the ice

cream hearts. No spoons showing. Nice. So much for that. Now for this other business. "Kitty, is that the last load?" Sally asked as her willing helper appeared with plates.

"The last. These berries and things can go back now, can't they?"

"Take the cakes and ice cream to Mrs. Andrews. She might like them," Sally called after her. They were making progress.

She grabbed up the sheet of instructions—rosebuds around bride's cake? Heavens! "Demmy, help me hoist this thing up on the table, will you? And hand me the bride and groom. Thanks." Center back. Where's that florist's box? Lovely small pink buds and leaves! Sally took time to sniff. How carefully Jo had planned yesterday and the day before to have everything on hand. If she had a minute she could rave over that beautiful rayon damask cloth—ice blue. Lovely with the pink roses. But she had no time to stop. A rosebud, a leaf; a rosebud, a leaf, around the base of her triple decker— Was that right? Looked pretty, she guessed, but her enthusiasm was running thin.

Now the salad tray. Center front, pale pink glass plates, delicately etched, forks. The sandwiches could go on either end. "Hand me that sandwich tray on the box back of you, Demmy, like a good lad, and I'll be through in a jiffy." She held out her hands to receive it, but too late! He let go, thinking she had hold of it. (At least she *guessed* he thought so. Surely he couldn't be so mean!) Sally grabbed frantically, but to no avail. Over went the tray, face down, on the dirty floor! Her hand went up to her throat. "Oh!" she gasped. "Oh! Why did you let go so quickly, Demmy?" she wailed.

"Why didn't you hang on, butter fingers? Now what are we going to do?"

Sally bent down and scooped up the remains. Tears
blurred her eyes. She was *so* tired. She was so *tired!* She
blinked fast and swallowed. "I'll have to make more. It—it
won't take me very long. I'm sorry," she said dully, and
made her weary way back to the kitchen. Her lovely tray!
A mess.

And she suddenly remembered, just to cap the climax, that
she couldn't make more sandwiches. She had only three
slices of bread left and almost no filling! What could she
do? It was after five now. Kitty had cleaned up and gone.
Well, she'd just turn those sandwiches other side up—dirty
side down on the tray! Rinse off the garnishes and use them
again. But the cheese molds were a total loss. She scraped
them into the garbage and looked hopefully in the icebox.
Here were three that hadn't been used. They would do for
one end anyhow. She'd have to take a few from the other
tray. Fill in with parsley—more radishes, more celery curls.
Thank goodness for them! Back to the studio. "There!" She
surveyed the reconstruction.

"Go ahead, Demmy. That's the best I can do, I guess." It
was really lovely, but she was too tired to see or care right
then.

"You *can* move when you have to. I'll hand you that
much," Demmy remarked, grudgingly. "The dame has
spunk—and pluck, at that," he mumbled to himself.

The camera clicked. Sally began her backward trek. Five
trips in all. The flowers and the table would have to stay as
they were till morning. She put away what food she thought
might be used again and dumped the rest into the garbage. It
was after six and she'd be too late for dinner at the cafeteria,
but she couldn't eat those sandwiches—not tonight!

The dishes finally washed and the kitchen tidy, she took

herself down the deserted hall, to find her wraps—where? She remembered that she had tossed them on a box in the studio. She snapped on the light. There was the wedding cake still bedecked in glory, the little bride and groom still standing on the top of their world. Okay for them. But nobody could ever give *her* a wedding breakfast—not for a gift! She and Alex were getting *married*. Anybody else could have the frills!

Young Mrs. Judy Martin of San Francisco Heights, coming out onto her small veranda that overlooked the City and all the Bay clear out to the Golden Gate, paused a minute to enjoy the view. She never tired of it. There was always a thrill, in fog or sunshine, and today it was spring in California and everything was at its loveliest. A meadowlark sang on the tip of a eucalyptus tree farther up the hillside and California poppies ran riot at the foot of her steps. They were the never-failing gold of the California hills, coming as sure as sun and summer.

Judy loved the City. It was an exciting place to live in. There was tang and snap and sparkle in the air. You wanted always to be up and doing—and she usually was. This afternoon she taught her homemaking class at the 4H Club. Her girls had done well this winter. They had kept house and marketed and learned about budgets by trying to stay inside one. They had cooked and served two suppers for the mothers' group—no mean achievement for girls under fifteen. But it was a real job to be their leader, Judy found. She had thought it most worth-while but she would have to give it up in the fall, for the stork was coming to her house, flying nearer every day. She rather hoped for a Bill Jr., but no matter—either one. She smiled happily.

But there was the postman climbing up her path. That rocky way, though charming and picturesque and her special delight, was tough on mail carriers. She'd wait and see what he brought. She went down the steps to meet him. Looked like a lot! She ran through the pile; a catalogue for Bill; mercy, she'd forgotten that cleaner's bill completely; an invitation to a tea, and—Sally's familiar scribble. She hadn't had a real letter from her in weeks. She sat down on the steps to enjoy herself. Sally's letters were always something to look forward to. Happy and excited, or discouraged and blue they might be, but never dull. Judy opened the envelope and read:

On My New Job

Hi, Mrs. Martin!

I hustled back from lunch early today so I could begin to catch up on letters. The fact has been borne in upon me of late that if I don't write any I don't get any!

I've been on this new job for over two weeks now and does it keep me stepping right along! The first week was sort of hard, especially the day that my instructor fainted and left me with a wedding breakfast to dish up for the photographer. (He's a fresh young smarty, too!) *I*, who scarcely ever attended a wedding much less know anything about how things for one of these fancy affairs should look. (Why it is called a *breakfast* in the first place when it is eaten nearer noon is beyond me!) Fortunately, Jo Daniels who was taking me over the bumps had things planned carefully and had all but drawn a map for me, so I could go ahead when she cracked up. Everything would have been all right, too, if one of my stylish platters of sandwiches and what-have-yous that we'd sweat, bled and all but died for, hadn't gone face down on the floor at the last minute! By the time damages were repaired and the picture finally taken, any

interest I ever had in weddings was gone for keeps. Justice
of the Peace for me and he can make it snappy, too!

But next day things went better. Even though Jo was out
I made a really elegant cocoanut cake—seven-minute icing
piled high—and a bowl of homemake fresh strawberry ice
cream in our refrigerator for the girl graduate's party and
set the table for it, too, with a suggestion or so from Miss
O'Hara, the foods editor! When the color plates came out
for all these June festivities she seemed delighted—at least
she said so—and believe me I didn't tell her that half her
wedding sandwiches came up off the dirty floor!

Already this week I've tested out twelve dessert recipes
sent in by readers from all over the country. You get five
dollars if yours is the best of the lot for the month or a dollar
if you are an also-ran. Better send one, Mrs. M. and see what
luck you have.

It is quite fun for me to cook again, and am I getting
trained! The desserts were a pleasure (I found one or two
good ones I'll pass on), not only because they were pretty
when they were done but because this is the first time the
tasting squad has descended on me. I was petrified at first,
but curiosity to see the big ones in action sort of made me
forget. They can all tell you what's right or wrong, too, even
Mr. Drake, the editor-in-chief. But they were very nice. It
was always the recipe that was at fault, not the cook!

Next week I have cold drinks to work on for July! I hope
it will be warmer than it is now. There were snow flurries
this morning when I was coming along the street. It's funny
always to have to be working so far ahead of the season. You
just have to remember back how hot it was last Fourth of
July and imagine what you'd like to eat and where you'd
rather be.

I've never been in a big organization like this before, so
many people to come in contact with. Four or five editors,
with people under them, a flock of stenographers, big adver-

tising department, and the circulation office that I don't even know about. All this to show housekeepers how to keep house better and do it happily. How to make their homes pretty and get fun out of doing it.

This business of homemaking—it's a real career, don't you think it is, Judy? I never really thought about it till this year but I'm finding out.

Lunch hour is over. Have to check a lot of bright ideas that have come in for Miss O'Hara, and write up the list of "Did You Know Thats" for the next issue.

No household is complete without *Your Home*, Mrs. Martin. "Subscribe for this magazine if you do not take it already, or buy a copy at your favorite newsstand and treat your family to the treats it contains"—and think of your little friend cooking in its kitchen. It's a lot of fun really!

As ever,
Sally

Judy folded her letter and looked off at the hills across the Bay. It *was* a career to make a home. She had found that out already. To keep your family happy and content and still have a chance to develop yourself; to make your house comfortable—charming if you could; to keep the food up, the budget down, and above all find fun and adventure in doing it. Hm-m. It certainly was a career. Had been so far. Next year she'd probably be so busy she'd think it was a three-ring circus! Judy's eyes came back to the letter in her hand. She read parts again. Her Sally was growing up she decided with a smile.

CHAPTER XV

"Leg Work"

"WE need to know what's new in the shops, Miss Lewis," Miss O'Hara said to Sally one afternoon some weeks later. "I shall be tied right here for another week on this material. You are pretty well caught up on the most necessary recipe testing for a few days. I wish you would make the rounds of the stores tomorrow and see what you can see. There's a food fair on at Gordon's and a kitchen equipment exhibit. Go there. Also stroll through their linen department and through Ellery's. Pick out three or four items you think entirely new and unusual and have them sent up on approval. We need picnic and outing things for August. Look in Dennison's. Take notes. Can you draw?"

"Only a little," Sally answered dubiously.

"Well, if you can, try to sketch the gadgets you think useful. Write down name, price and number and where you saw them so we can borrow if they seem worth while. Orrington's always have new things and Biddle and Burns run to the unusual in household equipment. Good night."

Hooray! A vacation. Sally tripped home feeling more lighthearted than she had for some time. Why it would seem like a holiday in the middle of the week! What could she do to celebrate? She hadn't seen Lou for two months. Maybe she could catch her before her rush hour for dinner began if she called right away. She fished a nickel out of her purse and stopped at the telephone booth in the lobby of the Y. She called the restaurant at the Barbarole and waited

—and waited.

"Hi, Lou! Did I call you from the depths of the store-room or somewhere? Cook out sick? Oh, I *am* sorry. I won't keep you a minute. Just wondered if you would like to go to the movies or something tonight, or will you be tired? What? A date with Speedy? I was afraid of that! But good for you. Give him my greetings. See you soon. Bye!"

Nothing doing there. That Speedy was certainly living up to his business! Well, she'd stroll down to the cafeteria and see what Clara had on her bill of fare for the evening. Maybe she could go. But again no luck. The "cousin"—they were going to the theatre. She was sorry. She'd go tomorrow night, Clara said.

Dates, dates. Everybody had a date but her, thought Sally. She went back to the lobby and was starting for the elevator when she remembered that she hadn't asked for her mail. Ah! That would be Mr. Alexander Merrill's writing. She would read the letter upstairs. In her room she threw off her coat, sailed her hat onto the bed and sat down, the letter in her hand, a smile in her eyes. At the salutation the smile spread over her face. Alex was such a dear. Did she care now that she was staying home alone? Not one bit. Further-more, she had a sudden urge to study that new booklet on room interiors that Mrs. Andrews and Jo had just finished for *Your Home*. She must get ideas for private consumption.

Miss Lewis breakfasted leisurely next morning. She was going on an expedition "for look see," as her Chinese boys used to say. Most of the stores weren't open before nine or nine-thirty. She could just take her time. She'd have one of Clara's big baked apples with cream. They had that lovely golden, glazed look on top that came only with long, care-ful "doing" under the broiler, with much sprinklings of sugar. She had watched Rosa do them many a time at the little Pudding Pan and heard her fuss and fume over the same. So long ago, it seemed!

She, Sally, was in New England now—and cooks fumed just the same as they did in California, she opined. It was a blessed good thing nobody had seen or heard *her* just day before yesterday, when the bottom fell out of that quart jar of ripe olives and let the whole black mess all over the floor! She could grin now at the picture.

But she must get on with her breakfast or Clara would be chasing her out.

It was a lovely day—for a change, thank goodness! Miss Sally wasn't so enamored of New England winters but she brightened and beamed when the sun shone. It was doing that today, and she set forth perkily, dressed in her best, for wasn't she going to stop 'n' shop? She was off to the Food Fair in the pride of the morning.

A crowd of women were standing in front of Gordon's waiting to get in when Sally arrived and most of them seemed to be heading for the same spot that she was, Sally found, as they all surged through when the doors opened.

Almost an entire floor of the big store was given over to displays of packaged foods—fancy, unusual and different— and to kitchen utensils such as Sally had never seen. Young women, many not so young, in white uniforms demonstrated their wares at every table.

"What adorable little jars of jams and jellies!" Sally exclaimed at the first display that caught her eye. Clear and sparkling in their odd-shaped glass jars and packed in such cunning boxes. Who wouldn't love to have one of these for a gift? Here were slim little pottery pitchers in lovely colors, filled with mustard sauce and mint, their slender necks corked tight. They would be so pretty for ornaments when they were empty.

"They are *charming!*" Sally said to the girl in charge.

"Yes, aren't they?" The salesgirl answered. "We usually carry these only at Christmas time, but they have been so popular that we sell them all the year round now. The woman who makes them runs a tearoom in the summer up in Vermont. The Syrup Jug, the label says."

Here was an idea! Sally whipped out her notebook and leaned against a counter. She had had drawing in school. You did get some art work if you majored in home economics, but if she had it to do over again she'd take all there was to be had! She'd see whether or not she could sketch a box of those cute jellies so Miss O'Hara could tell what it was, and a tiny pitcher. She scratched and scribbled industriously, unmindful of amused glances around her.

On to the next table. Things from Cape Cod. She knew about codfish cakes and clam chowder and Boston Brown bread in tins, and she even passed by an alluring brown stone crock of beans with only a nod of appreciation. Her eyes were on the Indian pudding that the demonstrator was taking out of a *can!* Shades of her great-grandmother! That must be all but sacrilege to an old-time New Englander. But think of the hours saved in baking—not to speak of the gas. You stirred a little milk in this and baked it thirty minutes or so! Sally took the taste offered her. Wel-l, yes, it was good, but The Spinning Wheel could beat it and she was sure that The Syrup Jug could, too! She guessed maybe she herself would stick to the ways of her forebears on that dish, but she scribbled a note on it just the same.

Right next to that table were all the frosted foods in a lovely case—broccoli and cauliflower and corn on the cob, steaks and broilers that made your mouth water—but everybody knew about them already so she didn't stop. Now, here was something. All sorts of fancy crackers and mixes for cocktail sandwiches and hors d'oeuvres! Thinsies and crispies and wheaties and whimsies. Some that looked like tiny waffles, with cheese or plain. And here was a large hammered aluminum tray filled with a very special kind— crescents and diamonds and squares, spread with pink caviar (Speedy and The Russian Bear!) and the black kind, bordered with cream cheese or tiny circles filled with anchovy. It looked lovely. If she had had those things now for that wedding breakfast—but why bring *that* up! She sketched two or three of the fanciest crackers, took the name, price and manufacturer, and traveled on.

Women, housewives she guessed, were buying everywhere. Bargains at every table.

Ah here, now what? Ice cream mixes in little cans? Maple walnut, caramel and ginger, and— Yes she knew about those, She had used one herself for the fresh strawberry ice cream she had made for the girl graduate's party. But this other? Panocha and fudge mixtures! "Add a little milk and cook as usual." Well, maybe. The condensed milk recipe she already used seemed just as easy. Pass that one. Good, but not good enough.

What was it that woman was serving out of the electric double boiler over there? Sally circled round.

"Will you try some of this chicken and noodle soup? It is a dehydrated product. Comes in an envelope. This ten-cent size will serve four. Add a quart of hot water and boil ten or fifteen minutes." The demonstrator ladled out a tiny cupful for Sally. There was parsley in it and onion. It was delicious! Now that was a real find. Into the notebook.

"Continental Chicken and Noodle Soup. Silver envelope. Comes in large size also, to make gallon," Sally wrote. "Cheap, convenient, new and *good*."

There were a dozen other tables and counters. Sally lingered a minute at one where relishes were displayed in very pretty trays of spun aluminum with glass containers. That red and green pepper hash was delicious, and the spiced apricots. Here was mango chutney from Hawaii! And salted macadamia nuts and candied ginger. Would these be new to someone else? She didn't know. She'd sketch a set and let Miss O'Hara decide.

This would do for the food. She must get on to the equipment. Everything was done by electricity now, it seemed to Sally as she moved between tables showing sandwich toasters, juice squeezers, beaters and coffee makers. These trays for the automatic toaster to set on, equipped with gay pottery or glass jars for jam or marmalade, were nice. And will you look at these electric roasters! They can be set on a table and you just plug them in anywhere and do a whole oven dinner. Besides, they will bake pies and cookies and biscuits! That was a slick thing. Sally scribbled swiftly. Sort of expensive, though, for poor folks, she thought wistfully.

Here was a whole case of small gadgets. This was her dish! She glued her eyes to the glass. There was a knife sharpener that should be worth something! A small four-sided piece of whetstone shaped down to a point and set in a gay handle—red or blue or green or ivory. "That's just the thing!" Sally decided. She did so hate a dull knife—worse than anything! This gadget was handy and handsome to boot. Check.

And behold, the thing the country needed most: a really good can opener! Small, compact, no pounding with your

fist. Foolproof—if you could work it! And here was one
that was a prize for prying off the metal caps on glass jars,
the kind that stick so fiendishly. Hooray! Check and double
check.

But she must move on. Here was a table of tin and aluminum things. Who would think there could be so many
different kinds of molds! Certainly no woman need stick to
the same old rounds or ovals. Here was one shaped like a
fish, if you please. And cutters for cookies! Look! Gingerbread men and sunbonnet girls, Christmas trees and valen-
tines, wreaths and stars and diamonds. What fun! Were
these old stuff? New to her anyhow. A note in the notebook.

Twelve o'clock? How could it be! Why she was just
getting started. There was a little coffee shop and lunch
counter right on the same floor, Sally remembered. She
perched on a stool. Fresh orangeade and a sandwich? Good
enough. She was full of pep yet. There was so much to see
and learn, why waste time on lunch?

"Where do I go from here?" She looked at her list as
she swung down off the stool. "Linen department? Fourth
floor. Take the escalator on your left," a clerk directed.

"I love to ride on these things and look all around a store,"
Sally thought as she moved up the incline. "I'm not so
grown-up as I think I am, I guess," she chuckled, as she
stepped off at her floor. "Now what do I look for?" Up one
aisle— "Oh, what lovely lunch cloths!" she exclaimed involuntarily at a display of rayon satin damask. In all the
pastel shades and so delicate. Faintest peach and green and
yellow and mauve! Jo must have found that ice blue cloth
here that she used for their wedding breakfast. Though why
she should keep remembering that affair was beyond her!

"Let it die in peace, for mercy sake, Sally," she scolded herself. These cloths wouldn't be "news" probably, but she'd just take a second to price them. She turned over the tags: Three ninety-eight and four ninety-eight. Maybe she might afford *one* for herself. And while she was right here she'd look at the sheets and blankets on the other side of the aisle. How lovely and soft the blankets were! Cedar rose, heather mist, camel color were the shades named on the tickets— twelve dollars, fifteen. They would be! Sally sighed, then jerked herself up short. "Hey, Miss! You are working for *Your Home*, not your home. There's plenty of difference in those capital letters, too, don't forget."

Her eyes roamed. Tea towels. Perhaps there was something here. She went over to a special table. "These are *very* pretty—white ones with borders of rainbow stripes. Nice with any light color scheme. Oh, and the same design comes on all the standard colors." She was interested herself. Would anyone else be? That was the question. A line or two in the notebook, just in case.

Luncheon sets, runners and place mats. Here was a set woven from lauhala fibers. From the South Seas? No, indeed. Honolulu, of course! Just wipe off with a damp cloth. Grand for summer homes, and camps! Now there was *one* idea for August if she never found another. Check that. "Oh, these are darling!" Her eye, caught by some gay colors, traveled on over the counter. "May I see these please?" she asked the clerk, indicating a set of place doilies done in appliqué. Hollyhocks they were! How nice for breakfast or lunch. "Will you please send this set to *Your Home* Magazine, in care of Miss O'Hara?" Sally requested. Surely her boss would like these.

But she *must* get on with her travels.

Why not look in at the china department before she left this store? Gordon's was supposed to be extra good in that line. Here was the elevator. What an array greeted her eye at the eighth floor. What an intriguing array! But she mustn't linger, and *oh* and *ah* over every dish or she'd never get through. But wait. Pastels seem to be the order for the afternoon, for here was a breakfast tray, set up in pink dishes and blue dishes mixed together. "Or you may have yellow ones and green ones if you prefer," said the saleslady. "Dainty as flowers, aren't they?" exclaimed Sally. As soon as she could get away from that clerk she would write in her book!

What gay, pretty dishes one could get for as little as six or seven dollars a set! Plenty for four. Surely nobody need use ugly ones at that price, thought Sally. And yet, as she remembered the cupboards of relatives and friends, odd lots and a grand jumble seemed to be the rule. Scribble, scribble in the book. Probably wouldn't do any good, but she'd pass the thought on. Miss O'Hara would no doubt much prefer facts to thoughts, especially from a neophyte of her years and size! But, anyhow, she'd try.

These hostess trays had been on the market for some time, she knew, but weren't they nice! Here was an especially good one, with gay glasses on either end and a place for sandwiches or cookies in the middle. Grand for serving friends out on the lawn in summer, or for supper in the back yard. Sally drew busily in her book. Didn't look much like the original but maybe she could explain! But she *must* get over to Ellery's. The elevator was packed but she squeezed in and was shoved out at the first floor. She zig-zagged through the crowd across the store to the door and out onto the street and up three blocks.

Ellery's was a specialty house for lace and linen, an old

and well-established firm. There was a crest on the door and inside was quiet elegance. This was a lovely place to be in. Clerks grown white-haired in the business stood behind the counters. Sally strolled down the aisle. Everything was very choice—she hardly knew where to go or what to look for.

But she didn't worry too long, for all at once, right there in the middle of things, Sally felt herself beginning to wilt. Suddenly she was so tired that she couldn't look at one more thing, elegant or not! She sat down in the first chair in sight. Why, this was ridiculous! It wasn't three o'clock yet and she had only covered one store. Miss O'Hara would think she was a sissy. She couldn't help it. She was done for. She might just as well go home. And what's more, she'd take a bus or the subway, and if she had to stand it would just be too bad! Miss Sally dragged her weary self to the elevator, to the nearest subway, to the Y. Why in the world had she worn those shoes? Little goose. She deserved to be tired, she scolded as she kicked off the offending pumps, slid out of her best dress and lay down on her bed. What were those remarks she had made about a *holiday?* "That was *last* night," she groaned, as she stretched out and closed her eyes!

"What luck did you have yesterday?" Miss O'Hara asked as Sally appeared at the office in the morning to make her report. She dreaded to tell the truth, but she might as well

get it over with.

"I'm ashamed to tell you that I only covered Gordon's and barely got inside of Ellery's. I guess I spent too much time at the Food Fair. It was very interesting to me. I tried to see everything. It was noon before I got away 'from that. Then by the time I'd gone through the linen and the china departments and got over to the other store I was so tired I couldn't see anything and I went home. I didn't get to Dennison's, I didn't get to Orrington's, I didn't get anywhere near Biddle and Burns!" There, she'd said it.

A smile of amusement tugged at Miss O'Hara's mouth. "I'm not surprised," she said. "This leg work is one of the hardest jobs we have to do. But after you've been around a while you learn the shops; where to look for what and how not to waste time on non-essentials; how to pick and flit. All that doesn't come with the first trial, however. Let me see what you found."

Sally laid her folder on the desk. She had spent a lot of time after supper redrawing her sketches, rewriting her notes. She hoped—

Miss O'Hara's sharp eyes took in the pages quickly. One, two—eight, nine, ten items under food, she counted. The sketches, well, the ideas were there all right. The art department could fix those in a hurry. Two—four gadgets, three things under linen, two or three for the china, twenty items in all! "Hm-m no wonder her legs gave out," she said to herself. She turned back to read what Sally had written under each one. Where had she read paragraphs that sounded like these? The style was light—"Catchy, I'll declare if it isn't! Sounds like Miss Kitury's Kitchen of the morning *Star!* Of course!" She read on. "The girl has promise, I do believe." Miss O'Hara tapped with her pencil thoughtfully.

Meantime Sally stood and waited, her spirits going down, down.

Miss O'Hara looked up. "Now let's consider some of these things carefully. This might do and this. Leave in the Indian pudding. Some woman who works all day in an office and has to get quick dinners at night might like it very much. We must keep just those very people in mind more than we do in evaluating our recipes and in recommending equipment. One of these days I want to run a series of menus and dishes—very simple but very attractive—just for these 'career girl' cooks and their hurry-up meals."

Sally, still standing at attention, relaxed a bit. Surely Miss O'Hara couldn't think she had done too badly or she wouldn't be treating her to any such "disquisition," as Prexy used to say.

"But to get back to the gadgets," Miss O'Hara resumed. "Take these that I have checked (Sally's heart beat faster as the list grew), rewrite the paragraphs, keep the light, snappy style but cut them—one-half, anyhow—and see if you can still make women feel that it is an adventure to find such things for themselves." She looked kindly at Sally as she handed back the folder. "Leave them on my desk when you've finished." Miss O'Hara turned to her work, then added. "Tomorrow you might go to the places you missed yesterday. Our weary feet are the penalties of our business, you know."

Sally gathered up her folder and departed happily for her little sanctum on the sitting-room side of the kitchen. Perhaps Miss Kitury's training had stood her in good stead and maybe she wasn't such a bad picker after all.

CHAPTER XVI

Sally's House—It Was Cute, Sort Of

THE weeks went by with amazing speed at the establishment of *Your Home*. Sally was astonished when May appeared on her calendar and she awakened to the fact that there were only a few weeks left. Why she hadn't been there any time at all! She was just getting started—just getting under way. It was such a busy place. There were so many different things going on all the time. So much still that she wanted to learn—Jo's work, for instance, in home decoration. Why she had scarcely seen Jo or had time even to talk with her. They had both been on the fly, she guessed.

Sally certainly knew that she had not been in any one place for long at a time. She had cooked and cooked and cooked. They, she and Miss O'Hara, had done an outdoor buffet supper for the July color page, and set up the drinks besides. Hadn't she, Sally, run up and down the streets, hunting red, white and blue accouterments and the latest wrinkle in outdoor serving? She was very sure there wasn't one of those wire holders for carrying fancy colored glasses in town that she hadn't spotted. They were really lovely, too, and she almost believed that the Five and Ten had as pretty ones as any store—delicate flower patterns in pastels or black and white, a nice change from plain colors. For the magazine they had chosen striking ones with field flowers in red and blue and yellow, with green leaves and stems.

The August issue featured picnics—all kinds of picnics: Hamburgs and steaks and hot dogs, *shish kabobs* and pigs-in-blankets to cook out of doors in your own back yard or over a campfire by the side of the lake. Hot weather food—at home or on the road; salads galore and cold combinations, plus the one hot dish for every meal that Miss O'Hara insisted upon.

This week they were working on school lunches for September and ways to balance the family's vitamins, as well as the budget. There was going to be a very good article on the latter—Budgets for Home Defense—in the July number, Miss O'Hara said. Sally made mental note that she must be sure to get it for herself.

My, she did have so much to do before June really came. She hadn't shopped yet for clothes for herself (That wouldn't take long for *one* good reason!), nor for her house, to speak of. She had picked up a few things on the wing on some of the jaunts that she had made for Miss O'Hara (Don't tell!)—linen, towels, and such. She must make a list that very night of the things she still had to do. Her thoughts strayed away from sandwich fillings for Johnny's lunch, from thermos bottles of hot cocoa, to—

"Telegram for you, Miss Lewis." Miss Day appeared at the door of the little kitchen.

"Thank you. I wonder—" Sally wiped her hands and took the envelope. A night letter from Chelton! She hoped—she didn't know *what,* as she tore open the message.

Found house you may like. Can you come Chelton Saturday? Wire train.

Love, Alex.

Hooray! Now that was really luck. She had been afraid of some mix-up in the draft. Alex's number was a high one. They felt safe for a year anyway, but things could happen.

She sighed her relief. A house! She hoped it was small and cute; that it had solid shutters; that it had a fireplace; that there was a back yard; that— How could she concentrate on any youngster's school lunch box? Three weeks till June? She wished it were there right then!

Was there a lovelier month in the year than May? June, to be sure, and possibly October, but that was all—and Sally wasn't even sure about them, she decided, as she and Alex drove through the village on their way from the station on Saturday afternoon. It was such gorgeous spring weather and everything so fresh and new. Chelton was a charming old town. The elms and maple trees that almost met over many of the streets were delicately green with new leaves, some still faintly pink in many places, and spring flowers blossomed gaily on every lawn.

"It does seem so good to get out of the city, Alex. I've just been pining for the country. I've scarcely seen a tree or heard a bird sing. Look at the iris over there! And tulips! It's a beautiful day, isn't it? Alex, will our house have any trees and flowers around it? Has it a back yard? What color is it? We can go there first before going home, can't we? Let's hurry!"

Alex looked down and grinned. "You don't lose a bit of your pep, do you? Ping! That's Miss Bantam still."

"Can't we, Alex?"

"Can't we what?"

"Can't we see the house before we go on home? Your mother won't expect us much before supper time, will she?"

"Not much, knowing A. Merrill, and not much after either knowing my appetite—but—" Alex made a quick turn into a side street and slowed down before a small gray

shingled cottage, a For Sale or Rent sign on the fence. It
looked down-at-the-heels and deserted. Last year's weeds
were still standing and there were holes in the walk, but it
had an air.

"Seems a shame to let a place like this go to wrack and
ruin, doesn't it?" Alex commented, letting the car idle along
in front of it. He watched Sally closely from the corner of
his eye.

"Yes, doesn't it? It's sort of cute, too. Nice space all
around. Grand old trees. It could be fixed up. It has all the
makings. I wonder why somebody doesn't—"

"That's just what I wondered." Alex looked down cautiously at the lady beside him as he brought the car finally
to a stop.

Suspicion stirred in Sally. She looked up quickly to catch
Alex's grin.

"Alex, is *this* the place? Is it? Tell me quickly. Is it?" She
grabbed his arm and shook it.

"It is, ma'am. What do you think of it?" He opened the
car door. Well, what did she think? A shade of disappointment flickered over her face. She had expected—well, not
this certainly— And yet—it was cute, sort of. It might be
fun to fix it up—

"Well?" Alex asked anxiously when Sally didn't answer
at once. His hand was still on the door.

"I was so surprised Alex, that's all. I just have to take a
minute to turn myself around first. I—" She looked at the
scene before her with new and calculating eyes. There was
a front yard and a back yard; there were trees; there were
solid shutters, one hanging by a corner to be sure, and the
chimney, if a bit dilapidated, looked as if there might be a
fireplace. Excitement began to rise.

"It might do, Alex, at that. It might. Let's look!"

They jumped out and ran hand in hand down the path.

"Mrs. Andrews, if you had a house that looked like this, with a floor plan like this, what would you do with it?" Sally stopped in the office of the editor on house furnishing and decoration one afternoon some days later, and laid a couple of snapshots and a drawing on her desk.

Mrs. Andrews glanced at the pictures. "Is this a hypothetical question, or are you looking for real information by chance?" Her eyes held a twinkle as she looked up at Sally.

"Real—very real information, please. I hope to live in it, perhaps this next year," Sally offered a bit shyly.

"Well, now that's different! Sit down a minute while we look things over a bit. The house has nice lines. Tell me how it looks inside. Walls, woodwork, floors?"

"Awful!" Sally answered emphatically. "The paper is peeling off all over and the paint is terrible. But the rent is low and the man who owns it said if we would take it he would paint and repaper the living room and one bedroom. The other bedroom we'll just use for a storeroom anyhow this year, so that isn't important." Sally's words tumbled one over the other. "The kitchen is a dark little hole, but it will have to do for a while, I guess. Later on, perhaps we can— But, no matter! A good scrubbing will help it a lot right now. So what I really have to decide about are the living room and bedroom, and I don't know what to do." She paused for breath and looked anxiously at Mrs. Andrews.

"Well, now, let's see. What color is your woodwork?"

"Was white *once*, I guess. Will be ivory, I hope and trust."

"And the walls? Living room? Bedroom?"

"What would you suggest?" Sally asked. "We can choose the paper, fortunately, provided it isn't expensive."

"Good. That makes things easier. What's your favorite color? Blue, I'd guess. Matches your eyes."

"Right." Sally laughed. "And Chinese red and—"

"Hold on now! We'll let you have a lacquer bowl or something, maybe, but that's about all of that color." Mrs. Andrews held out a restraining hand. "And blue is better for accent, too. A chair, curtains possibly. Will you have any pieces of furniture at all to begin with or are you starting from absolute scratch?"

"Scratch, I guess. Oh, no, we aren't either," Sally remembered suddenly. "Alex has a little old walnut sofa that belonged to his grandmother, and two small chairs that go with it. Cute things they are, too. Mulberry covers."

"Well, now, that's a real start. It also eliminates any discussion of modern versus mahogany and antiques. The latter will be more appropriate for your house anyhow, so that's all right. Now," Mrs. Andrews' eyes narrowed, "how would you like soft peach-colored paper for the living room? Would you be shocked if I suggested a pale blue ceiling? A rose-beige rug in one of the new weaves—self-toned brocade would go well or perhaps you'd rather have a color similar to the sofa cover—darker or lighter? Bring me the wall-paper book and those rug samples from the workroom and let's see what we can find."

Together they turned the pages and flipped samples back and forth.

"Oh, wait! There's a lovely paper. Could I have that?" Sally asked eagerly. Peach it was, with a faint stripe.

Mrs. Andrews looked at the price. "Pretty expensive, I'm afraid."

"It would be." Sally sighed and turned on.

"But now here's one," Mrs. Andrews held up a page. "Almost the same tint. Costs half as much. I'd choose that if I were you. And this broadloom in a soft mulberry—mauve they call it—would be lovely." Mrs. Andrews held the materials off together to get the effect.

"You know, I think I've a sample of drapery material that would be just right with that. It came yesterday. It's a new type of sateen, almost like chintz but only about half as expensive." Mrs. Andrews opened a drawer of her desk and drew out a swatch of satin-like cotton. Sally was delighted. "Aren't they lovely!" she exclaimed. Mrs. Andrews' practised eye ran through the lot. "Here's the one I mean. It's a lovely soft blue, and see how this floral design picks up the colors of your wall and the rug. Can you sew? If you can, you could make them yourself."

Sally looked a bit worried.

"Here's our new curtain book, telling just what to do." Mrs. Andrews' voice was reassuring as she handed over the leaflet. "But if these seem too expensive or too difficult, there's nothing prettier or more appropriate for a little old-fashioned cottage like yours than ruffled organdy throughout—bedroom and all. Your house looks well inside and out. I'm not sure they wouldn't be better for you anyhow, at first. Well, that's a start on your living room. Now let's see about the bedroom."

Back to the wallpaper book.

"Oh, that's a sweet one! Could I please have that?" Sally's eyes were shining. Light blue it was, with tiny nosegays.

"That would be lovely. Not expensive either," Mrs. Andrews approved. "Tint your ceiling a faint peach. Organdy curtains would be charming with that. Would you like braided rugs? Blue and tan and rose? All right now. There you are. Borrow these samples if you like, and think them over. How much money have you got to spend? I should have asked you that question right in the beginning."

"I think about five or six hundred dollars, maybe a little more between us," Sally answered doubtfully.

"Well, that's going to take some doing, but it can be done, if you plan carefully. The thing to do is to take your three rooms and the bath and list the things under each that you can't get along without. Electric icebox and gas stove in the kitchen, for instance."

Sally groaned, "There goes plenty already, I forgot about them. Two hundred dollars right there?"

"Don't forget Sears-Roebuck. You can do a lot better than that. And don't forget the second-hand stores for furniture. Sometimes you can pick up real finds, if you know how to refinish and are handy with hammer and saw. Here, take this folder. 'Setting Up Housekeeping on a Shoestring.' There are lists in it of minimum essentials and approximate prices compiled last year that may help you. Study these over and see me again when you decide, or before if you get stuck."

"Oh, thank you very much. That's wonderful help!" Sally exclaimed gratefully as she gathered up the materials.

The light burned late that night in Sally's small room at the Y. She figured and figured and thought, and figured some more. If she spent ninety dollars for a rug and forty for a chair and eighty-five or more for twin beds and thirty-five or forty for a dresser and twenty or more for tables, could she still have curtains and dishes and pots and pans and sheets and blankets and—and—? "If you don't spend so much for this, you will have more to spend for that. Make up your mind, Miss Lewis." She argued pro and con, forward and back, until the figures swam before her and she fell into bed at last, wondering wearily how it would seem, just for once, to go into a store and buy what she wanted— If she were only smart enough to *know* what it was!

The last days of May flicked by, Sally grabbing frantically at each one as it flew. She had *so* much to do! Before she knew it here was the very last day and her stretch at *Your Home* was over. She helped Kitty tidy up the little kitchen for the last time and said good-bye to the staff—to Miss O'Hara and to Mrs. Andrews. They were such clever women. They had all been kind. It had been an interesting ten weeks and so helpful. Sally had learned even more than with Miss Kitury. If she weren't getting married, she would like to go right on in that field.

But she *was* getting married, just two days hence! Clara was going out to Chelton with her. Wasn't she good? Alex would meet them at the station. They would go at once to the little church in the village. Alex's father and mother would be there, and his friend Ralph Adams and his wife— And then away to the camp in Maine!

It scarcely seemed possible that the long year had come to an end. It had been hard in many spots but now that it was over Sally was very glad for it all. She felt immeasurably better prepared for her new life ahead. Her horizon was far wider than it had been the previous June. She had had glimpses of homemaking from angles she hadn't known existed. Vision and inspiration had come to her. The home *was* important. Oh, very! Miss Kitury had spoken the truth.

As the elevator landed her at the street floor and the brass-studded door closed behind her, Sally waved good-bye to the quarters of the little magazine where new vistas had been opened for her. *Your Home* would be her guide in all the years to come.

So much for that adventure; tomorrow she would be starting on another. Ah, but *that* was something different! She paused a minute to take a deep breath of the fresh June air and her heart quickened as she turned down the street toward the Y.

PART II

CHAPTER XVII

Little Grains of Kalsomine, Little Drops of Paint

"AL-L-EX, breakfast is almost ready."
It was Saturday morning. Sally, energetically making
muffins in the kitchen, called toward the bedroom door.

"*Uh-huh,*" came the sleepy answer and then suspicious
silence. Sally waited a minute, then listened. Only a steady
z-z-z met her ear. With a grin, she swooped through the
bedroom toward the sleeping giant.

"Alex, darling, wake up! It's nearly eight. Wa-ake up."
She shook him gently, running a finger through his rampant
hair. A groan greeted her, a stretch, one eye opened a crack,
then a long arm reached out and grabbed her.

"*Aw-w,* have a heart, Banty. It's a holiday—"

"I know, but you remember what we have to do. Besides,
we're having muffins for breakfast with some of your mother's strawberry jam. They'll be done in ten minutes, too. All
right now—one for the money, two for the show," she
counted, "three to make ready—and out—you—go!" There
was a tussle as Sally snatched at the blankets and ran.

"Slave driver! Wait till I catch you!"

"Want to eat in your bathrobe and slippers?" Sally
stopped in flight to ask over her shoulder. "Wash your face
and hands then, brush your hair and come a-running."

"Okay, boss."

Bright winter sunshine came in through the window and
Mrs. Sally whistled and sang by turns as she set the little
table in the kitchen. No time for frills this morning but she'd

peel the oranges, cut them in half and slice them thin, just for a change, and put two or three cut-up dates in the cereal. Saturdays and Sundays were the mornings when she usually tried to do something different, but no time this week end. Special business was afoot. They were going to paint the kitchen! Sally had planned in her own mind to wait till spring before broaching the subject, but the room was *so* dingy. It never looked really clean, no matter how much she scrubbed and scoured. She did so hate that dark varnished woodwork. And spring was a long way off.

One day while she was in the village hardware store buying some tacks she had priced ivory enamel paint, "just for fun." Three dollars a gallon? Um-m. How many gallons for a small room—walls one coat maybe, woodwork two or more? "Wel-l, perhaps two gallons," the clerk risked a guess. Chinese red would be pretty for accents, wouldn't it? Around the table edges, inside the cupboards. Or should it be turquoise blue? Anyhow, it would take perhaps a quart of whichever color—fifty or seventy-five cents? That made only seven or eight dollars. Sally leaned against the counter, her mind's eye traveling around her already new and resplendent kitchen.

"What about the ceiling, lady?" inquired the clerk.

"The ceiling? Mercy, yes, I forgot the ceiling. It's dirty as anything. What do you do to that?" Sally inquired.

"Kalsomine or muresco. Maybe a pound or two, forty cents. You mix it up in water, you know."

No she didn't know but she was finding out.

"Have you brushes? Forty cents for this narrow kind, a dollar for the wide. And you'll need a special one for putting on the muresco, besides a sponge for washing."

"All that?" Sally did swift addition. There went another

two-dollar bill and more. Maybe they could borrow a sponge and brushes, too. Perhaps from Mr. Black, their landlord. To be sure, she hadn't even asked his permission yet for anything, but he was a good-natured old chap. "If we furnish the paint and do all the work, he won't care. Anyhow, he did say we could fix things up to suit ourselves."

Ten dollars would probably cover the whole business. Wouldn't it be nice! They could get along without the other new chair a while longer. All excited, Sally flew home to think, to plan, to juggle the budget, to talk to Alex—to cajole. She promised apple pie often. "I'll help," she wheedled. "If you'll do the ceiling and the high spots, I'll bet I could do the rest myself. How's that for a bargain? I can so. I wasn't brought up on a farm for nothing. You watch!"

And now here was the day. The paint had come the afternoon before. The ivory and the Chinese red for the trimming *and* a small can of turquoise blue, just to do a cooky jar with or something! Alex had found a stepladder in the cellar. His dad had loaned the sponge and given good advice, and Mr. Black had sent his brushes and his blessing. As soon as breakfast was over they would begin.

Sally hustled the muffins out of the oven, loosened them from the pans, set them where they would keep hot and served the fruit, just as Alex appeared.

"Mornin', Mrs. Newly-wed. Full of zip this morning, aren't you? What's on your mind?" he teased, seating himself at the table.

"Same thing that's going to be on yours—if not in your hair—in about fifteen minutes! Little grains of kalsomine, little drops of paint—to make this ugly kitchen, look like what it ain't," Sally paraphrased glibly. "High places are calling you, Alexander. You ascend to fame on the stepladder, remember." Sally standing beside him, coffee pot in hand, tucked an arm around his neck while she filled his cup. "We'll be in an awful mess, won't we? But only for a week, and then everything will look lovely."

"Yes, I hear you, sireen." Alex buttered a muffin, spread on the jam and took a bite. "Good. Darn good," he commented. "Any fellow who draws a wife that can cook is just plain lucky, I'll tell him, even if she does work him for whatever she wants on the side." He grinned across the table. "Any more coffee in the pot, Mrs. Bantam?"

The next few minutes were devoted strictly to the matter in hand. "Well, if we have to paint we have to paint, so we had better get going," Alex said as he shoved back his chair. "I'll get into my duds."

Sally swished through the dishes and carried them all to safety on the buffet and dining table. She remembered the thrilling day when Alex spotted those in Levi's old shop in the village and the weeks they spent on them, scraping, waxing, rubbing. Her cupboards were bare, ready for business. She would paint the furniture while Alex washed the ceiling. She carried chairs to the living room, spread newspapers, saved for days, over the stove, over the floor, got out her red enamel and stirred with a stick as she had seen her father do many times, till it was well mixed.

Alex was already on the ladder, a pail of warm water and sponge beside him. They worked busily, and the morning flew by on wings.

"There's the telephone. *Oo-o*, I'm stiff." Sally got up with a groan from sitting cross-legged on the floor while she did the table legs—ivory with red bands. "It's for you, Alex," she came back to report.

Alex scrambled down from his perch, set his pail on the

floor and picked up the receiver.

"Yes, Doctor. I certainly am sorry to hear that. Yes, of course, sir. I'll call for your instructions and take the next train. Good-bye."

"Oh, Alex, what's wrong? What's happened?" Sally looked up anxiously.

"Just this—the Doctor expected to go to the city this morning for a very important appointment. He's been hoping that this man—he's an old duck with scads of money—would make a gift to the school. This trip was to clinch the deal, if possible. The Doctor slipped getting out to the street and strained his back. He'll have to be in bed for a week at least and he wants me to go in his place. May have to stay overnight, too. Golly the next train goes at twelve-thirty! I'll have to fly. I'm sorry, dear. Shove the things in a corner and leave them there. I'll finish Monday after school. Help me pack my bag, like a good girl." Alex was already undressing. "What I know about this job is less than nothing. That fellow's a hard-boiled egg, too, if I ever saw one."

"Oh, Alex, I'm sorry. But you'll manage him. I know you will." Sally snapped the bag shut. "Here's the taxi."

" 'Bye, Sweet. Better go stay at Mother's tonight. I'll call you or wire. Keep off that stepladder, anyhow. 'Bye." Alex kissed her, paint smudges and all, grabbed his bag and was gone. Sally's anxious eyes followed him down the path and a glow of pride stole over her. He was so good-looking. They had such fun together. And, furthermore, he belonged to her.

She went back into the kitchen and surveyed the scene dolefully. Well, was this a sweet mess or wasn't it? Alex had washed the ceiling and part of the second wall. She had so hoped they could get the ceiling all finished that day, or the next surely, but now if Alex couldn't get back till Sunday night they'd be in this state of chaos for days. What about this muresco anyhow? She picked up the package. "Mix smooth in warm water. Let stand overnight or for several hours before applying," she read. Let stand *overnight?* That settled it. She'd just stir the stuff up right now. It could stand all afternoon and then she would put it on before she went to bed, if she broke her neck doing it! Wouldn't Alex be surprised! He'd probably scold, too—but— Well, no matter, the job would be done.

"Anyhow, I'd just like to see if I can," she said to herself. So she dumped the powder into the pail, poured in water and stirred—poured in more water and stirred—more water and stirred again. "Worse than making gravy for fifty," she spluttered. But at last it seemed right and she stuck the batch under the sink to "set"—or whatever it was supposed to do.

Meantime she'd finish washing the wall, paint the table top, and do the outside of the cupboards—maybe. She'd go like the wind while the fit was on and see how much she could get done. It was such fun to paint. A flick of the brush and old, dingy things were bright and new! Time and lunch were alike forgotten in the consuming urge for creation.

A long ring on the front doorbell brought her to with a jump. Western Union messenger. "Sign here, ma'am. Okay."

Sally tore open the envelope.

Think I've nicked his shell. Back late tomorrow afternoon.   Love, Alex.

Hooray! Well, that settled the ceiling for sure then. She certainly wasn't going to wait all that time—and Sally went to forage in the icebox for her supper. She needed rest and inner fortifying for what was ahead. Verily, yes. A run around the block in the fresh air cleared her head and revived her waning courage. Those directions said "Let stand several hours." It was six o'clock now. She had mixed the muresco at noon. That made "several hours," surely. She stired the muresco carefully, round and round. Seemed awful lumpy. What did the directions say? "Mix—let stand," she read along. "*Um*—here it is—strain before using." So she hunted cheesecloth and strained. That was more than she bargained for—but then, she'd strained blackberries for jelly many a time. This couldn't be much worse, surely. It wasn't—much—and just about as good for the hands. Ugh! But ready at last, she pinned a towel over her hair, gathered up pail and brush and climbed the ladder.

Pooh, this wasn't so hard! Why did anybody think a girl couldn't do this job, if she had to? Plop, went a gob right in her eye! Served her right for bragging. *O-oops!* She nearly took a spill that time, bucket and all. Four trips down to move the ladder; four trips back up. Plenty of drips on the floor, and her hands were a mess. But small matter, she was almost through. One last "smoothover" across that dark streak. There! She straightened the crick in her neck and backed down to earth, covered with whitewash and glory. She was be-spattered and be-daubed but pride of achievement shone from her weary eye. Her ceiling was fair to look upon and one Michael Angelo had nothing on her!

Next day she was tired but had no time to think about that. Too much still to do. If she could whiten a ceiling, she could certainly paint woodwork, and away she went. Hard work? Yes, but fun—and after all, wasn't it her kitchen she was laboring on? At three o'clock she quit, put her brush to soak and tidied up, heated herself a bowl of soup, took a bath and put on her best housecoat and curled up to rest till Alex came. She shut her eyes. She was tir—

Heavens, the stepladder! It was dissolving beneath her

feet and the paint can was coming down on top of— But it never landed. She found herself snatched up by two strong arms.

"Why-y, Alex, darling! When did you come? I didn't hear you."

"Good reason why. Buzzing like a bumblebee. What else have you been doing while I've been gone besides sleeping?" he ruffled her hair.

"Three guesses—and the first two don't count. Come, I'll show you." And Sally pulled him toward the kitchen door.

"Why, you little scamp! Didn't I tell you to keep off that ladder? I've a mind to turn you over my knee." Alex grinned in delighted surprise. "Pretty good job, at that—for a half-pint," he conceded.

But the next morning the story was something different. The artist was dead to the world.

"Hi, Sally. It's half past seven," she heard but faintly and heeded less.

"*Um-m*," she groaned and pulled up the covers.

"Hi, there! Having breakfast with me or not?" Alex called again a half hour later, coffee pot in hand.

"*O-o-o*, Alex, my neck! I can't bend it. I don't think I'll ever be able to move again," Sally moaned.

"Yes, what did I tell you? You *would* paint the ceiling, and do everything else under the sun all in one day, wouldn't you?"

And being Sally, she would.

"Leave the dishes, Alex. I'll do them after a while," Sally called wearily, turning over slowly and with great care.

"Okay. I'll have to run, I'm afraid. There's coffee on the stove and orange juice in the icebox. 'Bye, old stiffy." Alex bent over her. "Go back to sleep now."

Sally listened till the front door slammed behind him, then sank into oblivion.

It was ten o'clock when she finally came to the surface. That late? Heavens above! She'd have to hustle, stiff or no stiff, to get the beds made, house tidied, go to market, get lunch and plan for dinner. Come to think of it, though, food for the latter was already on hand. Her Sunday dinner was still in the icebox. That was luck for her. A mixed grill she'd planned, too. Seemed like a week ago. There were lamb chops, mushroom caps, tomatoes and bananas to cut in half— all to be broiled at the same time, and there was broccoli to serve buttered. That was a really elegant dinner—too elegant —but she had planned it, she remembered, with an eye toward lessening any chance of an issue on the topic of paint! It could still serve the same purpose, for the job was not yet done by any means. Anyhow, she wouldn't have to go to market till tomorrow, which was a help.

Old-fashioned potato soup was on the docket for lunch. She had all the makings for that, she knew. Just potatoes and onions sliced thin and cooked together until soft, with top milk added and butter, salt and pepper—a little chopped parsley or green pepper, a dust of paprika to float on top. Made her think of home. They always used to have potato soup washdays on the farm. Hot buttered toast was good with it and a piece of cheese.

She still had some Chateau in the icebox. New York–made this was, but she had bought it because that kind had first been served at a famous hotel, the Chateau Frontenac in Quebec, from which the cheese got its name. (She had read all that on the label!)

Sally gazed out the window—lunch and paint for the minute forgotten. She would love to go to Quebec. Sounded picturesque and interesting. Maybe she and Alex—some vacation—after the war was over. And one of these bright days when she was all through fixing up her house and with nothing else to do, she was going to take time out and read up a lot about cheeses. They were very interesting food. So many different kinds there were that had been bound so very closely with the lives of the common people in many different lands. Sally had flattened her nose often on the glass of the cheese counters in the big city stores. There were the darling round bright red cheeses like the ones that used to come from Holland—that tidy little land with the scrubbed streets, the wooden shoes and the lovely tulip farms —before the war had ruined everything; there was her own favorite Roquefort, made now in America but carrying with it the lure of far-away France. She remembered the old story of the shepherd boy who left his sandwich of bread and cheese in a cave, returning days later to find that it was shot through with a green mould. Testing it cautiously, he found it so wonderful that he spread the news through the village and Roquefort cheese was started on its road to fame. And there were the Cheddar cheeses, made famous in England long ago. Hadn't there been a coffee house in London where Dr. Johnson went, called the Cheddar Cheese? Cute name for a coffee house!

Remember the dark, smelly little old Italian shop down near Faneuil Hall where the round cheeses hung by strings from the ceiling? She and Miss Mack had found it one day on one of their prowls while they were in college. They had stopped to "talka wid da boss" Angelo Pag—something-or-other. Miss Mack had giggled when Sally, dropping into Chinese pidgin, had been forced to retreat before Meester Angelo's, "Tha's kind Ingleesh, Meess, I no onerstan'."

One could go all over the world no doubt and find famous foods in each country—and probably everyone of them could be found right in our own U.S.A. It would be fun to travel around and find them, wouldn't it? Sometime, maybe.

Was it possible that Mrs. Sally had an itching foot? Tut—tut. A real New England housewife should be content in her own home town—or if one *must* travel, there was always Boston, far enough away to satisfy any mortal with sense! Yankees born and bred wasted no time hankering for furrin' ports—or didn't they now?

Sally leaned against the sink. Oh, yes, she was doing her morning jobs but she couldn't work up any speed to save her life, and her thoughts rambled far afield. Interest in the scene in front of her seemed a bit dulled for some reason or other. Too much paint yesterday and the day before? Well, maybe, if she had to tell the truth.

But her soup was cooking at last and the table set after a fashion. This getting meals in the midst of paint cans and stepladders with everything somewhere else! Where on earth had she put the sugar can? Under the parlor sofa? Like as not. No, here it was in the box with the other things.

"This afternoon I'm just going to rest myself—on both sides, as Aunty used to say, and let my courage gather till Alex gets home from school."

But after lunch and a good chat with Alex—all about the details of his trip to Boston, how the Doctor was that morning and how pleased he seemed with his assistant's work on the HBE (Hard Boiled Egg)—Sally felt better. Sap was beginning to run again and, to her great surprise, she was actually coming to life.

"Think I'll just skip up to the village and see if I can find some material for new curtains for that window over the kitchen sink." She thought wistfully of that new oiled silk so much in vogue, but jerked herself back from danger. "Can't have that till we're richer," said she. "Red and white checked gingham would be more to the point. Or better, how about unbleached muslin with many rows of red bias tape stitched across the top ruffle and bind the tie-backs with red? Just the thing! *Your Home* couldn't do better!" She was off. "Tomorrow I'm going to paint the bread box, the flour and the sugar tins—ivory, with red tops, I guess. I'll do a flower design on each. They have them at the Five and Ten. Do that fruitcake tin that we use for cookies in turquoise. Set that on top of the frigidaire. And while I'm in the village, I'll look in Mrs. What's-Her-Name's flower shop for a little wall bracket to hang on the window. I'll paint the flowerpot turquoise to repeat the cooky tin accent, and set a red geranium in it. Hooray!" Mrs. Sally's spark plug was functioning again. She was running in high gear once more.

"Mother Merrill, what can I do with our kitchen floor?" Sally, at her mother-in-law's home next day making her new kitchen curtains, stopped her whirring machine in the middle of a stripe to ask worriedly. They were in the sewing room. It was a cozy spot. Afternoon sunshine filtered in through the old maple outside the window to make a dappled pattern on the floor at Mrs. Merrill's feet. She was sitting in her low rocker, knitting placidly. She loved her new daughter-in-law—such a little flash-in-the-pan she was! So quick and snappy. She loved her sparkle—the swift affectionate ways. Alex was more than fortunate. Were there many girls these days who would be content to settle down and keep house after an exciting life, to make a home for their husbands? Many who would think it fun to wriggle a few dollars out of a scanty budget to do over a kitchen in a rented house just because she couldn't stand it to work in a dingy one? Alex was lucky. He was their only son. She and Father were so thankful he had found a good girl to help him. She smiled contentedly at Sally's perplexed face.

"I don't know, dear. What's wrong with it as it is? What would you like to do with it?"

"Well, you see when I started this painting venture I never thought about the floor. Now that we are almost finished and everything looks so bright and pretty, I'm afraid that old varnish stain is going to spoil everything. I'd love linoleum, of course, but we can't afford it. There's a piece in the village that just suits me, too. Black with cream and flecks of red—clouded all-overish pattern, you know. But it's *so* expensive," Sally sighed wistfully.

"I *had* thought of paint—black or dark blue, they are both used now—but footprints and every bit of dirt show so on a plain dark color," she added doubtfully.

"Why couldn't you use either the blue or the black and make your own 'all-overish' design, as you call it?" Mrs. Merrill was looking at the sunlight pattern at her feet. "I remember when I was a little girl, in my grandmother's house there was a floor that I always loved. It was painted black with fine spatters all over it—like a guinea hen's feathers. Cream-colored the spots were, mostly, but here and there were specks of red and green. It always looked clean and it fascinated me. It's an old New England custom."

Sally's eyes squinted reflectively and a dawning smile spread over her face.

"That's an idea, Mother Merrill!" she exclaimed joyfully. "That's a sure 'nuff idea. We've got ivory left from the walls and I've a little red still, and a bit of blue. Black floor enamel is all we'll need. Look, may I come back and sew tomorrow? I want to go to the paint store right now, then get home and clean up the floor so I can put the first coat on tonight. Alex has a meeting scheduled, thank goodness." Sally chuckled and confided as one woman to another: "He told me this morning he was going to leave me and live with the lunatics if we didn't get straightened out soon."

"I know. Men do hate a mess at home. But it doesn't hurt them once in a while. Let Alex help you. Don't spoil him. See you tomorrow then? You had better have Alex meet you here for dinner. That will give you both a little change. Good-bye, dear."

"Aren't you good to us! We'll be more than delighted. Thanks just heaps for the bright idea. You're such a wonderful help to Mrs. Newly-Wed. 'Bye." Sally kissed the soft cheek and skipped. At the corner she turned to wave a scarlet-mittened hand. Where did all these tales about mothers-in-law come from anyhow? Certainly not from the Merrill family.

A suppressed excitement about Sally that night at dinner caught Alex's attention. "Now what's up?" he wondered. But as the meal progressed she grew quiet and a worried pucker appeared on her forehead.

"Alex," she finally queried, "how do you put spatters on a floor?"

"Wha-a-t?"

"I said, how do you put spatters on a floor?"

Alex whooped. "You asking *me* that after Saturday night?"

"Yes, but these spots I'm talking about you have to put on on purpose." Sally wrinkled her nose at him, saucily but carefully explained his mother's suggestion for their kitchen floor—"With speckles 'like a guinea hen's feathers,' your mother said."

"Guinea hen's feathers! Horse feathers, you mean," Alex hooted, pushing back his chair. "When you and Mother gang up there's no telling what will happen. Dad and I had better take to the woods."

"No, but Alex, seriously, the floor will look nice when it's done. Your mother says spattered floors are an old New England custom. That ought to settle it for you." Sally squinted up at him. "I'll put the first coat of black on tonight. You'll be away at lunchtime tomorrow, too, so I'll have time to put the second on then. Your mother invited us to supper, thank goodness—"

"Now that *is* a break," interrupted Alex with a grin.

"And I'd like to spatter next day—if I were only sure how to go about it."

"Well, hon, I don't know either, but wouldn't a whisk broom do the trick? Mind how you use it, though! Your pet ceiling is only ten feet above, remember." Alex ducked for the door, "Wait and I'll help you Thursday night," he called, "unless the trustees take it into their heads to meet again. So long, Goofus Feathers."

" 'Bye," Sally called with a grin and prepared for business.

"Let's ask the Adamses over for Sunday morning breakfast, what do you say, hubs?" Sally asked as she leaned across the table. They were having supper in the new kitchen several weeks later. In fact, they had had all their meals there for some time past. Ever since it had been finished. For believe it or not, it was finished—from the last band of red on the chair rounds, the red and white curtains, the pot holders with the red borders that Mother Merrill had knitted, the new cherry-bordered tea towels on the red rack, down to the red dingle dangle on the light cord, and the crowning achievement of the spattered floor. Sally had been so thrilled she could hardly stay out of her kitchen long enough to make the beds or dust.

"I feel like celebrating," she went on. "The Adamses are very jolly. I like her a lot. Shall we?" Sally's face brightened as the thought expanded in her mind.

"Good idea," Alex agreed. "I've been trying to see Ralph Adams for a week about the gym and that softball team the boys want to organize. Ask them now and see what they say."

Sally made for the telephone.

"They say they'll come with bells on. I told them to wear slacks and shirts instead. Nobody will have to bother to dress. About ten o'clock will be a good time. Then they can sleep if they want to. Now I've got to sit down and think what we'll have to eat. Waffles, I guess (Mother Merrill will lend me her iron.), and tiny sausages—the cocktail ones that come in a can, and— Well, I'll see."

The next Sunday morning found Mrs. Sally up and doing shortly after eight-thirty. Not that there was so much to do. There wasn't. This was a very easy party—and no social obligations involved. A party just for fun, and she wanted time to be leisurely and enjoy herself. Bright red flannel shirt, sleeves rolled above the elbows; light gray flannel slacks, bright red socks and navy sneakers, fair hair curled high. She reminded herself of the weeks when she and Alex had camped up in Maine last summer.

It was a clear, snappy morning. Sun streamed in through the windows. Sally set her table with care and pleasure—

pale green linen cloth she had made herself, with small napkins to match. Her dishes were a soft pastel pink with white centers—so far, only enough to serve four but they were an open-stock pattern and she hoped to have a set of eight before another year. However, that matter was of small moment this morning. She was serving four—she had dishes for four. Check. A hammered aluminum plate—a wedding gift —piled with shining green peppers and lemons, topped with green grapes—did for a center piece.

She was having grapefruit—big pink seedless ones from Texas—with a tablespoonful of maple syrup in the center. These were already cut and in the icebox. The coffee was measured into the drip pot—one level tablespoonful for each measuring cup of boiling water to be added later. The little sausages were out of the can and in the frying pan. The waffle iron was set on a small table by her place where she could attend to it easily. She was having orange-honey syrup to drizzle over the waffles. She put this together now. The orange juice and honey, the melted butter and the grated orange rind, ready to heat.

Now for the waffle batter. Her's was the standard basic recipe. She ran over the amounts in her mind as she got out the materials. The method was easy. Just like making muffins, only the batter wasn't so thick. (Sally had a two-way sifter that did a double job with one pull, which she loved. Hadn't she tramped the streets for that for *Your Home?*)

Her mixing bowl matched her new color scheme—cream with red lines. This would set on a plate right by the waffle iron. She liked a bowl and spoon just as well as a pitcher for the batter. Saved dishwashing, and besides she didn't have a pitcher anyhow—yet!

Everything was ready as far as it could be. "On the Road

to Manda-la-ay" came a baritone solo from the bathroom. Alex shaving. So Sally made the beds and tidied the bedroom.

"Morning, Mrs. M. You look fresh as the dawn of day." Alex tweaked her ear as he passed en route.

"Same to you and many of them. You look fresh and you *are* fresh! But grab your house jacket, darling. I see Mabel Adams' bonnet bobbing down the path."

Greetings over and wraps disposed of, the men settled to talk while the ladies proceeded to get breakfast on the table. At sight of the kitchen, Mrs. Adams exclaimed in delight.

"What a darling place! I'll wager it never looked like this when old Parker lived here! When did you have it done over? Don't tell me you did it yourselves! I love the whole thing. And this floor! Will you tell me how you did this, if you please?"

"It was Mother Merrill's idea. Alex helped me put on the spatters. You have the paint quite thick so it won't run, take a little on the brush and then knock it gently against your left hand, and I mean gently! We did have sense enough to wait and paint the baseboards after the floor was finished or we'd certainly have had them to do over again. The whole project was so much fun. I don't know when I was ever more excited over anything." Sally beamed with pleasure.

"I don't wonder. It's as successful a piece of face lifting as I've seen in many a day. I feel inspired to try my hand, but you home economics girls sort of have the edge on the rest of us." Mabel Adams sighed in envy.

"Nonsense. Anybody can do this," Sally scoffed.

"Maybe. Here, hand me that grapefruit. I can take that in. Looks delicious." Mrs. Adams glanced down appreciatively at the plates in her hands.

"First call to breakfast, gentlemen," sang Sally, following

with butter and cream.

"Mabel, will you sit here? And Ralph, you here, please."

It was a jolly breakfast—easy and informal. Gay banter and friendly gossip. And the morning sped by before they knew it.

"Shall we move to more comfortable chairs?" Sally finally rose at the head of the table. The coffee pot was empty and the waffle bowl scraped clean!

"Let's do the dishes while the men smoke. I want to see more of that kitchen." Mabel Adams gathered up plates and cups and marched out through the door. "It's the nicest place in the house," said she.

Hours later, after the Adamses had regretfully left, Sally curled up on the sofa to rest. "Aren't they jolly, Alex, and didn't we have a good time? That's the way I like to entertain. Just have people in for fun." She lay quiet for a minute, relaxed and happy.

"Alex! I've an idea!" Sally sat up with a bounce. "You know what? I'm going to write up our kitchen and send it to Miss O'Hara for *Your Home!* 'Before' and 'After' you know. Won't she be surprised!"

CHAPTER XVIII

The Night Before Christmas

"DAD and Mother have to go to Florida the first of next week," Alex announced one night at dinner several weeks later.

"Oh, Alex, why?" Sally was all concern. "You mean they can't even be here for Christmas? They have counted so much on having us over there with them, you know."

" 'Fraid not, Banty. Dad isn't too well yet, and Dr. Anglin told him today that inasmuch as they were going later anyhow, they had better cut right out now before any more cold weather comes along. So they're leaving Monday or Tuesday."

"Oh, Alex, I'm sorry. I'll go right over tomorrow and see if I can help. Think they would let Hilma and me close the house for them after they go? That's such a chore. I expect your mother will want to see to things herself, though, but I'll offer anyhow. We'll miss them terribly, won't we? Right at Christmas time, too." Concern for Alex's family, disappointment for herself crossed Sally's face.

"No can help, I suppose, but the whole thing sort of changes everybody's plans, doesn't it?"

The next week was a busy one for Sally, filled with running back and forth between the two places. Helping Mrs. Merrill close the house, helping pack. Sally put gifts in each suitcase—small surprises. She pinned a joke to her father-in-law's shirt and left notes among their handkerchiefs. Anything to make them laugh. Finally she and Alex drove them to the train, settled them in their Pullman with magazines and pillows—with affectionate and comforting words. Mustering what gaiety they could, they said good-bye.

"Don't fall overboard fishing for skates, Dad, and for Pete's sake don't buy any lemon farms," Alex called. " 'Bye, Mother." They waved and kissed their hands, as the train pulled out of the station.

"Poor dears. I hope they aren't going to be lonesome down there." Sally tucked her hand in Alex's arm as they made for the waiting car—Father's, left for their use, which was a help!

"If we were rich, we'd go down for the holidays and give them a whirl, wouldn't we? Think you could stand it to dance 'neath a silvery moon once more?" Alex looked down.

"Next year maybe. This time we'll have Christmas in our *own home*. I'm going to decorate a Christmas tree, make a big candle for our doorstep and a swatch for our front door. I want to put candles in all our windows—and have a party!"

Alex gave her arm a quick squeeze. "You win, Sweet."

Sally took the letter the postman handed her and looked at the address: *Mrs. Alexander Merrill, Chelton, Mass.*

Her heart still quickened at the sight of her new name. She sat on the arm of Alex's chair and tore open the envelope. A note from Lou. She hadn't heard from her in months. A new job offered her with the Telephone Company? Run their big cafeteria! Wonder if she'll take it. Sally skipped down the page, many memories coming back to her—Lou and Speedy—they had all had fun together last winter. Why not have them out for Christmas Eve? Lou was off, she said. A good idea! She would write this very night.

The few days left before Christmas were filled to the

brim. To be sure, it was ever thus since Christmas Day began but the new homemaker was certain that she was busier
than anyone else had ever been before. In addition to planning for the usual gifts, there were all of Alex's family to be
remembered. The few dollars had to be stretched and then
stretched again. So much long division!

Then she had her dinner to think about and her home to
decorate. A swatch for the front door. How did one do that?
How about a branch or two from that small blue spruce in
the yard? It needed trimming badly. Maybe Alex could cut
off a few branches where they wouldn't show. She could lay
them together with a string of those silver and blue bells
from the Five and Ten and tie them with a smashing bow of
blue oilcloth. How about that? She'd get the things in the
village when she bought the candles and the lights for the
tree in the yard. Then she must take time and really decide
about dinner, so she could order the food.

Tuesday night she sat herself down with pencil and paper.
What for a first course?

"Alex," she called, "which would you rather have—
grapefruit decorated with maraschino cherry petals arranged to make it look like a poinsettia or—?"

"That's all right. Stop right there," Alex interrupted. "Are
we having turkey or roast chicken? I'd just as lief have
chicken, wouldn't you?"

"Love it. Capon, maybe, if I can get it. Want onions
baked or sliced in thin cream? And would you rather have
kernel corn sautéd with pimento or—well, kernel corn sautéd
with pimento?"

"Make it onions in cream and I'll take a chance on your
corn."

"Very good, sir. If we have stuffed celery and pickled

pears and cranberry and orange relish, do you want a salad? Hope you say no. I'm a bit shy on plates."

"Skip the salad. When I eat chicken, I like to eat chicken. At a time like this, salad's what old Prof. Nick used to call a supererogation."

"Whatever that is."

"Don't forget mashed potatoes," Alex reminded her. "Light like a feather. Those were pretty special last night."

"Thank you, husband. Now, in case you're interested, we're having a chocolate chip torte—first prize winner at *Your Home* last month. Maybe I can spring something new on Lou. That's all." Sally wrote with a flourish, doing the menu in style. "That should certainly hold us," said she.

"The cranberry relish I'll make in the morning," Sally planned. "It's better if it stands a couple of days. I remember when Mrs. Whoosis from somewhere sent that recipe in to Miss Kitury. I must write her a Christmas note—Miss Kitury, I mean." She scribbled along, mentally checking her supplies as she made out her market order.

"—and cream cheese to stuff the celery—almost forgot. I'll chop an olive or two to mix with it. These things I'll see about tomorrow and order the chicken from Tim at the market. And a yeast cake for the rolls. Forgot that." She propped the list against the kitchen window and got ready for bed. She had been on the run all day and tomorrow she would be busier still.

The day of the Christmas party found Mrs. Sally heels over head in dinner preparations. As a matter of training and from force of habit, she had mentally divided the work to be done into three parts: the things that could be made ready the day before, all that must be done in the morning of the day needed, and finally the actual cooking of the meal and all last-minute matters. The chicken she had washed thoroughly and put in the icebox when it was delivered late the afternoon before; also the celery now crisping in the icebox hydrator. She had made a little sugar syrup for the grapefruit.

And now, the day having arrived, with red and white apron tied over her blue morning dress, she was making things fly.

Already the dough for her rolls was rising in a big bowl over hot water. She had stirred that up early. The recipe was a good one that she knew by heart from college days, so she didn't have to bother with a cook book. And already the graham cracker crust for chocolate chip torte * was baking in the oven. Ten minutes for that, so she got the milk, the eggs, the sugar, and the gelatine ready for the filling, and measured out the chocolate chips. The whipped cream for the top would go on later.

Meantime, many other things could be done between tricks. The number one job was the dressing for the chicken. Crumbling the loaf of stale bread very fine after having shaved off the thin brown crusts, she stirred into it melted butter, a small onion minced, and the green branches of celery cut fine, about a quarter of a cup or so. Salt and pepper and poultry dressing and a little chopped parsley. Remember how many recipes for dressing came in to Miss Kitury's Kitchen last fall? Dozens. No matter. This was the old familiar way. Into the chicken it went—crop too—and then she sewed up the openings with coarse white thread. Suddenly she was a little girl again, perched on the wood box in the kitchen at home, watching her mother do just this. And again with old Ah Mon at Haiilani in Honolulu. Remember

* Note. Would you like to make this yourself? See the Notebook.

how he scolded when he couldn't find his needle that he sewed his turkeys with, suspecting her of throwing it out in one of her tidying raids on his private domain? And now here was she, married to Alex, stuffing her own chicken for her first Christmas in her own home!

She had come a long way since the day that she had been graduated from Wilmantic out on the Pacific Coast—her home economics sheepskin under her arm. The two loved years at Haiilani School in Hawaii; the summer at the Pudding Pan, that little tearoom in California where she worked like a whirlwind; her first year in the East and the lunchroom at Manfred Junior College; Miss Kitury's Kitchen of the *Star* and the magazine, *Your Home;* and now, married, getting Christmas dinner in her new kitchen—a new career—this time her real one, opening up before her! "It *is* a career to make a home. Don't let anybody tell you anything different," she harangued the chicken in front of her. "I know."

> A gas log and a cat
> Can't civilize a flat
> No! something more is needed for a home.

'Deed yes. To make her house pretty and pleasant with ingenuity and hard work in lieu of money; to keep her husband comfortable and well fed on a small budget; to bring up her children—if she should be so lucky—to be well behaved. She'd like three, please, and she'd ask the good Lord to let the girl have the curly hair, if it was just the same—and brains, please, for all. It frightened her. If she could only keep them happy, and teach them to be straightforward, self-reliant and jolly. Could she make their home the place where they'd rather be than anywhere else in the world? And she must keep Alex happy, no matter what. If she could just manage never to lose her sense of humor—or her "fig-ger" please! And never look like a rag—all washed out.

"*Hm-m*—" she thought dubiously to herself, "there have been many times when I've had the jitters at having to feed and manage for a hundred or so, or to talk before clubs or on the radio, but let me say I could have them a lot worse right now if I stopped to look ahead very far!" But Mrs. Sally plunked the chicken into the pan and prepared to finish her dessert, resolved to have fun first—at least on this Christmas —before she started worrying!

That simple job over, she peeled the potatoes and the onions, covered them with cold water, opened the corn and the pimento, cut the latter in tiny cubes and set it in the icebox, fixed the cheese mixture for the celery, opened and drained the peaches for broiling, with a dab of mayonnaise, under the gas, and cleaned up the kitchen. She and Alex were having a "hand-out" for lunch. This and that. No time wasted there—so she went ahead and arranged her table decoration. In a copy of *Your Home* she had seen an idea. (Mrs. Andrews was full of them. Sally wondered if Jo were still with her. Clever girl.) Shiny red apples with the cores removed made holders for ivory tapers, with rosettes and ivory crepe paper at the base of each candle. Three of these on her pet silver plate. Around the apples and the plate small spruce branches made the wreath that completed the picture. Pretty it was, too.

That finished, plus a similar group of candles on the man-tel, and the dirty work was done. She could rest until time to put the chicken in the oven at three-thirty. The latest ex-pert dictum on roasting being long slow cooking for every-thing—long and slow it should be.

"Why, Lou! How sweet you look in that outfit." Sally, just that minute dressed, answered the ring at her front door. "Put your things in the bedroom and come on out into the kitchen where I can see and talk to you. I'm deep in domestic duties right at present. Sit here where nothing can happen to that dress."

"Why, Sally, your kitchen! How nice!" Lou looked about her. "*You* did it, you say? My what marvels a can of paint can do, mixed with imagination and taste," she added admiringly.

"And elbow grease, don't forget," Sally put in. "Cheap, neat and tasty is our aim at all times. The first from necessity, the last from choice and I've been really pleased—also surprised—at this my major effort. You've no idea how much more fun it is to work out here now than it used to be. The dark woodwork and dingy walls that were here certainly did annoy me to death. Now I'm quite thrilled every time I wash the dishes or get the meals. It only nicked our budget for ten dollars or so. Cheap, don't you think? And they were dollars well invested, I claim. The hours we spent with the paint brush—skip. They never count, if you like the results, do they? If you love your job, it seldom seems hard—so the book says anyhow, or words to that effect." Sally ended with a flourish as she put the last slim crescent of cherry in the circle around the grapefruit.

"But speaking of jobs, I'm so interested in this new chance that has come your way, Lou. Are you really thinking of taking it?" Sally asked with interest. "It would be good experience if you want to go in that direction, wouldn't it?"

"Yes, very, and the pay is good, but—well, I think I'll stay where I am for a while longer."

"The only time to take a job is when it's offered," Sally

advised. *Hm-m.* She stole a quick look at Lou. "Speedy wouldn't be having anything to do with your decision, by chance?"

Lou flushed a bit. "Perhaps," she answered truthfully. "He is getting a fine start in his uncle's business. Prospects are good for advancement. Next year—maybe—if the war doesn't spoil everything—"

"Really, Lou? I *am* glad," Sally spoke warmly. "But didn't I hear Alex and Greg on the porch just now? They have had plenty of time to put the car away." She ran to the door.

"Hi, Greg! Come right in. Alex, dear, you'll take Speedy's coat and hat, won't you, and see that he and Lou are comfortable while I hustle dinner along?" Sally put her hand in greeting on her husband's arm.

"Let me help," Lou offered quickly.

"And me," Gregory spoke up. "I'm the best helper in captivity."

"Okay, then. Come on, the whole lot of you," and Sally laughingly led the way toward the kitchen.

"Everything's pretty well done except mashing the potatoes and making the gravy, and putting things on the table," she explained.

"Me for the potatoes," Greg made a swift choice.

"And I'll do the gravy," said Lou.

"Here are aprons, then. Greg, you take this one of Alex's, and here's a frilly one for you, Lou. I can't have you getting ruined with spatters. Experts don't spatter, of course—pardon me—but just in case! Safety first." Sally handed out aprons and opened the oven door a crack to see how her rolls were coming on. The chicken was already done and out, keeping hot on top of the oven, so that she could turn up the gas for the rolls. Greg and Lou sniffed appreciatively at the

savory smells as they started their jobs.

"This takes me straight back home. My mother 'larned' me to mash potatoes—I can't remember when. Boy! Lots of hot milk. That's what it takes. Then beat 'em like mad. Here we go!" Greg flourished the masher.

"Alex, you see if your mother's carving knife is as sharp as you like it, will you? I gave it a flirt or two on the steel, but you're better at it than I am." Mrs. Sally marshalled her forces—right in her element.

Before she knew it everything was ready. The peaches to garnish the chicken platter were browned under the broiler till the mayonnaise in the centers was puffed and golden. The stuffed celery, the cranberry relish, and the pickled pears were on the table; grapefruit around, water poured and candles lighted. Off went all aprons, and presto, in trooped a stylish company, adorned in their best.

"When I was a junior at college and lived with the President's big family for a while, we always sang *The Owl and the Pussy Cat* at Sunday or holiday dinners. The youngsters loved it and I can still see handsome and dignified Prexy turning loose on it, to the delight of the twins." Sally looked around the table with a wicked twinkle.

"Okay now, Mrs. Sally, I'll bet I can follow, if you can lead, believe it or not," challenged Greg and away they all went, at the top of their lungs.

"The neighbors will think we're crazy." Sally, flushed and laughing after her efforts, unfolded her napkin. Surely no one could feel anything but at ease after that piece of foolishness! Nor did they. Between one joke and another the food disappeared like magic.

"I rise and bow to your skill with that carving knife, Alexander. How come?" Speedy was watching the chicken wings come off with apparent ease under Alex's hand.

"Oh, I'm good," Alex boasted. "Ought to be, I've certainly watched my dad times enough."

"For which talent I give thanks," said Sally. "Roasts of any kind are just plain spoiled, I think, when they have to be carved in the kitchen. I was worried over the first one we had right after we were married. And did I ever heave a sigh of relief—I'd say pride if he weren't listening—when friend husband here swung into it with the carving knife like one to the manner born, as it were."

"Nothing to it. A mere twist of the wrist. What a young man should know about carving in one easy lesson. Kindly follow." Alex flourished the knife and settled down to business, as did they all when the plates were filled and passed around.

"Golly, that was a good dinner. Best I've had in months." Greg smiled at Mrs. Sally. Tapping and lighting the cigarette that Alex passed, he leaned back in his chair.

"Delicious!" exclaimed Lou. "That was super-elegant dessert. I love those crunchy pieces of chocolate all through it. Where did you get that recipe?"

"It drew first prize in the July dessert contest of *Your Home*. Ever hear of that magazine, by chance?" Sally laughed. " 'Tis woman's guide and friend."

Comfortable chat followed till Sally finally rose. "Will you please make yourselves quite at home," she said to her guests, "while I just clear the table and put the food away, then we can have a hand of bridge."

"Oh, no, let's do the dishes first. It won't take us long." Lou rose to help.

"I'm the prize dishwasher. They grow 'em bigger and better West of the Rockies." Greg was already peeling off his coat and rolling up his sleeves. "We'll hustle these out of sight in nothing flat. You can hold time on us, Alex."

"Good! Let the young ones do the work, wife. How will they ever learn what they need to know, if they don't?" Alex stretched himself out in his chair to smoke in comfort while Sally put things away.

"Close guessing. Nothing left but the running gears!" noted Sally, as she covered the remains of the chicken and put it into the icebox.

"When does that train leave that we said we would have to take? Soon, doesn't it?" Lou rose at the end of the second bridge rubber. "I've had such a jolly time I hate to go," she added regretfully.

"We're sorry, too," Sally spoke warmly. "But I know you have a long trip back."

"I'll call a cab for you," Alex said as he went to the telephone. Speedy helped Lou into her coat.

"We've had such a grand time, we'd like to come again," they both chorused. "Thanks heaps for the wonderful dinner. Good-bye and Merry Christmas!" They called again from the walk.

Sally and Alex, arm in arm, stood in the open door to light them on their way.

Hark! The chimes from the church in the village, where they had gone to hear the music a year ago—where they had been married in June. *It Came Upon a Midnight Clear* floated down to them on the frosty air. Their first Christmas Eve.

Alex tipped Sally's chin up with one finger and bent and kissed her.

"That was a perfect dinner, Banty. Merry Christmas!"

CHAPTER XIX

Spring Fever

SPRING was coming to New England at last. Sally, shaking her dust mop from her small back porch, stopped to drink in the clear morning air. For almost the first time in months the sun felt really warm. There were robins hopping over what should be their lawn and she had heard a song sparrow that very morning!

"Don't tell me there's a dandelion out already! Hooray!" Sally propped the mop against the railing and was down the steps in two moves. Wasn't it the gay, pretty thing? Pest or not, it was pure gold after the weeks and weeks of winter. Alex would be rooting it and all its tribe out with ruthless hand in a very short while, she knew full well, but right now it was a lovely herald of spring. She smiled down on it with affection.

"Maybe the tulips that I planted last fall are coming up, too." She found a stick and poked away the leaves under the front windows. "There they are! Bless their hearts, there they are. All choked up." There was a rake in the basement. In two minutes she was back with it, gently dislodging the leaves from her precious bulbs. Perhaps there were other things coming that she didn't know about. She went around the house, raking carefully. Ah, here in a shaded spot by the back door were lilies of the valley, just showing tiny sprouts, and there were iris by the front walk! She hoped they would be blue. Or maybe they'd be that lovely delicate orchid shade. Wouldn't it be fun to watch them open! She hoped they weren't those sickly white ones. Visions of the church in the country where she went to Sunday School as a child rose before her. Always on the edge of the platform there had been Mason fruit jars jammed tight with those iris and with snowballs and to this day she couldn't stand either. It would certainly be the irony of something or other if she were to find both of them right here in her own front yard! Sally leaned on her rake and looked about—housekeeping, the mop on the back porch, forgotten.

"My, this place certainly does need everything in the world done to it," she mused. "We'll have one busy vacation next week. While Alex paints the shutters and mends that walk again, I'll rake and burn the leaves. I love the smell." She sniffed in anticipation. "Then he'll have to spade up, re-seed and roll the lawn. The books say that should have been done last fall, but we didn't know about it then and besides we were too busy fixing furniture and what not. You know, I wish—" She squinted speculatively toward the back of the yard.

"You wouldn't be rushing the season, would you, Maud Muller?"

Sally jumped. "Why, Alex, how come you're home in the middle of the morning? Forget something?"

"Middle of the morning, what do you mean, woman? It's twelve o'clock."

"Oh, Alex, it couldn't be! Why I just came out here!" Rueful astonishment spread over Sally's face. "It's the first real spring day, darling, that's what did it. I was so busy scratching in the dirt like a hen and making a garden in my mind's eye, that I plumb forgot I was a married woman with a house to take care of and a husband to feed! Never mind," she took his arm and smiled up at him. "It won't take a jiff

to switch lunch together. Look, I've just been wondering—
Don't you think a latticework fence, not too high, stained the
same gray as the house, running from here to about there,
would be nice? It would divide the front yard from the
back, as it were. Then I could plant flowers on this side of it
—petunias, Rosy Dawn and Purple Prince, you know, and
we could have vegetables on the other side—radishes and
onions and lettuce, maybe? Then I wish we could plant
climbing roses over that back fence and have a row of asparagus in front of it. My father always said it took forever-
more for it to get started but once established it lived for-
evermore. Can't you just taste fresh asparagus right out of
our own garden? Makes my mouth water! And then I want
to plant herbs. (Shades of Miss Kitury!) I've got a pot of
chives on the window-sill already that I'll set out later. Mabel Adams said she'd give me a root of parsley. She has loads
and I've seeds to plant of thyme and marjoram and savory.
Do you like sage? We had to drink so much sage tea for
colds when we were children that I couldn't look it in the
face now! And then I'd like—"

"Hey, Banty, hold on! Back up a rod or so. What was that
fence idea?"

Sally, held in mid-air, laughed and backed up. "I saw a
picture of one I thought was very good-looking in *Your
Home* last week. *You* could make one like it easy as pie.
Come on, I'll show it to you right after lunch. Now rest a
minute or two, Mr. Merrill, and your tardy wife will have
the food on the table in two jumps."

Suiting actions to words, she lit the oven, fished left-over
corned beef hash out of the icebox, the mustard pot, the
horseradish bottle, and some American cheese that Tim had
sliced thin for her at the market. She spread the hash on slices

of bread, then a little horseradish and a little mustard over
that and topped the whole with a slice of cheese, put them in
a shallow pan and slid them under the broiler.

There was lettuce crisping in the hydrator. She broke
several leaves in pieces, rubbed the salad bowl with garlic,
put in the lettuce. Stirred a little anchovy paste into her
French dressing and poured it over the lettuce, turning and
lifting with spoon and fork. Set the kitchen table on the fly,
took the sandwiches out of the oven, poured glasses of milk
and called her husband to lunch. Fifteen minutes, flat!

Where had she learned these tricks? In college? In Hawaii
or at the Pudding Pan? Guess again. From Miss Kitury's
Kitchen of the *Star?* From *Your Home?* Right!

"Any more of those cookies you made yesterday, Sally?"
Alex was finishing his last bite of sandwich.

"Loads!" Sally took the turquoise-colored cooky tin off
the top of the refrigerator, filled a plate and passed it over.
They were her sister's pet hermits, spicy and moist, full of
nuts and raisins. It was a grand recipe, made a big lot and they
kept so well—if Alex didn't eat them all after school and
at bedtime! Heavens, she had promised to give the recipe to
Mabel Adams. She jumped up.

"I'll just scratch this recipe off quickly, Alex, while you
finish. I'm afraid I'll forget it again if I don't." Sally found
a sheet of paper, fished her worn notebook out of the drawer
and copied busily—and left it on the desk where she couldn't
help but see it.

She found the magazine with the garden lattice fence and
showed it to Alex. Heads together, they poured over the
drawings. How many nights that winter they had done the
same over the seed catalogues, planning for spring—and here
today she had arrived with pomp and splendor, trailing green

and gold over the countryside—at least one glorious dandelion's worth of gold. Next week they would go forth to
meet her with hammer and paint brush, with rake and spade
and—optimism. For the catalogue said that so-and-so had
beautiful flowers, that these tomatoes were of mammoth size
—easy to grow, simple as one, two, three—and even Sally,
farmer's daughter though she was, believed!

"Friday. And no school next week! Hear that, Mrs. M.?"
Alex stretching himself in the kitchen doorway, grabbed
Sally as she tried to slide under his arm en route to breakfast preparations next morning. "Let's celebrate. Go into
town for dinner tonight. Ask the Adamses if they don't want
to join us. It would be a shame not to take advantage of this
wonderful weather. May snow tomorrow, knowing New
England, so let's go now. What do you say?"

"All right! Let's hustle breakfast along. Then we can call
the Adamses before Ralph gets away for school." Sally wrig-
gled loose and put on the coffee pot. "You do the orange
juice, hubs, while I get the other things. Want bacon or
scrambled eggs or both?"

"Both. All or nothing today! I feel lordly and lavish. Any
money in the fun fund?"

"Five or six dollars."

"Um-m. Well we can't drink much champagne on that,
can we? We could have Chinese chow and drink tea, though.
We've hardly done that at all since we left Hawaii. Remember Hing Chow's parlor where we used to go so often? How
about that?"

"You know me. It's my favorite food. Hope the Adamses
like it. You either do a lot or you don't at all! Ask them,
Alex, like a dear, while I finish what I'm doing."

Alex went to the telephone.

"Hello, Ralph. Sally and I thought we'd drive in to the city tonight for a spree. Don't you and Mabel want to come along? Fine. Like Chinese chow? What? Okay. Right after school then. We'll call for you. Good."

"What did he say, Alex?" Sally asked, spoon poised in air.

"They're all for it!"

"But do they like Chinese food?"

"He said they'd risk it. They could only die once." Alex sat down at the table with a grin.

That afternoon at four o'clock Mrs. Sally was putting on the finishing touches. Her dark blue spring suit, freshly cleaned and pressed, looked trim and good as new. She buttoned it straight to the neck, pulled the round collar of her tailored blouse over it and pinned said collar with the silver filigree pin Alex had given her before they were married. A speck more powder on the nose—a little lip-stick, a critical look to the nails. "Pass—on a pinch," she decided, after a survey of what Aunt Ina used to call the "toot n' cymbal." She laid out camel's hair topcoat, blue hat and gloves. Alex should be home any minute now.

The front door slammed. Husband—flinging off hat and coat on the run.

"Hi, Sally. That my clean shirt on the bed? Thought I'd never get away from that office. Everybody wanted something at the last minute. Some of them didn't get it either, I pause to state."

"Four boys have to stay in the dormitory over the vacation," he called later from the bathroom door. "Live too far away to get home. Tough, isn't it? I felt sorry for the kids when everyone else was leaving. This coming Sunday will be the worst time for them, I suspect. I wonder if—"

Sally laughed softly to herself. She knew that sign well. "If they couldn't come here that day?" she supplied for him. "Surely, why not? How about Sunday night supper? Suppose they would like to cook it themselves?" Her precious kitchen rose before her and she groaned inwardly, but at that it might be easier than if she had to do the work herself, and more fun for the boys—maybe.

"Gee, Banty, you're a good gal. Are you all ready? Come on, let's get going then. Let's see first if I've got the keys to the car—and to the front door—and my money. All set. We're off."

"Golly, I feel years younger already," Alex, his passengers collected, swung himself behind the wheel and turned into the turnpike.

"You're not alone there, bud." Ralph Adams settled his legs under the dashboard and relaxed.

The two ladies on the back seat, being only wives and homemakers, winked at one another. At least this was one night when they didn't have to get dinner for their lords, praises be!

It was a jolly ride in, they felt free and gay.

"We'll probably have to park blocks from where we want to go. The streets down in Chinatown are so narrow." Alex began looking as they neared that crowded quarter. "Here's a parking lot. This will be better." He drove into the enclosure and took the ticket from the attendant. They all got out and tramped down the block.

Familiar sights and sounds greeted Sally. Her eyes sparkled. She was back in the markets of Honolulu!

"Look, Alex, look! Remember these things?" She pulled him to a stop in front of an open vegetable stall. "See the roasted pig skin, all crackly, hanging over there, and the dried duck. Remember these very long green beans and the funny squash and the Chinese cabbage? And look, here are water chestnuts!" She pointed to the bushel basket of small black balls—sniffing and peering about her in eager excitement.

Inside the shop were Chinese women in the well-remembered long black jackets and trousers. Their hair slicked back—jet and shining, into the familiar bun. Here was an older dame, gold and jade pins in her hair. Well-to-do Mrs. China, buying food for her household, and woe betide the luckless "veg'table" boy who gave her one leaf too few!

Sally sniffed. "The national air of China," she said, eyes sparkling, "you don't sing it, you smell it, as someone said."

Farther down the street was an embroidery shop. Mabel Adams was entranced but Sally was spirited far away from New England. She was again trailing up and down the streets of San Francisco's Chinatown for the first time. She had bought slippers for Judy in just such a shop as this the night before she sailed for Honolulu and her first job. It seemed long, long ago.

"So this is the place, Alex?" Sally asked as he turned in at a doorway, bedecked and much becarved with gilded dragons, that opened at the foot of a gaily lighted area, a few steps below street level. Red paper panels with bold black characters invited all and sundry to Wong Foo's—chop suey parlor to you. They stepped down and through the door into a rather dimly lighted room.

There were black wood tables inlaid with mother of pearl. There were pictures painted on glass in carved wood frames, and old and intricate Chinese lanterns hung from the ceiling. At one end of the room was the kitchen, just a low counter separating it from the diners, open for all to see. Sally was all eyes.

"This is really different from any place we've ever been in, isn't it, Alex? Look at that kitchen man slicing those vegetables, will you! Makes me think of old Ah Lin." Sally stood by, fascinated at the swift sureness of the big knife as it rose and fell in the cook's thin hand, leaving piles of celery, of green peppers, of water chestnuts, all paper thin on the block in front of him.

Huge steel cooking bowls fitted into the stove where rice steamed and the shredded vegetables cooked in proper Chinese style. A faint smell of peanut oil, of sesame and soy floated out into the air. The cooks, clad in sketchy garments, worked in stolid silence, their dead-pan faces registering not one flicker of interest in the onlookers. When they were finally seated, Ralph Adams scanned the menu before him. "My soul, how can you tell what you are eating from *this?*" he wanted to know.

"Read the little fine print underneath each thing," his wife instructed him. "See where it says 'bamboo shoot and fine chicken'? Listen to this one—'fry noodle, also mushroom,' and this 'Pekin duck very cost.'" Mabel went on down the line, enjoying herself hugely.

"What are 'spring rolls,' Alex?" Sally wanted to know. "Anyhow I vote for them—just to match the day. Usually each dish will serve four, so why don't we choose one or two things apiece and see what we draw? What takes your eye, Mabel?"

"I'll have that number three—'bamboo shoot and fine chicken with water chestnut.' I certainly never chewed on a bamboo shoot before." Mabel laughed.

"You're next, Ralph."

"Make mine number six—'fry fresh shrimp.' At least I recognize those words!"

"Let's have chicken chow mein with almonds, Alex. We used to love that, remember? You give the order, dear. You know how to do it in style. Don't forget sweet and sour spareribs!" Sally settled back in her chair, prepared to enjoy the evening.

Very soon their waiter appeared (so much like her precious Fan Yow of Haiilani days that Sally looked twice to make sure!) bringing in the first installment of their dinner. Very smooth, round mounds of rice in small blue Canton bowls—one for each. Flowered pots of oolong tea that grew stronger and stronger as the meal progressed. You had a fork and chopsticks beside you and as a special favor, plates to eat from.

Next came a tray stacked with covered dishes—the "coolie" china, green lined and odd-shaped that had intrigued Sally of old. Covers off, they viewed their food. There were the "fresh fry shrimp"—huge ones dipped in batter and fried in deep fat. And the "spring rolls"—meat chopped very fine, seasoned and mixed with pine nuts, was wrapped in very thin crisp pancakes. Delicious!

The proper procedure was this: You first put rice on your plate, then over that went something of everything in the dishes—the bamboo shoot with "fine chicken and water chestnut" (like white asparagus and thinly sliced sweet white turnip), the better known chow mein with small toasted almonds all through it, a little of the "sweet and sour spareribs" for a relish, and then soy sauce to flavor it all—and if you were a real devotee, you mixed mustard with the soy! Sally looked over at Ralph and laughed aloud at the dubious look on his face. Little handle-less cups of tea were passed all around. They were off!

"By George, this is really good! Pass me over some more of my 'fry fresh shrimp,' Mabel—there by your elbow." Ralph Adams was sold to the food of Wong Foo—and the party was a success!

Dish followed dish around the table. Teapots passed back and forth.

"You know, it's funny about Chinese food," Alex remarked at last when the spring rolls were no more and the chow mein dish was empty. "You always feel so satisfied and you never think about dessert. We *could* have canned lichees. They're like big, peeled grapes. Look lovely, but a snare and a delusion, I warn you. Anybody want to try 'em?"

"Not another bite for me." Ralph lit a cigarette and relaxed.

Mabel waved a languid hand.

" 'I sassify,' as old Ah Mon used to say." Sally grinned, and they all rested, chatting quietly or not at all, comfortable, at ease.

"Well, think we had better move on?" Alex asked at last, when the cigarettes were finally finished. "Saw one of those cooks looking this way as if he'd like to heave a cleaver at us, so maybe we had better go while we're still whole and can. Tough-looking birds, aren't they?"

They all donned wraps at last and trailed out into the noisy streets.

Beautiful porcelain and silks and jade lured them from one shop to another. Rice pattern blue Canton china and the fragile rose design in slender cups and saucers, in bowl and plate, drew wistful "ohs" and "ahs" from the two housewives. In and out of the narrow crowded alleys they wandered, fascinated by that small bit of an ancient and foreign way of life, set down in their own New England.

"We had a good time last night, didn't we? Seemed like old times," said Sally across the breakfast table to her young husband next morning. They were sitting—just sitting, enjoying the unwonted leisure of the first day of vacation and the beauty of a real spring morning. Birds chirped in the bushes out back—a flash of blue flew past the kitchen window, and the sun streamed in.

"I'd love to leave the dishes right here on this table and go rake leaves!" Sally stretched. "But I suppose if we are going to have those boys in for supper tomorrow night I'd better think a bit about what to feed them and get the orders in. If they are to do the cooking, things will have to be simple, won't they? Guess I'll get a couple of pounds of chopped steak, one or two of those big sweet Bermuda onions, a couple of dozen buns and they can have hamburgers. Fat dill pickles to go with them. Boys love hamburgers. They used to mob us on the days when we had them at Manfred.

" 'Bye, darling," Sally called to Alex, already backing toward the door. "Be out there with you in a short space." Sally went on with her planning. "Let's see, what else? Salads are off their lists—'rabbit's food'!—though they used to like a cabbage relish with a bit of onion, sugar, and vinegar that we sometimes had. I'll make a dish of that tomorrow. Open a can of those good baked beans, 'floss' them up with some bacon strips and catsup and bake them in a pan, I guess.

"Tomorrow morning right after breakfast, I'll make some applesauce and stir up that gingerbread 'mix' and put the

cream cheese and grated orange peel frosting on it that I remember from the days of Miss Kitury's Kitchen. Feel lazy every time I use any of these prepared 'mixes'—but tomorrow's Sunday and vacation—and today I want to make a garden!"

She called Tim, put in her order, after checking staples for the week end, cleared the table, stacked the dishes in the sink and went forth to dig in the dirt.

The smoke from the burning leaves rose straight in the clear still air. Sally and Alex raked and pruned and burned, cleared and trimmed and burned some more. They ate a snack off the kitchen shelf and returned to the scene of their labors. By late afternoon they were neat and unbelievably tidy, a bed had been spaded for vegetable seeds, and Mrs. Sally went in to rest, take a bath and get supper for a working man.

She was having fresh strawberry shortcake. The kind made with rich biscuit dough, baked flat in a tin, split and buttered hot, filled with lots of cut and sugared berries, covered with more on top and served country style with a pitcher of cream!

"Oh, I hate to get up." Sally stretched and opened one eye and squinted across at Alex's bed next morning. It was empty. "Must be late!" She fished her watch out from under her pillow. Eight-thirty. "Late enough!" She swung her feet out of bed into her slippers, reached for her housecoat and looked out the window. There was Alex, spading up the lawn. She tapped on the glass and waved to him.

"He'll be hungry as a bear by the time I get breakfast ready. Better have French toast and maple syrup. We haven't had that in a long time."

They lingered over their coffee. How grand not to have to hurry or do anything they didn't want to do.

"Well, this won't make the grass grow." Alex rose at last.

"Nor get things ready for those lads tonight—nor dust the hearth nor sweep," added his wife, "so we had better get started."

"Why do you bother with lunch, Bantam? Have just a

bite. You'll be cooking all morning long," Alex turned in
the doorway to ask.

"Suits me. We'll eat off the pantry shelf, thank you
kindly, sir."

"Good enough. Okay by me." Alex's whistle was already
floating back from the yard.

"Come in, boys, glad to see you," Alex greeted his young
guests, arriving at the door some hours later.

"Sally, I want you to know these boys, Peter, Edward,
William, and Donald. I think Peter here comes from your
side of the Rockies. Idaho, isn't that right, Pete? Land of the
big potatoes?"

"That's right. Sagebrush and rabbits, too." Peter, older
than the others, slim and dark and quick, acknowledged the
introduction politely and set the pace.

"Ever been in Spokane, Peter? That's where I went to
school. We were almost neighbors, weren't we?" Sally took
caps and hats.

"Let's look around the garden a bit while it is still sunny.
I need somebody to tell me how to plant beans." Alex led
the way outside.

"I know beans, Mr. Merrill. They're easy. We had a big
garden last year at home, Dad and I!" Donald broke in
eagerly—snub-nosed, freckled, dubbed Duck for short.

"My mother has lots of flowers in her yard. I helped her
one summer and we had marigolds—'way up to here!" Edward measured to his pocket.

"You're the lad for me, Edward." Sally smiled. "Better
come down this week and show me how. I have lots of
flowers to plant, and I don't know much about it either."

"Okay. Can Bill come, too? He's a good egg."

"He most certainly may. Why don't you all come? Wear your old duds. We'll garden and then picnic under the tree over there. Would you like that?" Sally looked inquiringly at each in turn.

"Sure, we'll come. How about tomorrow?" they chorused.

"Fine, if the weather is still nice. We'll look for you. Now I think we had better see about supper. I thought you would all like to help. Any of you boys belong to the Scouts?" Sally asked.

"Pete does, I know. You do, too, don't you, Donald?" Alex asked.

"Bill and I can cook. We helped in camp last summer," Edward offered. "Old Rose used to let me flip the hotcakes when we had them. Boy, was she black. Remember the day, Bill, that she chased us out a-flying for tying her apron strings to the chair and shaking flour over her cake instead of powdered sugar? But she was smart. Never got away with much without getting caught."

"All right. We'll go in now and you can all turn to." Sally led the way.

"Gee, this is a snazzy kitchen! My mother would like this."

"Hey, Duck, sit on a chair, not on the table, you big—"

"What do we do, Mrs. Merrill?"

"Now, Bill, you and Edward can be the cooks—you being experienced. There are hamburgers to fry and beans to heat up in the oven. Peter, you and Donald get out the dishes, serve the applesauce and cut the gingerbread. Want to eat on the dining table in style or perch around the kitchen, or on the back steps?" Sally already had meat, relish and pickles out of the refrigerator and was lighting the oven.

"Back porch for me."

"Me for the kitchen. Nearer the grub."

"Me, too. We get style at school."

"I'll say. Have to wear a necktie 'n' everything."

"So be it. Here are your hamburgers, Edward, and your frying pan. You'll find a piece of suet there to grease it with so it won't stick. The buns are in that box. You want to butter them, Bill, and then slice the onion and the dills? I'll show you about making coffee in the 'drip' when the water boils." Sally marshalled her crew. "Like Manfred lunch-room days," she thought happily. Chatter and fooling and cutting up. She'd forgotten how lively boys could be and how much fun.

But they were all for their jobs and in short order things were ready. The cooks served their wares from behind the kitchen table.

"Right this way, ladies and gents. Come and get it!"

Hamburgers from the frying pan to the buns to the plates.

"*Hey*, ladies first, you! There you are, Mrs. Merrill."

"Want onion on yours, Pete?"

"Sure."

"You, Duck?"

"You bet!"

"How about you, Mr. Merrill?"

"Give me the works. Those beans look grand, Bill. Have you boys left plenty for yourselves?"

"Leave it to us! Spear me that fat pickle, Eddie. Chef likes dills. And give me some of that relish. 'Atta' boy."

Milk from the icebox for the boys. Coffee for Sally and Alex. Draped over the porch rail, on the steps—in and out of the kitchen, there were boys, going out to eat, coming back for more.

"Bring on your gingerbread there, Pete. How's that apple-

sauce, Duckie? Service is lousy in this joint." Bill banged his fork on the steps, hollering for attention.

"Help yourself, chef. Pay more or eat less. We belong to the union."

Sally chuckled. "Cute, aren't they?" she said on the side to Alex.

"All hands on k.p. now." Peter took the helm when the plates were finally empty. "You go sit in the parlor, Mrs.

Merrill, and we'll have the dishes done before you can say Jack Robinson. *Hey,* stack those plates up good there, D. Duck."

Dishes done, games over, Sally and Alex, from the doorstep, were at last speeding their parting guests. "Good night, boys. See you all Monday?"

"Sure thing! Gee that was a swell supper."

"Good night. We had a fine time."

"Had a fine time, thanks."

"Fine time. Good night."

Suddenly shy, they made their adieus. Just as suddenly relieved to have their manners disposed of, they joyfully jostled one another down the walk.

"They *are* cute boys. I'd like two or three of my own just like them." Sally watched them go—a smile for their frolicking on her lips.

Alex's arm tightened around her shoulders.

"Me too, Banty."

And together they turned back into their house. Yes, something more *was* needed for a home.

PAGES
FROM
SALLY'S NOTEBOOK

Date Icebox Cookies (*Mrs. Hope*)

1 cup butter	1 cup dates
2 cups brown sugar	3½ cups flour
2 eggs	½ tsp. soda
1 cup nut meats	1 tsp. salt

Cream butter and sugar and add well-beaten eggs. Add nuts cut in pieces and the dates which have been put through the coarse food chopper. Add flour sifted with salt and soda. Shape in rolls, wrap in waxed paper and put in refrigerator for several hours. Slice thin and bake in moderate oven.

Spoon Bread

1 cup boiling water	2 tsp. butter
½ cup yellow corn meal	1 cup milk
1 tsp. salt	2 eggs—separated
	1 tsp. baking powder

Add corn meal, salt and baking powder to the boiling water. Stir well until smooth and thick. Add butter, milk and well-beaten egg yolk. Fold in stiffly beaten whites. Bake 50 minutes at 350° in well-greased casserole. Serve directly from dish in which it is baked. Lots of butter is called for, orange marmalade, winter weather and a good appetite.

Chocolate Drop Cookies (*First Prize*)

1 cup sugar	1½ cups flour
½ cup MyOMy shortening	½ tsp. soda
1 egg	1 tsp. baking powder
½ cup milk	½ cup raisins
1½ squares chocolate or 4 tbsp. cocoa	½ cup nut meats
	1 tsp. vanilla

255

Cream sugar and shortening, add egg and beat well. Add milk and melted chocolate. Add flour sifted with dry ingredients. Stir in raisins, nuts and vanilla. Drop by teaspoonfuls on cooky sheet and bake slowly at 325–350°.

Caramel Squares (Second Prize)

1 cup brown sugar
¼ cup butter and MyOMy, half and half
2 egg yolks
½ tsp. vanilla
1 cup walnuts chopped

1 ½ cups flour
2 tsp. baking powder
⅛ tsp. salt
Meringue: 2 egg whites
1 cup brown sugar, ½ tsp. vanilla

Cream butter and 1 cup brown sugar, add egg yolks and vanilla and beat well. Add flour sifted with the baking powder and salt and stir until well mixed. Pour into nine-inch cake pan. Spread nuts on top. Spread meringue over this made by beating the two egg whites stiff and adding slowly the other cup of brown sugar and the vanilla. Bake 30 minutes in moderate oven. Cut in squares or bars. Cocoanut may be used instead of nuts.

Icebox Cookies (Honorable Mention)

1 cup butter and MyOMy shortening, half and half
2 cups brown sugar
2 eggs—unbeaten
1 cup chopped walnuts
½ cup raisins

1 tsp. vanilla
1 tsp. salt
1 tsp. baking powder
½ tsp. soda
3 cups flour

Cream butter and sugar, add eggs one at a time, and beat well. Add nuts and raisins, flour sifted with the dry ingredients and mix well. Turn out on lightly floured board. Divide dough in several parts. Form into rolls. Wrap in waxed paper and put in icebox. Slice them as needed and bake in moderate oven 350°. Makes many!

Red Raspberry Bavarian

1 package lemon-flavored gelatin	½ cup orange juice
1 cup hot pineapple juice	1 cup heavy cream whipped
	1 cup crushed raspberries

Dissolve the gelatine in the hot pineapple juice, add the orange juice and chill till slightly thick. Beat until fluffy; fold in the whipped cream and the crushed raspberries. Chill until firm in large mold or in sherbet glasses.

Strawberry Puff (First Prize—Your Home)

Vanilla Wafer Crumb Crust

Mix 1 ½ cups vanilla wafer crumbs with
    ¼ cup melted butter, and
    2 tbsp. soft butter. Press this mixture firmly into an eight-inch cake pan.

Meringue: Add ½ cup sugar gradually to 4 stiffly beaten egg whites and continue beating until the meringue forms peaks. Swirl over crumb mixture and bake slowly (325°) for 20 minutes, cool; spread 2 cups sweetened strawberries over top. Whip one cup heavy cream; add one tablespoon sugar; spread over berries. Garnish with whole berries.

Blueberry Nut Bread

2 eggs	1 teaspoon salt
1 cup sugar	4 teaspoons baking powder
3 tablespoons melted shortening (MyOMy)	1 cup blueberries
1 cup milk	½ cup walnut meats— broken
3 cups flour	

Beat eggs and add sugar gradually; mix well, add milk, shortening and the flour sifted with the salt and baking powder. Mix only until blended. Fold in blueberries and nut-

meats. Pour into greased loaf pan and bake in moderate oven
(350°) for 50 to 60 minutes. This will make a loaf 5 x 12
inches.

Chocolate Chip Torte

2 beaten egg yolks
2½ tablespoons sugar
⅔ cup milk
Dash of salt
½ teaspoon vanilla
1 tablespoon (1 envelope)
plain gelatine

¼ cup cold water
2 beaten egg whites
2 tablespoons sugar
½ cup coarsely chipped
semi-sweet chocolate
1 cup heavy cream
whipped

Beat egg yolks and sugar; add milk and salt. Cook in
double-boiler until thick, stirring; add vanilla and gelatine
softened in the water. Chill until partially set. Fold in egg
whites beaten with the remaining sugar. Fold in chocolate.
Pour into Graham cracker crust. Chill till firm. Spread with
the whipped cream; sprinkle with fine chocolate chips.

Graham Cracker Crust:

Mix 1½ cups graham cracker crumbs and ¼ cup sugar
with ¼ cup soft butter. Add 1 tablespoonful water. Press
into eight-inch cake pan. Bake in moderate oven (325°)
10 minutes. Cool.

Hermits (Sally's Sister)

1 cup MyOMy shortening
2 cups brown sugar
½ cup coffee—warm
2 eggs
2 tsp. cinnamon
1 tsp. nutmeg
1 tsp. cloves (Ground)

1 tsp. allspice
3 cups flour
1 tsp. soda
1 tsp. baking powder
1 tsp. salt
1 cup raisins
1 cup nuts

Cream shortening and sugar, add coffee (left from breakfast) and eggs, one at a time, beating after each one. (A Speedy Mixer makes this easy!) Sift all dry ingredients together and add with the raisins. Stir in the nuts. Drop by spoonfuls on greased cooky sheet. Bake in moderate oven, about 350°. Makes a lot!